The
Ghostly
Guide
to
England

On the Trail of the *Paranormal*

Rupert Matthews

COUNTRYSIDE BOOKS
NEWBURY BERKSHIRE

First published 2006
© Rupert Matthews 2006

COUNTRYSIDE BOOKS
3 Catherine Road
Newbury, Berkshire

To view our complete range of books,
please visit us at
www.countrysidebooks.co.uk

ISBN 1 85306 988 4
EAN 978185306 988 8

Photographs by the author unless stated otherwise

Designed by Peter Davies, Nautilus Design
Typeset by Mac Style, Nafferton, E. Yorkshire
Produced through MRM Associates Ltd, Reading
Printed by Woolnough Bookbinding Ltd., Irthlingborough

Contents

Introduction 4
Bedfordshire 6
Berkshire 12
Bristol & Bath 22
Buckinghamshire 29
Cambridgeshire 36
Cheshire 43
Cornwall 50
Cumbria 63
Derbyshire 74
Devon 79
Dorset 85
Durham 94
Essex 97
Gloucestershire 102
Hampshire 109
Herefordshire 122
Hertfordshire 127
Kent 134
Lancashire 140

Leicestershire 147
Lincolnshire 152
London 161
Norfolk 170
Northamptonshire 175
Northumberland 181
Nottinghamshire 187
Oxfordshire 192
Rutland 198
Shropshire 200
Somerset 206
Staffordshire 212
Suffolk 217
Surrey 223
Sussex 227
Tyne and Wear 231
Warwickshire 240
Wiltshire 244
Worcestershire 248
Yorkshire 253

Introduction

England is a most beautiful kingdom, and a most haunted one. Wherever you turn there are ghosts, phantoms or spectres. The bleak moors are home to some spectacular apparitions that roam the high lands on their unending supernatural business. There are ghosts in the rolling fields of the lowlands and amid the soaring peaks of the uplands. There are ghosts on the open high road and in cosy streets. Old houses have their phantoms, but so do new buildings. The ghosts of England are no respecters of age or dignity. They crop up almost anywhere.

And the ghosts date back to almost any age of the past. There are ancient figures lurking amongst the standing stones that were erected by our ancestors some five thousand years ago. There are knights stomping in their armour and ladies in medieval gowns flitting about castle ruins. Tudor spirits are common, as are those of the Georgian and Victorian periods. Even our own age is well represented with ghostly ladies in mini-skirts and chaps in modern suits. All periods have produced their ghosts, and most of them are still active today.

But the vast majority of English ghosts simply potter about their purpose paying no attention to the mortals that surround them. They ride their horses, walk through their houses and wander around the landscape on whatever mysterious business brings them here. Those who live with ghosts in their homes or places of work tend to be quite relaxed about the fact. The apparitions have the power to surprise or startle, but very few have the power to do much more – though there are a few that are best avoided and one or two that are downright dangerous.

Indeed, the haunted places of England include in their number some of the most welcoming and relaxing you could hope to visit. Stately homes that have the ghosts of former owners striding about the place are all the more interesting for that. Lanes or greens that play host to local citizens of years gone by have an atmosphere not found in their less supernatural counterparts, and the haunted pubs serve good ale and wholesome food.

I would advise you, dear reader, to follow in my tyre-tracks and footsteps to visit these places for yourself. Of course, there are far more haunted places in the kingdom than are detailed here. I have included some of the most famous, most active or most dramatic hauntings in this book, but there are thousands more just waiting to be discovered.

So wherever you live in England – or if you are just visiting – check out the relevant county in this book and pop round to visit your local ghost. You might be surprised at what you find.

Of course, a book of this size cannot possibly be the work of just one person. I would like to thank all those who welcomed me to their premises and took the time to talk to me about their resident ghost or phantom. Thanks are also due to those who communicated by post or email, updating me on recent sightings and filling in background information that I was missing.

I would also like to thank Peter Kensell and Tim Brown who came along on some of my journeys to help with the navigation and research, especially at haunted pubs and hotels. My daughter, Bo, contributed with her many interruptions, questions and opinions – though being only two years old these tended to be limited to food and drink related items. And I must also thank my wife for her patience with my task and my many absences from home trying to track down some particularly elusive phantom.

Bedfordshire

The gentle landscapes of Bedfordshire are often heedlessly passed by. Far too many people rush through on their way to or from London, and many of the county's residents commute into London and so barely see their home county except at weekends. The unkindest slight of all is the dismissal of the county as 'Brussels sprout country', for its devotion to market gardening to feed the consumers of London. This is a shame, for Bedfordshire is one of England's most gentle counties and is filled with architectural and historic wonders.

And it is filled with ghosts.

One of the most terrifying to encounter is that of Sir Roland Alstons in Odell. It is not that Sir Roland himself was a particularly frightening character, though he was a quarrelsome fellow, it is what his ghost brings in its wake that causes the fear. It is best, all things considered, to make oneself scarce if this ghost is seen riding through the village.

Sir Roland lived in the 17th century and was a tempestuous man who gambled recklessly, brawled enthusiastically and fought frequent duels. Despite his wild ways he never came to serious harm and, it was whispered, he had the luck of the Devil. Then early one morning Sir Robert's body was found lying inside the village church, the door locked and bolted as if the man had been desperate to keep someone – or something – outside. And etched deep into the solid timber of the door were scorched claw marks as

THE HAUNTED PARISH CHURCH OF
ODELL STANDS OUTSIDE THE VILLAGE,
ITS TOWER BEING BARELY VISIBLE FROM
THE HOUSES.

if some gigantic taloned hand had scrabbled at the door, burning it with intense heat.

Sir Roland's servants had a disturbing tale to tell. The previous evening a tall, well-dressed man had come calling. The dark stranger had barely entered the house, before Sir Roland fled at high speed. The visitor followed, laughing and jeering and saying that Sir Roland could not break the bargain now the time had come to pay. Soon gossip had it that Sir Roland had sold his soul in return for earthly success and that the tall stranger had been the Devil come to collect.

The idea gained credence when the hauntings began. Sir Roland's phantom was seen riding at full gallop through the village towards the church, pursued by a dark, scurrying shape that might have been a man, but could equally have been a monstrously deformed beast with horns. Time and again the terrible chase has been played out in spectral form. And always the ghosts vanish as they reach the churchyard. Did Sir Roland escape his fate by reaching holy ground in time? We will never know.

* * *

Sir John Gostwick of Willington was nothing if not ambitious, but he relied on his brains rather than a pact with the Devil to gain his ends. The family estates he inherited at Willington in the early 16th century were fine, but hardly magnificent and much the same could be said for the manor house in which he lived. Sir John had his eyes set on grander things, so he went where all ambitious young men of good family went in Tudor England. He went to court.

Unlike the other dashing young blades, Sir John forbore from flashy clothes, poetry writing and excessive flattery of the rich and the famous. Instead he chose to do dull, repetitive work and to run errands for court officials. Sir John had shrewdly guessed that if he made himself useful to the officials they would ensure he was always on hand when work was to be done, and that was when he might take his chance. Things fell out much as Sir John hoped and he was soon both popular and always present. Thus he earned himself the post of Master of Hounds to King Henry VIII. It was not a very highly paid position, but it gave him the king's ear and many courtiers and businessmen were willing to present Sir John with gifts if he mentioned them kindly to the royal hunter.

With this money, Sir John transformed his manor at Willington. The house and its outbuildings were rebuilt in magnificent style. No expense was spared and the village gained fame through its mighty manor. However, Sir John's house has long since vanished. It was

THE MAGNIFICENCE OF THE STABLES AT WILLINGTON MANOR ATTRACTS THE RESTLESS SPIRIT OF THE MAN WHO BUILT THEM IN TUDOR TIMES.

consumed by fire in the 18th century and today only the dovecote and other outbuildings survive to display his taste and wealth.

The wraith of Sir John has been seen to return from time to time to inspect the site of his beloved home, and wander across the wide green towards the church where he is buried. He strides purposefully, dressed in the doublet and hose so fashionable in the days when he came back from court, his fortune made.

The Willington Manor that stands today is a pleasant Georgian residence with a small pool and fountain in the courtyard. Sir John has not been seen in the new house – perhaps he does not approve of it – but in the 19th century the manor was the centre of a remarkable haunting. So famous did it become that Bill Turner, a noted early psychic investigator, carried out a study here.

A male ghost stalked the corridors of the house, though nobody seemed to have any idea who he might have been in mortal form. The investigation took several days, and Turner was able to gather impressive sighting reports and other evidence of the ghost's reality. Not only was the ghost seen, but his heavy footsteps were heard, and the family's pet dog would sometimes unaccountably go wild in the early hours of the morning. Turner was, however, unable to find any cause for the haunting and left it a mystery.

Some years later, shortly before the outbreak of the First World War, the house was being renovated. The works involved taking down the outbuildings linked to the kitchen, including the old dairy. Buried beneath the stone flags was found the skeleton of a man. There were no possessions to give a clue to his identity, nor to what grisly fate had brought his body to be secreted beneath the floor. But after the bones were taken away for a decent, if anonymous, Christian burial, the hauntings abruptly ceased.

* * *

A burial that failed completely to put a ghost to rest was that of Black Tom, the local ne'er-do-well hanged for highway robbery in Bedford in the 17th century. His body was taken down from the scaffold in Union Street and thrown into a pit beside the crossroads

THE PAVEMENT OF UNION STREET IN BEDFORD
IS THE HAUNT OF A GRUESOME SPECTRE.

with Tavistock Street. It may have been because of the lack of respect shown to his body, or perhaps anger at the fact of his execution, but for whatever reason Black Tom was soon back on the streets of Bedford.

The ghost still appears walking down Union Street dressed in a long coat with embroidered buttonholes and high boots. A man who saw the ghost one Christmas in the mid-1990s described Black Tom as reeling down the road as if drunk. Indeed, he thought the figure was that of some reveller in fancy dress who had enjoyed too liquid a lunch. But there was something indefinably odd about the figure, which attracted attention. And then the ghost abruptly vanished. It did not slip behind a parked car or into a doorway. One second it was weaving along the pavement, the next it had gone.

Linked to the legal system in a quite different way is the ghost of Bedford's Mill Street. During the 1960s the staff of the Magistrates' Courts had their offices here in an old Georgian house of grand proportions. The activities of a ghost hit the local headlines when none other than Mr Derek Payne, Deputy Clerk to the Court, had an encounter with the phantom.

Mr Payne was in his office finishing off some work early one evening in December. He thought he was alone in the building, but heard footsteps approach his office, then there were two sharp knocks on the wooden door. Mr Payne got up and opened it, but nobody was there. A hurried inspection of the house showed that he was, indeed, alone in a locked building.

If Mr Payne could not explain this eerie experience, his staff could. They had long known about the ghost, even naming him George, as he marched about a Georgian building. Tall and

THE MAGISTRATES' COURTS IN BEDFORD ARE HOUSED WITHIN A FINE PUBLIC
BUILDING, WHICH THEY SHARE WITH AN ACTIVE PHANTOM.

apparently heavy, 'George' walked the house at all times of the day
or night, opening doors, twiddling door handles or causing
unexplained noises of all kinds.

When the story reached the newspapers, an elderly man who had
lived in the house as a child wrote in to confirm the stories. The ghost
had walked the house during his childhood, though his father had
always refused to talk about it or to accept the phantom's reality.

A final legal haunting in Bedford afflicts the Magistrates' Courts
in St Paul's Square. This ghost is generally reckoned to be a former
Clerk to the Court who dropped dead of a massive heart attack at
work one day. He is never seen, but his footsteps are heard and he
slams doors with unseen hands.

Berkshire

erkshire has the unique distinction of being a Royal County, due to the presence of the mighty royal fortress of Windsor Castle near its eastern boundaries. This did not save it from being seriously reduced in size during the reorganisation of England's historic counties in the 1970s. Large areas of northern Berkshire were lost to Oxfordshire. What remains is largely level land, spreading out beside the Thames and in many places covered with fruit orchards. It is a gentle region, but some of the ghosts are very different.

The road running out of Hungerford towards Andover and Salisbury climbs steeply from the River Kennet, which flows through the town, to the chalk hills. Atop the windswept heights, the road dips and turns as it pushes on across the open countryside. At night, or when dusk is closing in, a phantom coach pulled by four horses may suddenly emerge from out of nowhere and tear along at high speed. The horses are galloping wild-eyed and with flying hooves while the coachman stands at his seat wielding the whip with great ferocity.

This startling apparition is the ghostly echo of an accident that took place here about 200 years ago. Nobody knows quite what happened, for there were no survivors, but a stagecoach carrying passengers north towards Hungerford overturned on the road just before the long hill down into the town. The wreckage was found by a pair of farmworkers walking down into Hungerford for the

THE MAIN ROAD SOUTH OF HUNGERFORD IS HAUNTED BY A PHANTOM COACH.

evening. They hurriedly reported the catastrophe, but there was nothing to indicate what had caused the vehicle to swerve off the road and crash to destruction.

But if the evidence of the phantom re-enactment is to be believed, the coachman was whipping his horses to a frenzy in a mad desire for speed. Why there should have been such a fatal rush, nobody can say.

Another ghost seen here appears only during daylight hours. She is a lady dressed in a long flowing dress who rides a great grey horse. She ambles serenely along as if on a gentle afternoon outing. Who she is and why she haunts the same stretch of road as the madly careering coach is not clear, but local belief has it that the two spectres are closely linked.

* * *

While the A338 may boast two phantoms, it is Windsor that is the real ghostly capital of Berkshire. The town itself is remarkably ancient, but it is dominated, both physically and historically, by the mighty castle. Founded by William the Conqueror almost a thousand years ago, the castle guarded the western approaches to London throughout the Middle Ages. Charles II turned the grim fortress into a royal home, a transformation completed by George IV, who installed truly palatial rooms and buildings disguised as medieval fortifications.

It is none of these monarchs that haunts the castle and its park, but a forester whose startling spectre has become one of the most famous and terrifying ghosts in all England. This is Herne the Hunter, a ghostly presence not to be trifled with. Even soldiers who have served on war-torn battlefields have turned pale and fled when confronted with Herne the Hunter. And the officers know the ghost and his reputation too well to discipline the men for leaving their posts unguarded. Such is the power of this spectre.

Herne lived back in the days of King Richard II in the 14th century. Poor Richard seems to have been one of those people with the gift of doing the wrong thing at the wrong time and of rubbing up the wrong way all the people who might have done him some good and of being best friends with those who were only out for themselves.

In those days everyone hunted to keep the larders stocked. Kings maintained hundreds of staff to run the financial and diplomatic affairs of the country and to keep the royal palaces clean and properly maintained. All these people needed to be fed. At all the royal residences a staff of hunters had to see that there were always plenty of deer, boars, birds and so on available and healthy to be hunted and eaten. They also needed to make sure that there were horses to be ridden, hawks to be flown and dogs to chase and corner prey.

Being a hunter was a skilled and important job for the local lads. There was competition to be accepted by the in-crowd and then to rise to the top with all the perks of good cuts of meat, accommodation in cottages, sturdy uniforms and hand me downs from royalty for the wives and children.

Herne was one such hunter at Windsor Castle. He was good at his job and pleasant in his manner. The king took a fancy to him and whenever Richard came to Windsor and wanted to go out hunting, he always chose Herne to ride with him. Herne showed him where to find the best stags and Herne's two black hounds ran them down and lined them up. When Richard came up to shoot the stags he could scarcely miss.

Herne could flush out a wild boar. He knew where to dig out a badger or start a fox or startle an otter. Instead of using each of the hunters in turn, starting with the longest employed and most important, Richard always chose Herne. Jealousy prevailed.

One day the king, the Earl of Oxford and various others were out hunting a hart. Oxford, like most honest noblemen, despised Richard and wanted nothing more than to see him removed from the throne. The chase went on and on, with the king and Herne outstripping everyone else. When the stag finally turned at bay, only the king and Herne were in the clearing. The desperate stag gored the king's horse and was about to gore the king, when Herne flung himself from his horse, put himself between the king and the stag and took the stabbing horn in his own body.

Even though badly wounded, Herne pulled his knife, killed the stag and generally behaved in the heroic successful way that was getting him hated by everyone – except the king. Richard was of course very upset to see his favourite wounded and bleeding. He rode off looking for help and blowing Herne's hunting horn to attract attention. Soon the Earl of Oxford and some of the other hunters caught up

Richard told them how Herne had taken the blow meant for him and had thus saved the royal life. The Earl of Oxford did his best to seem pleased. The hunters, who were genuinely pleased that Herne had caught a mortal wound, did their best to look sorry.

By this time Herne, though still alive, had fainted. The chief keeper, Osmond Crooke, drew his hunting knife. 'Poor Herne,' he said, 'even if he survives he will never be fit and strong again. It would be merciful to kill him now.' Osmond leaned forward to the approving murmurs of his fellow keepers and hunters and was about to kill Herne, when the king stopped him.

'You cannot kill the man who has just saved my life,' he said.

The Earl of Oxford's comments go unrecorded.

'Why,' went on King Richard, 'I would give a huge reward to anyone who could save Herne's life.'

At those words, a strangely dressed, tall dark man mounted on a black steed rode into the clearing, dismounted and said he would take the king up on his offer. He said his name was Philip Urswick and that he could cure Herne. Richard promised him a huge reward and pardon for any former crimes and the deal was made.

Then to everyone's surprise, this so-called Philip Urswick cut the head from the fallen stag at the place where the head meets the neck. Then he sliced it down from the lower lip to make a wide opening, put it on to Herne's head and bound it firmly into place. He said that Herne would be well again in a month, but that he must be taken to his, Philip's, hut where he would look after him in person. So poor Herne was carried off to the small hut in the middle of Bagshot Heath.

Now all this while Philip could hear the other hunters muttering that they wished Herne had been killed and that they were rid of him. So wanting to make all he could out of the event, Philip asked the hunters what they would give him to finish forever the triumphs of Herne. The outcome was that Philip said he must keep his bargain with the king and Herne would recover, but a spell would be on him, so that he would lose all his former skills.

So it happened. At the end of the month Herne was thin and pale, but on his feet again and seemingly recovered. The king was pleased, gave Philip a purse of gold coins and a silver bugle and the happy hunting started all over again.

However, nothing went right. Herne had lost all his skills. After a while King Richard said he would have to dismiss Herne from his service. Crazed with disappointment, Herne rushed away into the forest. As darkness fell he came galloping back with a chain wound round his arm and the stag's head rammed once more on his head. He had fetched it from Philip's cottage and was now wearing it like a helmet. All the other hunters laughed at him and Herne rushed away once more. A while later he was found hanging by a rope from the mighty oak tree that now bears his name.

When he was told of the death, the king asked the priests to say prayers for the repose of Herne's soul, but they refused, as Herne had apparently taken his own life. When the keepers went back to the oak tree to cut down the body of Herne, it was gone and it has never been found. Anyway the keepers managed to control their sorrow. They had other things to think about as the worst thunderstorm anyone could ever remember descended that night on Windsor, and the oak on which Herne had hanged himself was struck by lightening.

When the storm was over, Osmond, the head keeper, got his old job of chief hunter back, as Herne was no longer there to do it, and the other hunters and keepers got their promotions. King Richard went on his way to another part of the country.

Unfortunately, however, Osmond and the keepers found that they also had lost their powers and were no good as huntsmen. Fearing to lose their jobs, they went to consult Philip Urswick in his cottage on Bagshot Heath. He told them that Herne's blood was on their hands and they must placate him. They were to go back to Windsor and go to consult Herne at the blasted oak where Herne had hanged himself. Back they went, arriving at midnight.

It was pitch dark, but they picked out the oak because of the white part where a branch had been torn off by the lightning. A blue flame like a will o' the wisp danced three times round the tree. Then Herne was standing in front of them, rattling the chain on his arm and with the horned stag's head rammed down on his own head.

Herne screamed with terrible laughter and told the hunters that the next night they must return dressed for the hunt and bring horses and dogs as if they were going hunting with the king. When they did so, Herne greeted them chanting strange spells. He mounted his horse, ordering the others to follow him, and galloped at breakneck speed through the forest towards the marshes, where he halted by a huge beech tree.

Here Herne, dismounting, said magic words and conjured the Devil, who had the features of Philip Urswick.

'Welcome, Herne, King of the Forest,' said the Devil. 'And welcome to you, his comrades and followers,' the Evil One went on, looking at Osmond and the others. 'From now on you must be the band of Herne the Hunter and continue to obey him.'

17

So every night the terrified huntsmen rode out with Herne the Hunter to slaughter the king's deer. Some weeks later King Richard came back again and wanted to know who was hunting and taking all his best deer. The hunters, led by Osmond the chief huntsman, told him their story, and next midnight King Richard insisted on riding out to the blasted oak himself to see Herne the Hunter with the horned stag's head stuck on his head.

Well the story goes that he did see Herne and asked him what it was all about. Herne said that although he had hanged himself he wanted revenge on the other hunters for their behaviour. King Richard agreed with Herne. Next day he had all the other hunters and keepers strung up on the same oak tree on which Herne had hanged himself.

Herne was not seen again in the park during the reign of Richard, but came back again when Henry IV was on the throne. Again deer were hunted. People were hanged, but Herne himself was never caught.

WINDSOR GREAT PARK IS HOME TO ONE OF THE MOST FAMOUS – AND MOST TERRIFYING – OF ENGLISH GHOSTS.

To this day Herne still haunts the park and it is said he will do so as long as any part of Windsor Forest remains. During the reign of Henry VIII when the Earl of Surrey was travelling towards Windsor Castle, through the park and near to the blasted oak, he saw a mysterious blue light and then a weird figure clanking a chain and wearing a horned stag's head on its head. The young earl said his prayers and the figure disappeared.

One night the Duke of Richmond saw a horned figure dressed in deer skins, riding a black horse with an owl flying ahead of him and two black hounds running at his side. He disappeared as he leapt some fencing.

And so the sightings go on and on, right up to the present day.

At midnight at times of the full moon Herne stands under the lightning struck oak tree with the horned stag's head rammed onto his head. He looks towards the windows of Windsor Castle and waits and waits for King Richard to come down and hunt with him, as in the days when he was young and successful and handsome and alive.

WINDSOR CASTLE IS RUMOURED TO BE HOME TO SEVERAL ROYAL GHOSTS, BUT NONE HAS BEEN RELIABLY REPORTED IN RECENT YEARS.

But it never happens and he turns sadly away.

If Herne is the most persistent and terrifying of the ghosts at Windsor, he is by no means the only one. Queen Elizabeth I is rumoured to walk the castle library, though nobody seems to have seen her in recent years, and the ghost of George III in the royal apartments is equally unwilling to put in an appearance as the 21st century proceeds.

*　*　*

Outside Windsor Castle, however, the ghosts are rather more active. The Theatre Royal faces the castle across Thames Street, which runs down the hill to the bridge across the river. The current building replaced the original Georgian structure, which burned down in 1908. A young girl named Charlotte died in the fire, her poor charred body being found by firemen after the flames had been subdued. Her ghost is here still, drifting slowly and sadly around the new theatre.

WINDSOR'S THEATRE ROYAL HAS A QUIET, CONTEMPLATIVE GHOST DATING BACK TO A CATASTROPHIC FIRE IN 1908.

During the days of King Charles II, the professionals who attended the king lived in Black Horse Yard. There these men of some means built themselves solid town houses, which afforded them gracious living, while being close enough to the castle to attend the king whenever needed. Among those living here for generations were the doctors that looked after the royal health. Windsor tradition has it that the good

A MEDICAL GHOST WITH ROYAL SIGNIFICANCE HAS BEEN SEEN EMERGING FROM
BLACK HORSE YARD, WINDSOR.

doctor who attended Charles II on his deathbed became so devoted
to his task that he continues it in spectral form. Whenever the
monarch is dangerously ill, it is said, the good doctor will emerge
from Black Horse Yard, dressed in sombre clothing and riding in an
open coach. He will then gallop off to wherever the sick monarch
happens to be. He was not reported when King George VI died in
1952, so perhaps he has finally given up his job. Time will tell.

Other Windsor ghosts are more active, but less well known. The
ancient Elizabethan House in Peascod Street is haunted by heavy
footsteps, which plod up and down the staircase, though nobody is
ever seen. Similar footsteps are heard at Hadleigh House in Sheet
Street, though these are accompanied by the smell of cloves. Sir
Christopher Wren's house, near the river, has a phantom gentleman
who lurks in the upper floors, though whether it is the great man
himself is unclear.

Bristol & Bath

The two cities of Bristol and Bath were lumped together by the 1974 reorganisation of local government in England – though quite why is something of a mystery. Historically they have been in separate counties (Bristol in Gloucestershire and Bath in Somerset) and their characters have always been distinct. Bristol has been a port and industrial city for centuries, while Bath has been a graceful leisure centre since Roman times.

Such decisions may baffle the human inhabitants of the cities, but the ghosts don't seem to mind. They continue to go about their supernatural business heedless of such mundane matters.

In Bristol, All Saints' church harbours a phantom with a story to tell, though he has remained mute to date. This is the ghost of a monk who has been on duty here for over four centuries. The church was once the main building of a wealthy monastery, but it was closed down by King Henry VIII along with all the other monasteries in England. Hoping that the religious upheavals would prove to be only temporary, the last abbot hid the monastery treasures somewhere in or near the church. When the king's men came calling neither treasure nor abbot was to be found. They searched diligently, but discovered only a few oddments, not the store of gold and jewels they expected.

When one monk remonstrated with the angry soldiers for their supposed impiety, he was struck so hard that he fell back and smashed his head on the pavement. He died soon after, and his

A PHANTOM MONK GUARDS A CENTURIES' OLD SECRET AT ALL SAINTS' CHURCH IN BRISTOL.

ghost began to walk. It is generally supposed that the ghost is guarding the great treasure hidden thereabouts. Whether he is trying to lead people to it, or guard it from prying eyes, nobody is entirely certain. He vanishes almost as soon as he appears.

Another monkish ghost haunts the cathedral in Deanery Road. This mighty church was once a priory, which, like All Saints', was closed down by King Henry. There are no stories to account for this ghost, though doubtless he is a monk from medieval times. He is seen most often in the afternoon, his appearance coinciding perhaps with the time of one of the monastery services.

* * *

A quite different spirit, recalling Bristol's industrial past, haunts Leigh Woods at Clifton. In the 1840s this was a very different place from the quiet wooded park that it is today. The merchants of Bristol had collected £10,000 to build a bridge over the nearby Clifton Gorge and in 1830 a design competition was won by the outstandingly gifted engineer Isambard Kingdom Brunel. In 1831 the foundation stones were laid and work began.

No sooner was the base for the west tower completed, however, than the workmen went on strike. The labour had been drawn from the Bristol Docks and unrest there led to the bridge labour force downing tools. Brunel was furious, but left to work on equally impressive projects elsewhere. Twice the work began. Brunel returned to Leigh Woods to stalk among his workforce, hurrying them along and watching out for signs of unrest. But twice more work was halted. Finally, in 1852 the merchants sold off for scrap the mighty iron chains that Brunel had manufactured so lovingly.

Brunel strode one last time around the abandoned works, then left Bristol. He died in 1859. The following year work began again to Brunel's original plans and the bridge finally opened for business in 1864. Unsurprisingly, the tall, dark-suited figure that strides purposefully through Leigh Woods is identified as Brunel. The ghost was first seen just a few weeks after his death and has continued to be seen off and on ever since.

Sadly he is never seen on the completed bridge, which might bring his ghost some happiness. He walks only at the scene of the industrial unrest that ruined his plans while alive. Many would think that one of Britain's finest engineers and architects deserves better.

* * *

Bath is far more sedate and elegant than bustling Bristol. And nowhere is the town more distinguished than in the Royal Crescent. This magnificent terrace of grand town houses was built in 1767 by the architect John Wood, who was responsible with his son for most of the rebuilding of Bath in the 18th century. The terrace is arranged in a great semi circle that looks out across a large park, which seeps down to the River Avon and the town centre. The houses themselves were grand, but made grander still by being linked together to form one of the great architectural masterpieces of England.

One of the wealthy families who lived here in the 1770s were the Linleys of No 11. Sir Thomas Linley was a gentleman of great wealth and owner of spreading acres. He was also the father of a young, beautiful and spirited daughter – Elizabeth. Around Christmas 1771, Sir Thomas became aware that his daughter was seeing rather a lot of a young man named Richard Sheridan. The youthful Irishman was pleasant enough and an entertaining companion, but his father was an actor and he had barely enough money to pay his tailor's bills. In February, Sir Thomas stepped in firmly to forbid his daughter from seeing the young man who was, quite clearly, not a suitable match.

On 18 March 1772 Sir Thomas came home to No 11 Royal Crescent to be told by the servants that a coach and four had called that morning carrying a message. Upon reading the note, young Elizabeth had ordered her maid to pack a trunk and had fled.

Guessing what had happened, Sir Thomas raced round to the rooms rented by young Sheridan only to find that he had vacated them that morning. It took some weeks, and much effort, for Sir Thomas to find his daughter and by then it was too late. She had married her handsome, witty and penniless Irishman. The details of the confrontation between father-in-law and son-in-law have not been recorded, but it ended with the young couple moving to London to live on a small allowance.

Then, in January 1775, Sheridan saw a play he had written put on at Covent Garden. *The Rivals* was an instant and massive success. Later that year, Sheridan had two more comedies on the London stage. Soon the money was pouring in, and so was the approval of his father-in-law. In 1778, Linley went so far as to buy a half share in the Drury Lane theatre and installed his now beloved son-in-law as chief producer and playwright. Sheridan went on to become a Member of Parliament and a minister in the Navy Office. Linley was totally won over.

Sadly, Sheridan did not enjoy a comfortable old age. His beloved Elizabeth died in 1792 and by 1809 he was in serious financial difficulties. He died in 1816 in poverty alleviated only by the generosity of his friends.

Soon after his death, Sheridan returned to Bath in spectral form. A phantom coach was seen to draw up outside No 11 Royal Crescent. Out stepped a footman, who entered the house, leaving a short time later with a beautiful young woman on his arm. There could be no doubting the identity of the couple. Perhaps they had come back to Bath to relive the first excitement of their loving life together. These days the coach alone is seen rather more often than Sheridan or Elizabeth. It pulls up outside the house, waits awhile and then moves off again.

THE BEAUTIFUL ROYAL CRESCENT IN BATH IS HAUNTED BY ONE OF BRITAIN'S
FINEST PLAYWRIGHTS.

Recently one witness called into the museum at No 1 Royal Crescent and asked which film was being shot in the area. He had seen the ghostly carriage and was so convinced of its reality that he assumed it was a prop for some movie. Needless to say, no film was being made.

So successful was the Royal Crescent, that the Woods then built The Circus a few yards away. This equally impressive terrace takes the form of a complete circle of elegant houses facing in towards a circular garden, broken only by three roads giving access. The houses here are smaller, but just as splendid as those of the Royal Crescent, and they are likewise haunted. The ghost is of an amiable and quiet elderly lady dressed all in black. This lady lived here throughout her long widowhood and died in 1883. A week after her funeral, her family were understandably shocked to see her potter quietly along the pavement and approach the front door of her old house. She has been seen infrequently ever since, walking slowly and with care around The Circus.

* * *

Rather more active is the notorious 'Man in Black', who frequents the area around the Pump Room. Built in 1789 to cater for the genteel folk who came to Bath to take the waters, the Pump Room is a masterpiece of Georgian architecture. The Man in Black, however, seems to be rather older. He wears a short cloak, which billows around him in even the calmest weather, and has a tall black hat. His dress seems to date him to the later 1600s, when Bath was a quiet county town with no sign of the elegant fashionable grandeur it would soon acquire.

Nobody knows who this phantom might be, but all who encounter him agree that he is a rather unpleasant fellow. He has a scowl upon his face and exudes a feeling of malevolence. It is this that attracts the attention of some people, thinking he is in a bad temper and might be best avoided.

THE AREA AROUND BATH ABBEY AND THE PUMP ROOM IS HAUNTED BY AN ANCIENT AND MALEVOLENT SPECTRE.

If the Man in Black is anonymous, the opposite is true of the ghost of Great Pulteney Street. This is the spectre of Richard Earl Howe, one of the great naval heroes of the 18th century. He joined the navy at the age of 13 and commanded his own ship at the early age of just 20. He fought in the Mediterranean, the Atlantic and the Pacific, but his great moment came in 1793 when he led the Channel Fleet to a spectacular victory over the French in a battle that quickly became known as the Glorious First of June.

Wealthy, ennobled and famous, Howe then retired from the sea to his house in

Bath. He seems to have liked it so much that he has stayed on long after his death. He appears in a cocked hat and long cloak, beneath which can be glimpsed the glitter of gold braid and jewelled medals. He was happy here in Bath and appears in his finest outfit.

Another beautifully dressed ghost is the gentleman who appears at the Theatre Royal and the next door Garrick's Head. The haunting dates back to a tragic game of cards held in the Garrick's Head in 1812. Among the men playing was the husband of an actress who was appearing in the Theatre Royal, and the man he suspected of being her lover. The two men had both been drinking and began gambling for increasingly high stakes. Finally the drunken husband suggested they play one last hand for possession of the woman they both loved. The handsome lover agreed, and promptly won. At this the wronged husband drew his sword and before anybody could stop him had plunged it into his rival, killing him instantly. At this point the actress wife arrived, took in the scene at a glance and fled. She was found some time later having hanged herself in the theatre.

Both victims of the tragic evening have returned in phantom form over the years.

RICHARD EARL HOWE, A NAVAL HERO OF THE 18TH CENTURY WARS AGAINST FRANCE, RETIRED TO BATH AND HIS GHOST REMAINS THERE STILL.

Buckinghamshire

'Beechy Bucks', as this lovely county is known to its inhabitants, is both one of the smallest and most engaging of English counties. It takes its name from a tribe or people known as the Bokki who came here during the earliest days of the Dark Ages, when the Angles stormed across the North Sea to take control of crumbling Roman Britain. Roman mosaics, roads and coins turn up time and again when the rich soil of Buckinghamshire is ploughed, but it is these early English who have really left their mark here. It was they who named and built the towns and villages that spread across this county. They took the chalk hills of the Chilterns and planted them with beech, oak and hornbeam when they did not graze sheep upon them.

It is those beeches, in the shape of the famous wood of Burnham Beeches, that take the county into the supernatural. The great 600 acre wood is famously home to hundreds of ancient beech trees of enormous size. In the distant past many were pollarded, but now have been allowed to grow wild for generations, resulting in their having bizarre and twisted shapes. Local legend has it that the pollarding was done by Roundhead troopers acting on the orders of Oliver Cromwell. When Cromwell died, Charles II came back to the throne and ordered that the trees be left to grow wild. Until 1883 the area was remote and rarely visited except by foresters. Then it was purchased by the Corporation of London, which promptly drove a road straight through the woodland.

LEGENDS SWIRL AROUND THE ANCIENT, GNARLED TREES OF BURNHAM BEECHES.

Despite this, the area is deeply atmospheric. As a child, I would spend my summer holidays with my grandmother near Burnham Beeches. She told me that the wood was haunted and that I was not to go there! It has also long been rumoured that the wood is the location of perhaps the most powerful witches' coven in England. Strange tokens and signs that look as if they are left over from witches' ceremonies are sometimes found by ramblers and walkers. The wood is an eerie place.

* * *

Rather less peculiar is the charming village of Haddenham. This little place usually features in guide books because of the spectacular dragon carved onto the medieval font of its church, but otherwise is dismissed with few words. One specialist in church architecture noted the dragon, then unkindly continued, 'Apart from this Haddenham need not detain us. The church was over-restored in 1864.' But no amount of restoration could rid Haddenham church of its ghost.

THE GHOST OF A MURDERED MAN WALKS TO THE CHURCH AT HADDENHAM, PERHAPS TO FIND HIS GRAVE.

One day in 1828 a Mrs Edden of Haddenham suddenly fainted. When she came to, she announced to the villagers who had gathered around her that her husband – then out working the fields – had been murdered. Moreover, she said, she knew who had committed the crime. The villagers were understandably reluctant to believe the vision Mrs Edden claimed to have had, but one man ran off to the fields to check on Mr Edden. He was found dead with his throat slashed. A hue and cry was raised for the alleged killers, who were swiftly arrested and found to be in possession of Mr Edden's rent money. They were duly hanged, though the vision was not given in evidence at the trial.

Soon afterwards, a ghostly Mr Edden was seen walking from the spot where he was murdered to Haddenham church, where he had been buried. He continues to pace the route, undeterred by passing years or the restoration of the church.

* * *

One of the first towns to be founded in Buckinghamshire by the early English was Amersham. It stands beside the River Misbourne, beside a steep hill, and preserves houses, shops and pubs from many different periods. It also preserves its ghosts.

The oldest are to be found at the Chequers pub, just outside the town proper. During the 16th century, religion was a fraught subject. The Catholics persecuted the Protestants, and the Protestants returned the favour. At the Chequers a particularly brutal crackdown led to hauntings by both the persecuted and the persecutors.

A Protestant by the name of William Tylsworth lived in Amersham. Soon his outspoken views attracted the attentions of the Catholic government. Soldiers came to Amersham with orders to arrange the trial and execution of Tylsworth and his supporters. A court was convened, with a jury packed with Catholics and guarded by armed men. The verdict and sentence were a foregone conclusion, so Tylsworth and six of his followers were found guilty and condemned to be burnt at the stake. The night before the execution they were locked up in the stout outbuildings of the Chequers.

Meanwhile, in the bar, the commander of the soldiers was drinking to celebrate a job well done. Named Osman, this was a brutal man. The torture of death by burning was not bad enough for the heretics, Osman decided as he drank. He added a refinement of his own to their punishment. Next day the seven men were taken to nearby Rectory Woods to be burned. At the last moment a screaming teenage girl was dragged forward by Osman. It was

THE CHEQUERS AT AMERSHAM IS HOME TO AT LEAST NINE GHOSTS.

Tylsworth's own daughter. At swordpoint, Osman forced young Joan to light the fire that took her father to eternity.

Delighted by his macabre jest, Osman returned to the Chequers to buy his men more drinks before returning to London. He was destined not to leave alive for as he boasted of his deeds, he suffered a massive stroke and fell dead in the bar.

It is Osman who haunts the bar area of the pub. He is seen most often near the fireplace, dressed in dark clothes and seeming to stare morosely at the fireplace or out of the window. Perhaps he is finally repenting for his deeds. His victims also haunt the building, or more properly the outbuilding where they were locked up before their execution. They are not seen, but heard. From time to time patrons have thought they heard a person calling for help from behind the pub. Those who go to see what is happening find themselves confronted only by silence. The ghosts are beyond any human assistance.

A HAPLESS GROUP OF PRISONERS WHO WERE KEPT LOCKED IN THIS OUTBUILDING CALL FOR HELP MANY YEARS AFTER THEY WERE TAKEN OUT FOR SUMMARY EXECUTION.

Yet another ghost lurks upstairs in a small attic room used by staff for paperwork or to rest between shifts. This lady in white is usually identified as poor Joan Tylsworth, who was forced to kill her own father. She stands quietly by the window for a few seconds, then fades gently from view.

Other pubs in Amersham are haunted, though these ghosts are not encountered as often as are those at the Chequers. The Boot and Slipper is rumoured to have a ghost in the cellar which visits as an invisible man who pushes past staff who go down to change barrels or otherwise care for the excellent ale served here. The Elephant and Castle, meanwhile, is the haunt of a lady wearing a dark brown, or black, dress. She is seen most often in the kitchens and the dining area, but nobody seems to know whose ghost she might be.

* * *

Very clearly identified is the unfortunate ghost haunting the George and Dragon at West Wycombe. This is the phantom of Sukie, a barmaid who lived and worked there in the 18th century. She was, everyone agreed, an extremely attractive girl. And she knew it. She decided that she was destined for higher things than to become a farmer's wife. She turned down the advances of all the local lads, and instead flirted outrageously with the rich gentlemen who stopped at the George and Dragon as the stagecoaches travelled to and from London. Not that she was loose in any way; young Sukie knew that if she wanted to talk one of these rich gentlemen into matrimony she had to keep herself free of scandal.

Finally, one regular traveller of obvious wealth seemed to be very taken with Sukie. After one of his visits, Sukie announced grandly that the man had proposed marriage and that she would soon become his lady.

Three local farm boys were both jealous and annoyed by the news. Sukie had turned them all down and they resented the fact that her grand

THE GHOST OF A FORMER BARMAID HAUNTS THE GEORGE AND DRAGON AT WEST WYCOMBE.

airs and ambitions had won her a rich husband. They decided to play a cruel trick on the hapless girl. They forged a letter from her betrothed, begging her to meet him at the caves just up the road from the George and Dragon. The note asked her to come with all her baggage and dressed for a wedding. The excited girl did as the note said, but instead of meeting her beloved found only the jeering local boys. Angry and furious, she slipped on a stone as she turned to leave, and fell badly.

Suddenly worried by the turn of events, the three young men carried Sukie's senseless body to the George and Dragon. She never recovered consciousness and died next morning.

Within days, Sukie was back. Her graceful form appears dressed as she died – fit for a wedding. She seems to prefer the early morning for her visits, and is usually seen in the kitchens or nearby corridors where she spent most of her life.

Cambridgeshire

C ambridgeshire is a county of two halves. To the south lies a stretch of chalky hills and ridges that have for centuries been the home of scattered villages and patches of woodland. To the north lie the flat expanses of the fens. These vast marshes were drained only in recent times, so there are few villages but many scattered farms and houses. And right at the border between the two lies the county town of Cambridge, more famous for its university than anything else.

The first of several haunted colleges in Cambridge is Christ's College. At any time of the year a visitor to the college may come across a stooped figure shuffling quietly around the Fellows' Garden, most often near the mulberry tree. This is the penitent ghost of a Fellow from two centuries ago, named Christopher Rounds. He killed another Fellow of the college on this spot and, although he escaped the noose, his spirit returns still in the hope of achieving forgiveness.

Also haunted by a Fellow, but for very different reasons, is Clare College. In 1730 Dr Robert Greene died leaving some rather strange conditions in his will. He bequeathed his house in the town and a sizeable share of his wealth to the college on the sole condition that his body be dissected, the flesh and organs burnt and the bones put on display in the college library. At that date the college would have been breaking the law in carrying out his instructions, for bodies had to be given a Christian burial unless

A MOST PECULIAR SET OF INSTRUCTIONS LEFT IN A WILL LED TO THE PERSISTENT
HAUNTING OF CLARE COLLEGE.

they were those of a criminal condemned to hang. Greene's family promptly buried the deceased. Legal wrangles ensued, with the result that in 1742 the good doctor's bones were exhumed, packed in a trunk and sent to Clare College along with the promised money and deeds to the house.

Whether it was because the will took so long to sort out, or because the college promptly lost most of the bones, is unclear. But whatever the reason, Dr Greene's ghost stalks the library where his bones were supposed to rest.

Corpus Christi College can boast three ghosts. The first is the sedate spectre of Dr Butts, the master of the college from 1626 to 1632. This blameless phantom potters about the upper storey of Old Court, where he had his chambers.

Rather more dramatic are the ghosts that lurk in the old kitchens and nearby rooms. Between 1667 and 1693 Corpus Christi had as its

THE GHOSTS THAT LURK IN AND AROUND THE KITCHENS OF CORPUS CHRISTI
COLLEGE RECALL A TRAGEDY FROM LONG AGO.

master one Dr Spenser, whose wife died during his term of office, leaving him with a teenage daughter to bring up. Dr Spenser proved to be a harsh father, so the college staff turned a blind eye when the girl found solace in the arms of an undergraduate. The father managed to find out about the affair and disapproved most strongly of his daughter wasting herself on a penniless young student. He banned the two from meeting, but still the lovers would find a quiet corner where they could be together while the staff bustled about their duties.

One day the pair were exchanging sweet nothings in the kitchen when Dr Spenser himself happened to walk in. The furious father snatched up a kitchen cleaver and ran at his daughter and her companion. The young man fled, while the girl tried to slow her father down. By now in a towering temper, Dr Spenser pushed his daughter aside. Though he did not realise it, she struck her head on the corner of a table as she fell and suffered injuries that led to her death a few hours later. In those few seconds of delay, the student had got away. Spenser angrily searched the building, but could find no trace of the young man. As he calmed down, the staff called him back to care for his dying daughter, and the escaping miscreant was forgotten.

The boy was remembered two days later when a kitchen maid found him in a heavy chest used to store the college's finer tableware. It seemed the lad had leapt into the chest to escape from Dr Spenser but had then been unable to lift the lid from within and had suffocated to death.

Almost as soon as the tragic lovers were buried, the haunting began. Over the years it has faded somewhat in both intensity and frequency. The girl is seen only rarely, while the student appears as only a dark shadow or silhouette fleetingly glimpsed moving across the room. Noises are heard rather more often, usually taking the form of a spectral argument or struggle complete with shouts, oaths, blows and falling furniture.

The Grey Lady of Girton is seen so often that the main staircase at the college goes by the name of Grey Lady Stairs. The ghost is said to be the unhappy spirit of one Miss Taylor. She passed the entrance examination to become one of the very first young women to be allowed to study at the university, but then fell sick and died before she could arrive at the college. Her phantom, it seems, is determined to be here in death when she could not arrive in life.

Also greatly devoted to his college is the phantom of Dr James Wood, who haunts St John's College. When he arrived here as an undergraduate in 1779, young Wood was famously intelligent and talented, but just as famously poor. He could afford neither candles by which to study nor coals to warm his room. During the long winter evenings, he would sit on the staircase to use the lamp placed there by the porters as light by which to read. And on chilly evenings he would stuff his thin coat with straw to keep himself warm. Wood's dedication and intellect paid off and he went on to enjoy a glittering career. Eventually he rose to be Master of St John's College. It is said that as old age caught up with him, Wood would often pause by the spot on the stairs where he had sat as a young undergraduate and pause in thought.

DR JAMES WOOD REMAINS DEVOTED
TO ST JOHN'S COLLEGE, CAMBRIDGE,
CENTURIES AFTER HIS DEATH
(JONATHAN WOODS).

His ghost returns there still. One must wonder what he makes of the dedication of the present day generation of students.

Rather more bizarre is the ghostly disembodied head said to haunt Sidney Sussex College. This is one of the older colleges at Cambridge and it was here that a youthful Oliver Cromwell studied around the year 1620. Cromwell went on to lead the Parliamentarian armies to victory over those of King Charles I in the Civil War in the 1640s, crushed an Irish uprising in 1649 and defeated Scotland in 1650. In 1653 Cromwell was declared to be the Lord Protector of England, using his dictatorial powers to reform government administration, introduce religious tolerance and reorganise Parliament.

After King Charles II was restored to the throne in 1660, he ordered that Cromwell's body be dug up and hanged at Tyburn as a traitor. Cromwell's head was then hacked off and stuck on a pole outside the Palace of Westminster. In 1680 the head was taken down and put on display, after which it disappeared into private hands. In 1960 it was presented to the college for Christian burial by its then owner, Dr Wilkinson. The head was promptly buried in a secret location and a simple plaque put up in the college chapel to record the event.

Almost at once a phantom severed head began to be seen about the college. It is glimpsed most often floating a few feet above the ground in the southern part of Chapel Court. This may indicate where the head is now buried, but some suspect the tales are simply undergraduate inventions.

Similar suspicions surround the ghostly screaming child of Trinity College, the phantom man hanging from the bell rope at Peterhouse and the numerous stories of the supernatural that surround Newnham College.

* * *

Outside Cambridge, to the south, stand the Gog Magog Hills, which rise dramatically from the otherwise flat Cambridgeshire landscape. The hills take their unusual name from the pair of giants who legend says once lived here and are buried beneath the hills. Until the area was incorporated into the landscaped grounds of Lord Godolphin in the 18th century the figure of a large giant was carved into the southern slopes.

On the summit of the little range of hills stands Wandlebury Camp, an ancient hillfort, thought to have been a stronghold of Queen Boadicea's Iceni tribe. It is here that the ghost is to be found. The phantom figure appears only at the full moon and on the few nights that follow. He comes in the form of a gigantic warrior dressed in glittering armour and mounted on a great black charger. He rides around the hillfort, patrolling his domain and challenging any trespassers to battle, then vanishes.

It is said that more than eight centuries ago a Norman knight named Osbert was staying in Cambridge. Hearing of the ghostly knight, he decided to ride out to Wandlebury Camp and challenge the mysterious stranger to battle. The fight that followed was long and arduous, but in the end Osbert managed to unseat his rival. Grabbing the reins of the black charger, Osbert rode off. But as he left the earthwork, the fallen warrior got to his feet and threw a spear that plunged into Osbert's thigh.

Nothing daunted, Osbert rode back to Cambridge. He was put to bed while a surgeon was called and the magnificent stallion was put into the stables. Next day great crowds gathered to look at the beautiful horse, which stood calmly in its new stall. That night, however, the stallion grew restive. It pricked its ears as if hearing a distant call, then kicked down the stable door and galloped out into the wan moonlight. It galloped back to the ancient hill where, presumably, its owner awaited it. Osbert recovered in due course, but every year on the anniversary of the fight on the Gog Magog Hills his wound broke out afresh.

This warrior from the Gog Magogs is not a ghost to trifle with.

* * *

The casual passer-by would be unwise to do anything to antagonise the spectre that lurks around the village of Balsham. The white lady who walks the lane that runs from this village to West Wratting appears harmless enough at first sight, but appearances can be deceptive. If she is approached she will transform herself into the terrifying supernatural beast known as the shuck-monkey. This appalling creature is a gigantic black dog, said to be a favoured pet of the Devil himself, which has the face of a monkey.

However, a witness who saw the white lady recently reported her to be a rather tall figure walking along the road towards Balsham. As he approached in his car, the figure merely turned off the road and vanished. The man slowed down in confusion for the roadside hedges do not allow anyone to pass through them, but the figure had gone.

Perhaps he had a lucky escape.

Cheshire

The county of Cheshire has long guarded the northern end of the border between England and Wales. Even before the two nations existed, the Romans built a mighty fortress here to block the wild mountain tribes from raiding the rich lowlands. The English King of Mercia, Offa, built his dyke here for much the same reason and medieval kings of England dotted the county with castles.

In these peaceful days the fortresses have long been abandoned. There are prosperous farms where the rich red soil is ploughed for arable crops, and the flourishing towns of Tatton, Runcorn and Chester give the county a more modern, urban face.

The ghosts are fairly widespread across the area, but do tend to congregate in the older towns and villages. The ancient county town of Chester boasts perhaps the oldest in the form of a Roman soldier. This ghostly legionary paces endlessly between the ruined Roman tower beside Newgate in the city walls and the excavated ruins of the amphitheatre.

Local tradition has it that he was stationed here soon after the Roman conquest. He fell in love with a local girl and was in the habit of slipping out of the fortress city, then known as Deva, to meet her. Unfortunately a band of tough Celtic warriors got to hear of this and, one evening, followed the girl to her secret assignation. As soon as the decurion appeared, the warriors pounced on him, bundling him into a ditch while they slipped into the city through

AN ENDLESS PATROL OF
SENTRY DUTY IS THE FATE FOR
THE PHANTOM ROMAN
SOLDIER OF CHESTER.

the open postern gate to steal and plunder as much as they could. The soldier broke free and rushed to raise the alarm, but was then cut down by a Celtic sword. His route is presumed to be that along which he ran while trying to save his comrades.

* * *

Scarcely younger is the ghost that lurks around the ruined priory of St John, just outside the city walls. Strangely this haunting began only in 1881, though the ghost itself is much more ancient. It was on 14 April that year that the church tower suddenly collapsed. The priory church had been in ruins for centuries, but even so the crashing to earth of the tower still came as a surprise.

Even more of a surprise was the fact that a ghostly monk at once began to be seen in and around the ruins. So solid and apparently real was he that at first the townsfolk took him for some prankster in fancy dress. Only when one or two witnesses saw him vanish into thin air did it become clear that this was a ghost. The falling tower must have disturbed him in some way, and he has not yet found rest, for this phantom walks the area still.

The ghost at once revived an old legend in Chester. During the later 11th century the priory attracted a tall stranger who begged to be admitted as a reclusive anchorite. He was taken in and allowed to build himself a small cell in which to devote his life to prayer and to study. The man was clearly a nobleman from his bearing and education, while the scars on his body showed that he

THE RUINED PRIORY AT CHESTER IS HAUNTED BY A GHOST WHO MIGHT BE A
FAMOUS HISTORICAL FIGURE.

had fought in more than one battle. In particular he had a jagged
scar down one side of his face and had lost an eye.

Perhaps inevitably gossip circulated that this was none other
than King Harold Godwinson. Harold had been killed at the Battle
of Hastings after being severely wounded in the eye by an arrow.
The good folk of Chester came to believe that their anchorite was
the former king, who had somehow escaped death and now sought
the consolation of a holy retirement after a lifetime of fighting and
ruling. When the man died at a great age, he was buried in the
priory graveyard.

* * *

One of the more active ghosts in Chester is the spectre that haunts
the Blue Bell in Northgate Street. This is, perhaps, appropriate as

the restaurant is the most ancient surviving domestic building in the city. This dates back to the 11th century though it is thought that the oldest part still standing was erected around 1250.

During the Civil War of the 1640s the cellars were commandeered by the Royalist garrison of Chester as an ammunition store – and it was this that led to the haunting. One of the cavalier officers in charge of the gunpowder and bullets stored below took up lodgings in the inn, then known simply as the Bell. He spent several happy weeks there with his lover, a lady of good family named Henrietta.

Then, on 24 September 1645, orders came to muster for battle. The cavaliers filled the street outside as they drew their ammunition, mounted their horses and rode off to do battle against the advancing forces of the Parliamentarian army of General Poyntz. The need was desperate. The Royalist army under Sir Marmaduke Langdale was in retreat after being defeated at Rowton Heath early that morning. Only the swift intervention of the men in Chester could avert disaster.

As Lady Henrietta watched from an upstairs window at the Bell, the Cavaliers trotted off over the cobbled streets and out of the city gates. Hours passed, gunfire was heard and the wounded straggled back. Langdale's army had been saved from catastrophe, but the cost had been high. As evening closed in the Royalist army marched back into Chester. Lady Henrietta peered from her window to search the faces for her beloved. But he was not there. His body lay stark and cold on the field of battle.

Finally a comrade came to the Bell to break the bad news. Henrietta was distraught, locking herself in her room. The landlord tried to talk to her, but she kept the door firmly shut. The following night, when everyone slept, she slipped out of her room and walked quietly to the cellar where she hanged herself.

It is the sad phantom of Lady Henrietta who haunts the Blue Bell to this day. Many passers-by have seen her pale face peering out of the upstairs window. Her strange clothes identify her as being no mortal, though some have taken her for a guest in fancy dress. She has also been seen walking through the restaurant and up the stairs.

Dressed in a beautiful full-length gown of rich velvet, she is unmistakable.

Jonathan Gilliatt, the manager in 2005, confirmed the ghost's existence and that several members of staff had seen her in the past year. Indeed, the sad presence of Lady Henrietta is felt rather more often than she is seen.

* * *

Perhaps Chester's most famous ghost is Sarah, who haunts a shop in Eastgate Street that has been various things, and now sells chocolate. Sarah, the charming and attractive daughter of the shopkeeper in early Victorian times, had the misfortune to fall in love with an utter rogue. The man, a native of Runcorn, jilted the girl just days before their wedding. Distraught, Sarah hurried home and hanged herself in an upstairs room.

The most haunted part of the shop remains the upstairs room where Sarah died, though the cellar is also visited by the ghost and the shop itself is the scene of ghostly disturbances. Gloria, who managed the shop in the 1990s, knew the ghost well. On her first day in the job, she went up to the haunted room on an errand, and came back down singing an old song and holding out her hands as if lifting a heavy silk dress free of her legs. Only when a member of staff asked her if she was all right did Gloria realise what she was doing.

On another occasion the ghostly Sarah caused an electrician to flee the room. The man declared that something was watching him, and could not be persuaded to return. He sent for a mate to complete the job. The ghost seems to have taken a dislike to the more romantic chocolates. Heart-shaped boxes or those inscribed for Valentine's Day are routinely thrown about the shop.

More dramatically, Gloria came to work one day to find a rear window had been forced. She hurried down to the cellar to inspect the overnight safe. The safe door was secure, but scattered around it were burglar's tools. These carried fingerprints and the Chester police were able to find the criminal responsible. Asked why he had fled the shop in such haste that he left behind his tools and fingerprints, the man replied that he had been disturbed by a lady in a long dress. The burglar was convinced he had seen the shop manager, but Gloria was at home and so were all her staff. Only Sarah was in the shop.

* * *

A few miles south-east of Chester lies the village of Bunbury, which has a most spectacular ghost. This phantom dates back to the late 14th century. Sir Hugh de Calveley was a famous knight and one of the most feared warriors in Christendom. He stood 7 feet tall in his armoured boots, with broad shoulders and muscled arms, said to be able to hold an anvil above his head. He had followed King Edward III to victories in Scotland and in France, and had ridden off on adventures of his own in Spain and Italy.

THE CHURCH AT BUNBURY IS DEDICATED TO THE SAXON SAINT BONIFACE, BUT IT IS A MEDIEVAL KNIGHT WHOSE GHOST WALKS THERE.

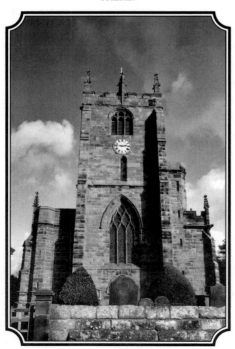

Finally, advancing age caught up with even the gigantic frame of Sir Hugh, and he may not have cared for the capricious new king, Richard II. Sir Hugh came home laden with honours and wealth. He decided to devote some of his money and time to establishing a chantry college. He chose nearby Bunbury, where the church was in poor repair and the priest had recently died.

In 1388 Sir Hugh persuaded the Bishop of Lichfield to appoint Thomas of Thornton to be the new priest and to allow the church to be rebuilt in grand style as a chantry for the Calveley family and as a college. Work progressed rapidly and before he died, Sir Hugh had the joy of seeing his dream fulfilled. He was promptly buried in front of the high altar in the church, his magnificent tomb topped by a life-size alabaster effigy of the giant knight.

But this was not enough for Sir Hugh. The church plays host not only to his tomb, but also to his ghost. Mounted on a magnificent charger and dressed in the rich velvets and furs of a retired knight, Sir Hugh rides along the lane from his old manor at Calveley. He trots up to the church porch, dismounts and walks into the nave, where he vanishes.

The church has two other tombs of note. Sir Hugh would no doubt have approved of the highly decorated tomb for Sir George Beeston. This redoubtable knight took command of the warship *Dreadnought* in the battles against the Spanish Armada in the year 1588, when he himself was over the age of 80. He survived to celebrate the victory and return home to Bunbury. The other tomb may have given the ghostly Sir Hugh pause for thought. It stands today in the north aisle, but originally stood close to that of Sir Hugh in the choir. This is the tomb of Jane Johnson who died on 6 April 1741. It carries a standing statue of the deceased, which does not hold back in celebrating the lady's voluptuous curves. In 1760 the then vicar thought the statue improper and suspected that it was distracting his male parishioners from his sermons, so he had it removed and buried in the churchyard. In 1882 a gravedigger came across the hidden statue, and it was placed back in the church for all to see.

In 1940 a stray stick of bombs landed beside Bunbury church, courtesy of Hitler's Luftwaffe. The blast shattered the roof and crushed the organ. The church has since been repaired. Sir Hugh returns still, so presumably he approves.

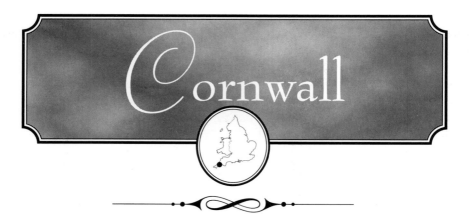

Cornwall

Beyond the Tamar lies Cornwall, once a fiercely independent Celtic kingdom and now a Duchy long since incorporated into England. And yet the Cornish are a distinct people and some Englishmen may feel that they are entering a slightly foreign country when they come into this wildly scenic land. The red on white cross of St George is replaced on boats and cars by the white on black cross of St Pinon, and there are still a handful of people who speak Cornish and erect signs in their ancient tongue.

And when it comes to the supernatural, Cornwall is in a league of its own. There is a greater variety of ghosts, spooks and otherworldly creatures here than in almost any county in the kingdom. Certainly they are packed densely together. And nowhere more so than at the Jamaica Inn at Bolvenor, high on Bodmin Moor.

The inn is famous as the setting for the classic novel by Daphne Du Maurier, but has recently gained fame for its ghosts. Nobody is entirely certain how many there are lurking in this welcoming ancient inn.

Given its naval connections, it is not surprising that one of the ghosts at Jamaica Inn is a sailor. He sits on the stone wall outside the pub as if waiting for a coach or a friend to come along the main road from London to Penzance. If so, he waits in vain. The road outside the inn is no longer the main highway, for a modern bypass takes the hurtling traffic a few hundred yards to the north. Which makes this

THE ANCIENT JAMAICA INN STANDS HIGH ON BODMIN MOOR AND HAS COLLECTED A GREAT NUMBER OF GHOSTS.

a more peaceful place than it would otherwise have been.

The sailor is, however, rarely seen. Far more active is the man in the tricorn hat, who haunts Room No 5. This is on the first floor in the oldest part of the inn. The room dates back to the 16th century, so a gentleman in 18th century clothing would be quite at home.

Glen, the general manager, recently reported, 'He appears by the window, usually in the small hours of the morning. Then he walks across to the cupboard and vanishes. He can muck about with clocks and watches. In the autumn, a lady staying in this room was late to breakfast because her alarm clock had stopped in the middle of the night. That would be the ghost. She didn't see him. But it was him. He likes stopping clocks.

'Down in the bar is a corner table where the old man sits. He has grey hair and is dressed in dark, old-fashioned clothes, which are a bit shabby as if they are wearing out. He just sits there and stares out the window. We don't like him much. We had a psychic in here a little while ago. She said he was dishonest and shifty – a real crook.'

Val worked at the Jamaica Inn for nearly 30 years as the cook and knows the ghosts well. She said that another ghost lurks in the restaurant. 'We sometimes see a smoky shape of a human at the far end. Can't make out if it is man or woman, but it drifts about like it is looking for something. But the real ghost appears in the doorway to the car park. It's a man in a green jumper – yes, modern like. Sort of thing people wear these days. I saw him one night when we kitchen staff was sitting here eating our meal after a big do. He

THIS CORNER TABLE AT THE JAMAICA INN IS THE HAUNT OF AN OLD MAN IN THREADBARE CLOTHING.

THE BEDROOM AT THE JAMAICA INN WHERE A GHOSTLY TRAVELLER IN A TRICORN HAT IS SOMETIMES SEEN.

just stood in the doorway watching us. Then he turned round and walked out to the car park. Gave me a real turn it did. I had locked that door shut just five minutes earlier. And it was still locked shut when we tested it. Very odd.'

There are other phantoms at Jamaica Inn. Some are seen rarely, others are only heard. Some put in an appearance once, then are not seen again. The Ghost Club, founded in 1862, is a much-respected society dedicated to the investigation of the paranormal anywhere in the world. A few years ago they carried out an investigation here and reached the conclusion that the inn is a major centre for psychic energy. Perhaps this is because it stands at the centre of a whole network of ley lines, those ancient lines that link sites of sacred importance.

* * *

A MODERN PHANTOM WEARING A CASUAL GREEN JUMPER APPEARS IN THIS DOORWAY AT THE JAMAICA INN.

But the most famous ghost of Cornwall is a phantom of the open air, and he is particularly active around the village of St Germans. Dando was a monk at the Augustinian priory of St Germans in the Middle Ages. And a very wicked monk he was too. He came from a wealthy family and had taken holy orders to avoid secular justice for one of his many sins. It is possible that he may have originated in northern Italy, where the name of Dandolo is not uncommon.

THE BEAUTIFUL AND ANCIENT CHURCH OF ST GERMANS EARNED NOTORIETY FOR THE BEHAVIOUR OF ONE OF ITS MONKS.

Having arrived in St Germans, Dando saw no reason why an oath of poverty, chastity and holiness should stop his pleasures. He had brought his private money with him and spent it freely on a pack of hounds for hunting, on luxurious foods for his private rooms and on enormous quantities of drink in the local taverns. Nor was he averse to purchasing the attentions of the less respectable local girls.

His debauched lifestyle would have been a disgrace to any normal young man. For a monk of holy orders – it was the scandal of the county.

Retribution was, however, on Dando's heels.

One day he was out hunting with a bunch of his cronies. Luck was with Dando and he caught a fine stag just before noon. The huntsmen halted for lunch, which Dando attacked with his customary vigour and called for ale. Nobody had brought any because it was Sunday – and Dando fell into a rage.

AN EVIL MONK WAS DRAGGED DOWN TO HELL AT THIS SPOT, BUT RETURNS FROM TIME TO TIME TO TERRIFY THE LOCAL POPULATION.

'Damn your Sabbath Day,' Dando yelled. 'Someone fetch me some ale.'

At that moment another hunter appeared, dressed all in black and leading a pack of black hounds. He pulled up alongside Dando and leaned down to offer a large flask filled with ale.

'Had much luck with your hunting?' asked Dando, pointing to his own stag.

'Not until now,' declared the stranger. He grabbed Dando by his collar and hauled him up onto the saddle bow and galloped off. Followed by his great, black hounds, the stranger rode straight into the River Lynher, where the waters closed over him, his hounds and the sacrilegious Dando in a boiling confusion from which steam and fire erupted.

It was not long before Dando came back from the Hell to which he had condemned himself. This time he led the pack of great black hounds as they raced over the Cornish countryside. But he did not hunt stags or deer. Not any more. Now Dando was after the souls of the damned to take back to his master the Devil.

* * *

To be avoided just as carefully as the deadly Dando and his dogs is another phantom hound. The B3254 from Liskeard to Launceston is a pretty road, popular with the motoring tourists who come to Cornwall for just such picturesque drives. It is also a haunted road for this is the path taken by Carrier, one of the more active of the many Lane Dogs of Cornwall.

Carrier is typical of the Lane Dogs. He is big, black and sinister. He is seen loping along the road oblivious to everything in his path. He takes as little notice of modern cars and lorries as he did of horsemen and coaches in days gone by. Drivers have been forced to swerve out of his way to avoid colliding with this great dog with shaggy hair and staring eyes. Carrier's single-minded pursuit of his journey is all that counts.

Unless, that is, somebody is foolish enough to block his path.

A BLACK DOG ENCOUNTERED AT BERIOWBRIDGE IS BEST AVOIDED.

If Carrier is stopped from following his ever-repeating journey up the B3254 he becomes angry. Stopping in his tracks, the dog snarls maliciously. His eyes glow a fearsome red – like hot coals it is said. In most instances this has persuaded the person blocking the path to get out of the way, but the damage has been done. Bad luck will inevitably come to anyone who dares to cross Carrier.

This fearsome dog is seen more at Beriowbridge than at any other spot along the road. He comes down the hill from Middlewood at a steady run and lopes over the bridge before continuing up the hill the other side towards Launceston.

* * *

Very different is the genteel ghost to be found in Luxulyan, a charming village perched on a hilltop and surrounded by the fertile fields for which Cornwall is so renowned. St Cyor, or St Cyr, was a local man, and very holy he was too. He came here when Cornwall was a pagan Celtic kingdom after the collapse of Roman rule in the 5th century. He converted the local people and baptised them in the

THE ANCIENT BAPTISTRY AT LUXULYAN IS HOME TO A PHANTOM FORMER VICAR.

waters of a natural spring just downhill from the modern church. The spring was covered by a stone baptistry in the 15th century. Although the waters no longer flow – having been cut off by the building of the railway embankment in the 19th century – the baptistry remains.

During the 18th century one of the vicars at Luxulyan was the Reverend Cole, a dedicated parish priest who cared assiduously for his flock. Even after he died, his spirit continued to look after the parish. His ghost was seen several times wandering the lanes near the church and the baptistry. Indeed, Mr. Cole was seen more than once in the churchyard itself and appearing from the baptistry.

* * *

Just as beautiful a little village as Luxulyan is Lanreath, but it harbours an altogether more disturbing phantom. The story began back in the 18th century when the vicar of Lanreath was an elderly widower of untidy habits, but some personal wealth. He was, therefore, the ideal target for local matrons with daughters to be married off. In time the vicar chose one such young girl, who was admirably trained in domestic skills and could be counted on to keep a tidy house and minister to the sick.

Then a handsome young curate arrived. Before long village gossip had it that the young wife and the young curate had taken to each other rather too warmly. The old vicar, it was said, was being betrayed under his own roof.

Gossip turned to deep suspicion when the vicar suddenly died. He had been dining with his wife and curate when he realised there was no wine to hand. The vicar headed for the cellar, but fell down the steep stone steps and broke his neck. Did he fall or was he pushed?

The suspicions of the village were enough to drive the young widow back home, but the curate stayed on to minister to the parish until a new vicar arrived. He even officiated at the funeral of the man he was suspected of killing.

And the very day after the funeral, the trouble began.

A huge jet-black cockerel arrived in the village. Nobody knew where it had come from. And it was bigger than any cockerel anyone had ever known. It was also downright evil. It hung about the churchyard and the vicarage. It would burst into raw-edged screeching whenever the curate came into view, puffing its feathers and flapping about in a fit of fury. If anyone approached the bird, they were driven back by a frantic onslaught of pecking beak and tearing claws, which drew blood and inflicted pain. Soon the bird grew bold enough to attack anyone it could reach.

There could be little doubt. This was the spirit of the murdered vicar come back to wreak his revenge.

Finally, the villagers had had enough. They gathered together with nets and sticks, determined to capture the cockerel. They cornered the bird against the churchyard wall and threw their nets. But the bird flapped into the air and escaped through the open window of the Punch Bowl Inn. It flew across the bar and into the oven by the fire. The quick-witted kitchen maid slammed the oven door shut, trapping the irate bird. And there it has remained ever since. None dares to open the oven door in case the vengeful spirit trapped within breaks loose and plagues the village once again.

Debbie, the landlady of the Punch Bowl, still keeps one particular bar door firmly locked shut, especially after the spooky trouble the pub suffered a year or two back. She reported that the door in the corner of the bar is meant to lead to a tunnel that descends down to

A VERY OLD BREAD OVEN AND ONE PARTICULAR BAR DOOR AT LANREATH'S
PUNCH BOWL INN ARE NEVER OPENED ...

the church vault. 'Some of the village lads wanted to explore the tunnel. They came over with torches one evening and I opened the door for them. They went down and found the tunnel extended for some distance, deeper and deeper, but was blocked by a fall. They said they would come back a few days later with shovels and props to clear the blockage and get further down the tunnel.

'Then the trouble began. Stuff was moved around in here. You know, glasses and furniture and stuff. Then I was hoovering one day and the hoover just stoppped. It had been switched off at the wall, but nobody else was in here. Then one of the staff heard voices even though the room was empty and locked at the time. I wasn't having that. I locked that door and blocked it up with a heavy wooden settle. Things quietened down after that. I'm not opening that door again, I can tell you. And I'm not taking chances with the oven either!'

* * *

THE CALM WATERS OF TALLAND BAY HAVE BEEN TROUBLED BY A NOTORIOUS
GHOST SHIP.

Chances should not be taken with the old *Jack Harry* either. This ghost ship is seen from time to time off the south Cornwall coast. A typical tale of this dangerous vessel is from Talland Bay. In the 1890s a moderate gale, nothing special by Cornish standards, swept the area. A small sailing ship was spotted in Talland Bay. It was in difficulty and seemed to be floundering. Fishermen put off from Looe and Polperro to try to rescue the crew and any passengers, but the ship always seemed to be out of reach. Finally a boat from Looe managed to draw up close and a fisherman threw a rope to the men and women on board, but the rope just fell straight through the ship. It was the *Jack Harry*.

* * *

Much more welcoming is the Bullers Arms in East Looe, a fine old pub, formerly favoured by fishermen but now catering for tourists as much as for the locals. It also welcomes its ghosts with some regularity There are three of them.

The first is sensed near the back door of the pub. He often opens toilet doors and the back door, letting them bang shut. He was a bookies' runner in the days when offcourse betting was illegal, and often used to dodge in and out of the pub avoiding the authorities and the landlord, whose wife he was rumoured to be seducing.

The second is a more playful spectre; he frequently stalks the bar, tapping shoulders on the way. He will also rearrange flowers, for which he appears to have a strange liking, and may move the beer or belongings of someone who does not do things the Cornish way, 'dreckly'. He once threw a slice of freshly cut birthday cake across the room in front of many guests.

The third form of phantom activity is associated with the smuggling traditions of Looe. Muffled whispers can be heard late at night when the staff are clearing up the empty bar. These are thought to be the murmurings of spectral smugglers plotting their next enterprise. In the old days of the 'fair traders', as they called themselves, the Bullers Arms was something of a centre for these men. It was here that they would meet to arrange rendezvous points and prices for their contraband. The pub was favoured because it was so small that any strangers, who might be informants for the Revenue men, would have been easy to spot.

THE BULLERS ARMS AT LOOE IS HOME TO NO LESS THAN THREE GHOSTS.

If you tap the slates at the window end of the pool table you will hear the hollow echoes of a former tunnel used by the smugglers to gain access to the beach.

* * *

BURIED IN A VALLEY SLOPE BELOW
PELYNT IS THE NATURAL SPRING SACRED
TO ST NUN, AND BELOVED OF THE
LITTLE PEOPLE.

Generally just as harmless are the piskies of Pelynt, though they should not be antagonised. So the wise visitor will bring a pin or other small piece of metal to leave as a gift for the piskies at St Nun's Well. But one local farmer a couple of centuries back became greedy and forgot to treat the piskies with proper respect. And he suffered for it.

The farmer decided that the stone bowl that catches the spring waters was just the right size to serve as a pig trough at his farm. He brought along a pair of oxen, yoked them up to the stone bowl and set them to heave. The strong oxen dragged the bowl to the farmyard, and the farmer was proud of his work.

The piskies, however, were angry. They loved St Nun's Well as it was and believed they owned the ancient stone bowl. That night they rolled the bowl back to its rightful place at the well. The next day the irate farmer yoked up his oxen and again dragged the stone bowl to his farmyard, only for the piskies to return it a second time.

The third day the farmer again removed the bowl, but this time the piskies had had enough. They came to the farm in numbers and not only recovered the stone bowl, but struck the farmer raving mad and made the oxen so sick they died within the week.

Needless to say, nobody has dared move the piskie-loved bowl since. Like much of Cornwall, it is best enjoyed by visitors as it is.

Cumbria

The scenically magnificent county of Cumbria takes its name from the Celtic people, the Cymry, who made this area their own and held out for centuries against the advancing English who invaded and conquered post-Roman Britain during the Dark Ages. For visitors, Cumbria means the Lake District, where towering mountains are reflected in the calm waters of Windermere, Coniston and Ullswater. But there is more to Cumbria than the Lake District. To the north, rolling hills stretch to the Scottish border at Carlisle. This is an area of rich farmland and gently flowing rivers.

The ghosts of Carlisle itself began to roam only after 1835, when alterations were made to the castle keep that involved taking down an interior wall. Inside the wall was a small chamber some 3 feet wide and 6 feet long. Sitting in a chair was the skeleton of a lady who had been dressed in a long silk tartan shawl or cloak, resting her feet on a stool covered in the same fabric. There was nothing to indicate her identity nor how long she had been there, so the body was taken away for a decent, if anonymous, Christian burial.

This does not seem to have been good enough for almost immediately afterwards a phantom lady dressed in a tartan cloak began to be seen about the castle. In 1842 a newly posted soldier made the mistake of challenging the ghost, thinking it was some unauthorised intruder. When he received no answer, he approached with bayonet raised and was surprised when the lady kept on

A GRIM DISCOVERY AT CARLISLE CASTLE HERALDED AN INTENSE PERIOD OF
HAUNTING.

walking towards him. His surprise turned to shock when she
walked right on to his bayonet, and then through him. The poor
man fled, bursting into the guardroom a gibbering wreck. He never
recovered from the shock and died soon after.

The second ghost of Carlisle wanders the town walls near to the
castle. He is a cavalier wearing a large, plumed hat. It is unclear if
he is connected to the lady at the castle, or to an indistinct and
shapeless figure that is sometimes seen at the cathedral. A favourite
theory is that this is a ghostly monk, but it never seems to appear
clearly enough for anyone to be certain.

* * *

To the south-east of Carlisle, in Geltsdale, there used to stand an
unpretentious manor by the name of Croglin Grange. The house
was for many generations home to a family called Fisher, but in the
1820s was rented out to the Cranswells, two brothers and a sister.
One summer evening soon after moving in the sister was watching
the sunset when she saw somebody, or something, moving in the
graveyard that lay in the valley below. The figure seemed to be

approaching the house, but the sun set and the girl lost sight of whoever, or whatever, it was.

That night she awoke to see an apparition scratching at the windows of her room. The figure was vaguely human, but had glowing eyes and long, claw-like fingers. While the horrified Miss Cranswell watched, the figure unlatched the window and sprang into the room. It grabbed her and bent over as if to kiss her, at which point she screamed and fainted. The brothers raced into the room and gave chase to the strange creature, which fled into the night. The girl was found to have bite marks on her neck.

After various events and alarms, the creature was tracked down to the Fisher crypt at the church. It was lying asleep in a coffin surrounded by the debris of various night excursions. The thing was dragged outside and burned to ashes.

Quite how true this story might be is unclear. Its provenance is dubious and it reads far too much like a horror story relating to Transylvanian vampires to have much to do with the more domestic phantoms of England. But it remains the most famous ghost story of Cumbria.

* * *

Running Croglin Grange a close second for fame among the Cumbrian supernatural is Corby Castle and its Radiant Boy. The castle, located at Great Corby, was for generations home to the Howard family, and the boy is thought to have been one of their number who passed away at a very young age long, long ago.

The ghost was not seen often, and indeed has not been seen for at least 100 years, but was said to be a phantom of unusual power. Those who saw the Radiant Boy were said to be doomed to a life of wealth and power, followed by a tragic and early death. In the 1780s the Howards were visited by Robert Stewart, the unremarkable teenage son of a well-to-do Ulster landowner. On coming down to breakfast, Stewart asked about a servant boy who had come into his room in the night. He said that the experience had been odd for two reasons. First the boy said nothing and did nothing, except to enter and look at Stewart before walking out again. Second the boy had been dressed all in white, which seemed to be reflecting a bright light that Stewart could not see.

The hosts at once recognised the Radiant Boy and reluctantly told their guest about the legend attached to the ghost. The young Irishman laughed and went home thinking no more of the experience other than that his English hosts were a superstitious lot.

Soon afterwards, the Radiant Boy's power became manifest. Stewart was elected to the Irish Parliament in 1790 at the age of just 21. In 1797 he entered the government. After the Irish and British parliaments merged, Stewart entered the British cabinet as Minister for War, rising to become Foreign Secretary in 1812. In 1816, through inheritance, he became Viscount Castlereagh, under which title he attended the Congress of Vienna that redrew the map of Europe after the Napoleonic Wars. It was an impressive career for an apparently unremarkable Irish landowner. But then in 1818 Castlereagh suffered an illness that plunged him into depression and madness. After four years of alternating lucidity and insanity, he killed himself.

His rise and fall followed a pattern that was typical for those who met the Radiant Boy of Corby.

A rare contemporary record of the ghost comes in the form of a diary entry kept by Ernest Rhys, who was renting Corby Castle at the time:

Sept. 8, 1803.—Amongst other guests invited to Corby Castle came the Rev. Henry A., of Redburgh, and rector of Greystoke, with Mrs A., his wife, who was a Miss S., of Ulverstone. According to previous arrangements, they were to have remained with us some days; but their visit was cut short in a very unexpected manner. On the morning after their arrival we were all assembled at breakfast, when a chaise and four dashed up to the door in such haste that it knocked down part of the fence of my flower garden. Our curiosity was, of course, awakened to know who could be arriving at so early an hour; when, happening to turn my eyes towards Mr A., I observed that he appeared extremely agitated. 'It is our carriage,' said he; 'I am very sorry, but we must absolutely leave you this morning.

We naturally felt and expressed considerable surprise, as well as regret, at this unexpected departure, representing that we had invited Colonel and Mrs S., some friends whom Mr A. particularly desired to meet, to dine with us on that day. Our expostulations, however, were vain; the breakfast was no sooner over than they departed, leaving us in consternation to conjecture what could possibly have occasioned so sudden an alteration in their arrangements. I really felt quite uneasy lest anything should have given them offence; and we reviewed all the occurrences of the preceding evening in order to discover, if offence there was, whence it had arisen. But our pains were vain; and after talking a great deal about it for some days, other circumstances banished the matter from our minds.

It was not till we some time afterwards visited the part of the county in which Mr A. resides that we learnt the real cause of his sudden departure from Corby. The relation of the fact, as it here follows, is in his own words:

'Soon after we went to bed, we fell asleep; it might be between one and two in the morning when I awoke. I observed that the fire was totally extinguished; but, although that was the case, and we had no light, I saw a glimmer in the centre of the room, which suddenly increased to a bright flame. I looked out, apprehending that something had caught fire, when, to my amazement, I beheld a beautiful boy, clothed in white, with bright locks resembling gold, standing by my bedside, in which position he remained some minutes, fixing his eyes upon me with a mild and benevolent expression. He then glided gently towards the side of the chimney, where it is obvious there is no possible egress, and entirely disappeared. I found myself again in total darkness, and all remained quiet until the usual hour of rising. I declare this to be a true account of what I saw at Corby Castle, upon my word as a clergyman.'

THE MAIN HOUSE AT CORBY CASTLE IS HOME TO A STRANGE AND
TROUBLING SPIRIT.

The current owner spoke of a haunting that continues with great regularity. The ghost appears in a bedroom on the third floor known as The Boudoir. This is the apparition of a distinguished-looking, balding gentleman of upright, military bearing who sits in a chair in a corner of the room drinking quietly from a glass. The description fits almost exactly that of a retired army officer who was allowed to live here during the 1930s, occupying the room in question. He was in the habit of taking a nightcap up to his room when he went to bed.

'All sightings are described as friendly,' says the current owner who has had his own experience with the supernatural at Corby Castle. The castle is open by appointment only rather than at regular opening times.

* * *

At Thirlmere there is not just a single ghost, but a whole host of them, together with a phantom castle. The Castle Rock is steep and sheer, and remained unclimbed until the 1920s. Despite this a castle is seen on top of the rock from time to time, and it seems that some great celebration is taking place to judge by the banners and numbers of people that are present. There is no one left alive who can tell the story of who these people are.

* * *

Another mass haunting took place at Souter Fell, a hill near Saddleback. In 1735 two farm workers walking home in the early evening were startled to see a column of marching men coming over Souter Fell. The men were five abreast and dressed in a colourful uniform. Though they were a mile or more distant, the soldiers and even a couple of officers riding alongside were clearly visible.

Thinking that an army was approaching and fearing that an invasion by the French had taken place, the men raced to give the alarm. Messengers were dispatched to the nearest town and riders

sent off to keep watch on the mystery army. But nothing could be found. The soldiers had vanished.

Three years later, they were back. Again it was early on a summer's evening when the column of men came marching down Souter Fell. This time no less than thirty people saw the soldiers, and one man timed how long they were in sight. It was two hours. In 1745 the

A TOWERING PHANTOM CASTLE HAS BEEN SEEN AT CASTLE ROCK HIGH ABOVE THIRLMERE.

phantom army was back a third time, sparking fears of a Jacobite uprising in support of Bonnie Prince Charlie, then raising troops in Scotland.

It is not recorded that any army has ever come to grief on Souter Fell, so there is no explanation for these ghostly goings-on.

* * *

Equally mysterious are the events that led to the haunting of Greystoke Castle, west of Penrith. In the 17th century this castle was owned by Charles Howard, Duke of Norfolk, who came here two or three times a year to enjoy the good hunting to be had on the estate. He usually brought a group of friends and relations with him. On one visit a guest vanished without trace. His bed had been slept in and his clothes lay neatly folded, but of him there was no sign. Diligent searches turned up no clue as to the man's fate, but his ghost soon returned. It walked the chamber where he had slept and was seen descending the stairs and leaving the building.

The ghost is still witnessed from time to time, but if it seeks to lead a human to solve the mystery of the disappearance it walks in vain, for nobody has yet been brave enough to follow.

* * *

A phantom haunts Irton Hall at Holmrock, in the north of the county. This lady in black is Lady Ann Lamplugh. In 1464, during the Wars of the Roses, a man arrived unexpectedly at the gates of Irton Hall. He was dressed in a torn coat and was mounted on an exhausted horse. He was alone, apart from a single servant. The man announced himself to be King Henry VI and asked for a bed for the night, as he was fleeing for his life from the Duke of York. Lady Ann did not believe the stranger and turned him out into the gathering darkness of a rainy night.

It was not until some days later that news arrived from Muncaster Castle that King Henry had arrived there after spending a night alone in the rain-sodden forests. He had been fleeing the disastrous Battle of Hexham. Lady Ann was distraught at her mistake. She took to her bed in depression and died soon after. Presumably her ghost walks the castle seeking forgiveness for her act.

* * *

Muncaster Castle, near Ravenglass, has ghosts that are the victim of a crime and its perpetrator. Sir Ferdinand Pennington of Muncaster Castle had a servant named Tom the Jester. Although Tom's official job was as an entertainer, he was a big, tough man with few scruples about the tasks he carried out for his master. When a carpenter from the local village became too familiar with Sir Ferdinand's pretty daughter, Tom was sent to teach the man a lesson.

Sir Ferdinand later claimed he had meant the carpenter to receive a beating, but in fact Tom administered a hunting knife between the ribs. The 'jester' then cut off the man's head and carried it back to

MUNCASTER CASTLE, ONE OF THE PREMIER STATELY HOMES OF CUMBRIA, HIDES A DARK SECRET FROM PAST TIMES. (© *MUNCASTER CASTLE*)

THIS PROTRAIT OF THE JESTER TOM AT MUNCASTER GIVES LITTLE CLUE TO HIS MURDEROUS NATURE. (© *MUNCASTER CASTLE*)

Muncaster Castle as proof of his work.

To this day the headless figure of a man walks at Muncaster Castle, and the phantom of Tom the Jester is also seen, though more rarely – but his spirit continues to play tricks on people here.

Hauntings often occur in the Tapestry Room. Visitors complain of disturbed nights, hear footsteps outside the room, see the door handle turning, and the door opening although nobody is there. A child is frequently heard crying towards the window end of the

THE MUCH-HAUNTED TAPESTRY ROOM AT MUNCASTER CASTLE IS NOT A PLACE WHERE MANY PEOPLE WOULD CHOOSE TO SLEEP THE NIGHT.
(© *MUNCASTER CASTLE*)

room, and sometimes a lady is heard singing, comforting a sick child. Visitors have also felt cold in the room for no apparent reason.

Other stories concern the 'Muncaster Boggle' or white lady who haunts the gardens and roadways around Muncaster. She is supposedly the ghost of Mary Bragg, a young girl murdered in the early 1800s on the road near the Main Gate. The castle is open to the public and organises all-night ghost hunts for those brave enough to indulge.

* * *

Also open to the public is Lanercost Priory, a partly ruined monastery with an attractive line in local crafts. These days it is quiet, but in the 19th century the ruins and surrounding area were famous for the boggles. These little people were known to play numerous tricks on the hapless humans who crossed their path, though they could be deterred by a Bible or silver crucifix. They have not been seen much in recent years, allowing visitors to enjoy the peaceful rural setting of this lovely old building.

THE RUINS OF LANERCOST PRIORY WERE ONCE HOME TO MISCHIEVOUS SPIRITS.

Derbyshire

Derbyshire is famous for its scenic Peak District. This is now a National Park, crisscrossed by public paths and subject to the sorts of rules and regulations that are loved by some and hated by others. The scenery is nevertheless spectacular, with craggy hills and bleak moorland. In some valleys lie cosy towns that have found renewed vigour from producing bottled spring water.

The largest town in the county is, by a wide margin, Derby, which industrialised rapidly in the 19th century and is still a major centre for business and population – and for ghosts. The town began as a fortified Roman camp and was favoured by the Vikings, who made this one of their five major settlements in England. It received a market charter in 1154, and the beautiful St Peter's church two centuries later, but thereafter little of note happened until the wild Highland clans of Bonnie Prince Charlie arrived in 1745, only to turn back towards Scotland and eventual defeat.

The most ancient ghost in Derby dates back to the very earliest days of the town's history. At Chester Green pedestrians out late at night have heard the sounds of a marching column of men, complete with jingling armour and stamping feet. Usually the sound swells and fades as if a body of invisible troops has marched past. Just occasionally, however, a ghost is seen. Though the sounds are of a number of men, only one appears. He wears chain mail and an iron helmet, with a square shield on his left arm. He is usually said to be a Roman legionary.

Almost as ancient is the black monk who haunts the aptly named Friary public house in Friar Gate. So frequent are the visits of this phantom cleric that the pub has taken to calling itself The Scream. Not that the ghost is particularly frightening, as with most ghosts, he is more likely simply to startle people than terrify them. He is seen most often in the corridor behind the bar, which is frequented by gentlemen on their way to spend a penny.

Slightly less ancient is the ghostly gentleman wearing a powdered, curled wig and dressed in rich velvet who walks up to the cathedral, pauses a moment and then enters only to vanish abruptly. Not far away the sounds of invisible men have been heard shouting, clashing steel together, and all against the background of neighing horses and pounding hooves. These are both thought to be ghostly echoes of the visit here by Bonnie Prince Charlie and his ferocious army of Highland Scots.

As heir to the Catholic Jacobite claim to the thrones of Scotland and England, young Charles Edward Stuart had invaded Scotland early in 1745 with a handful of men. He raised the Highland clans and marched south, brushing aside the government army sent against him. As he advanced into England, the Prince found that the English refused to rise up and follow him as he had hoped and expected. Instead they shut their doors and awaited the arrival of a new and much larger government army gathering around London. Charlie reached Derby before reality dawned on him. No French invasion of southern England had taken place and he was heavily outnumbered.

After attending a service at the cathedral, Bonnie Prince Charlie mustered his men and began the long retreat to Scotland. His campaign would end in defeat. He would spend the rest of his long life as a wandering king without a kingdom, begging support and help from other monarchs while drifting into despondent drunkenness. His followers were lucky if they escaped with their lives.

No wonder the ghosts of these would-be victors return to the spot where their hopes of success turned to dust.

A century after the Scots left Derby, a dedicated gardener was tending the lawns and flowerbeds of Pickford House. He is there

BONNIE PRINCE CHARLIE AT THE HEAD OF HIS ARMY. THE SCOTTISH PRETENDER'S STAY IN DERBY HAS LEFT ITS GHOSTLY MARK ON THE TOWN.

still, causing visitors who come to admire the gardens to jump in alarm. Also remaining behind from Victorian days is the lady who haunts the Assembly Rooms. She is a curious spectre, for she is only ever seen from the waist upwards, but for good reason. The Assembly Rooms that she would have known were gutted by fire in the 1960s and almost entirely rebuilt. The corridor along which she walks has a floor two feet higher up than it was in the old building.

In Sadler Gate is a public house that has changed its name in recent years to match changing fashions for Irish theme pubs or trendy cocktail bars. But it was known as the George Hotel when a grisly discovery was made here just after the Second World War. Some damaged floorboards were being replaced, when a human skull was found beneath them. The skull was pronounced to be that of an adult woman, which is odd, as it was the ghost of a man that promptly began appearing.

Dressed in a long blue coat with bright golden buttons, the man has long hair cascading to his shoulders. He has been noticed upstairs in the corridor as well as in the downstairs bar where the skull was discovered. Although not seen in the kitchen or beer cellar, he seems to be active there. Beer taps have been turned off, or on, by unseen hands and kitchen items frequently go missing for a few days only to turn up again.

Who the man in blue might be and how he is connected to the skull remain absolute mysteries.

* * *

Outside of Derby, perhaps the most active ghost is the phantom pedlar of Darley. This unfortunate man was murdered beside the churchyard in the early 17th century for the money that he was carrying home after a successful journey selling his wares in the villages of Derbyshire. His spectre stumbles down the lane as if badly wounded, and more than one person has hurried to see if they can help, only to find that the supposed person vanishes into thin air. The lane has been aptly renamed 'Ghost Lane' in recent years.

* * *

Seen less often is the phantom – or rather phantoms – that lurk at the Castle Hotel in Castleton. These ghosts are linked to a minor tragedy that took place here in late Victorian times. A local couple were due to wed and had hired a room at the Castle Hotel, in which to entertain their guests after the service. Quite what happened is unclear, but the girl was jilted at the altar, and returned here to weep while her errant fiancé fled the town never to return. Unlike other such tragedies that end in hauntings, the girl did not come to a swift, untimely end but got over her heartbreak and went on to live an apparently contented life.

But soon after the bride's death in middle age, her ghost began to walk at the Castle Hotel. She appeared as she had done on her wedding day, full of the bloom of youth and dressed in her long white dress. Perhaps she had not got over the blow after all, and in death returned here to mourn her loss.

Whether the spectral man in a smart suit and accompanied by a ghostly dog has anything to do with the lady in white is unclear. He does not appear with her, but at other times and less frequently. Perhaps he is to do with some other incident. He is just another of Derbyshire's many ghosts.

* * *

Rather more malevolent is the spectre that lurks beneath Swarkestone Bridge. This gruesome monster is said to demand three lives each year, or it will cause the river to flood and carry away the wealth of the village. The creature is now powerless, the locals say, for the bridge was built by two young sisters of Swarkestone who saw their lovers drowned when crossing the ford that stood here in the 14th century. The girls inherited a fortune and paid for the construction of the bridge. They put a small chapel on top of one of the bastions and provided enough money for prayers to be said weekly by a priest. The religious side of the bequest was abolished in the Reformation, but the more material side of it survived until 1795 when the mightiest flood of the Trent ever known washed away the central span. New moneys had to be found to replace the span and the girls' old legacy was not enough.

A VICTORIAN VIEW OF THE BRIDGE AT SWARKESTONE, WHERE A MOST DANGEROUS PHANTOM IS BEST AVOIDED.

Devon

The county of Devon is a land of two parts. There are the grim, windswept uplands of Dartmoor and Exmoor, which contrast starkly with the 'Red Lands', those lowland areas boasting a rich, red soil that is among the most fertile in England. For many centuries this was border country. The Romans built a mighty fortress at Isca, now Exeter, to serve as a base for the army that kept order among the Celtic peoples of the area. Centuries later the invading English shifted the border to the Tamar river, fighting numerous wars with the Cornish until an accommodation was reached around the year AD 900.

Warfare has returned to the gentle Devon countryside periodically since, and one clash has left its ghostly mark. The little town of Chagford lies tucked away in a fold of Dartmoor, which offers soft rural scenery that contrasts spectacularly with the wild, desolate splendour of the high moors. Chagford was formerly one of the four stannary towns of Devon, where the prosperous tin-mining industry, once the source of the town's wealth, was regulated. The town itself is clustered around the ancient Market Square.

It was this wealth that brought the dashing young nobleman and poet Sydney Godolphin to Chagford in February 1643. These were turbulent times for the Civil Wars between the Roundheads who supported Parliament and the Cavaliers who supported the king were just beginning. The king had charged Godolphin with securing all government property in Devon before Parliament could get its hands on the wealth and weapons at stake. As a stannary town, Chagford had a fair amount of government money and stores, so Godolphin rode into town at the head of his small band of Royalist cavaliers.

Unfortunately for Godolphin, the local Roundheads had thought of the same idea. They had arrived in Chagford a few minutes earlier and were waiting for the Cavaliers. As the Cavaliers rode into the Market Square, the Roundheads opened fire. In the short, but savage fight that followed, Godolphin was unhorsed. He held off the Roundheads attacking him with skilful swordplay and backed into the stone porch of the Three Crowns, where the walls afforded him some protection. He was not safe enough, however, and a musket ball brought him down.

THE STOUT STONE PORCH OF THE THREE CROWNS AT CHAGFORD WAS THE SCENE OF A CIVIL WAR SKIRMISH THAT CUT SHORT THE LIFE OF A POET.

The wounded man was carried into the Three Crowns, but nothing could save him and he died a short while later. His body was taken away by his wealthy family to be buried at Okehampton, but his ghost remains. The phantom Cavalier is seen most often in the porch or the room where he died, but he has been spotted in all parts of the hotel from time to time. One guest who saw him was an amateur artist who did a quick sketch of the ghost, which can be seen at the Three Crowns.

* * *

The charming little town of Totnes stands on a hill above the River Dart. The hill is crowned by the ancient castle

THE SKETCH OF THE GHOSTLY CAVALIER AT THE THREE CROWNS IN CHAGFORD.

that guarded the bridge over the river, and it is around this castle that the town has grown. The most famous ghost, and the most often seen, dates back well before even the castle. It is a grey lady who loiters around the ancient spring of fresh water known as the Leech Well. Today the spring is tucked away down a footpath, but time was when this was the main source of water for the town.

The Grey Lady of Leechwell may materialise beside the well at any time of day or night. Often she slowly takes on solid form, only to fade away again a few minutes later. Some believe that she is no phantom of a mere mortal, but the shade of the ancient goddess of the well. Certainly this is a magical place. The three stone basins into which the water splashes are said to cure respectively snakebite, skin disease and eye problems.

When the Grey Lady walks away from the Leech Well, she goes slowly downhill to Moat

THE LEECH WELL IN TOTNES IS HOME TO WHAT MIGHT BE THE OLDEST GHOST IN DEVON.

Hill and then Warland. There used to be a small chapel in Warland that dated back to medieval times, so perhaps she is walking between the two holy places: from her sacred well down to the chapel. Some claim she was a nun who was particularly devoted to the needs of the sick who came to the well in search of a cure.

* * *

Another grey lady haunts Torre Abbey, not far from Totnes in the heart of Torquay. The welcoming town draws in thousands of holidaymakers during the summer, and quite a few have seen a ghostly female figure walking the grounds of the old abbey, now a museum. This unfortunate girl was a Spanish lady who dressed as a man to accompany her lover, an officer in the Spanish Armada of 1588. The task of the Armada, with its vast array of warships and transports, was to conquer England. The officer was one of those who would have been responsible for organising the administration of the kingdom, once it had been conquered, and he was expected to be away from Spain for years. So his lover chose to follow him.

Unfortunately, the ship on which the two sailed was badly damaged in the fighting with the English ships. It was captured and brought to Torbay, with the crew held prisoner in the large barn of the abbey. The poor girl had been injured badly in the fighting and passed away in the barn. Only then did her lover reveal the truth. The girl was quickly dressed in lady's clothing for her burial. So far from home, her spirit seems to be restless. It flits around the scene of her death and is seen with some regularity.

* * *

Rather less harmless is the Blue Lady of Berry Pomeroy Castle, which stands between Torbay and Totnes. The ghost here has a sad story behind her, but a vengeful and violent presence. In life the Blue Lady was the daughter of one of the de la Pomerai lords who owned this castle for 19 generations to 1548 and who gave their name to the place. While still a young teenager she gave birth to a

THE PRETTY GHOST OF BERRY POMEROY CASTLE IS BEST AVOIDED, FOR SHE IS A
VENGEFUL SPIRIT INTENT ON LURING MEN INTO TRICKY SITUATIONS.

baby, local gossip had it that the birth was the result of an
incestuous relationship with the girl's brutal father but that is not
certain. Whoever the father was, the girl was distraught and
unhappy. One tragic night she smothered the baby then threw
herself from the battlements, being found dead the next day.

The poor girl found no peace in death, but returned to the castle
in spectral form. She was seen first on the day her father died and
returned thereafter whenever a male resident of the castle was to
die. But she is not just a harbinger of death. Her hatred of men
seems to motivate her to lure visitors to dangerous parts of the ruin,
or to lead them away from their companions.

This ghost is that of a pretty young girl dressed in a long blue
dress, sometimes described as being purple. Few people get close to
her, but one who did so in the 1990s said that there was something
quite disturbing about her eyes. They were somehow blurred, and
it was impossible to focus on them clearly. This particular witness
was so taken aback that he did not follow the ghost any further.
Given that others have been lured towards sheer drops and
crumbling masonry, he had a lucky escape.

* * *

In the late 19th century the body of a woman, dressed in rich clothes was washed up on the beach near Teignmouth. There were no documents to indicate who the unfortunate lady might be, though her clothes seemed to be of foreign origin. It was presumed that she must have fallen overboard from a ship, or that a vessel had foundered for some reason. It was confidently expected that, sooner or later, a lady would be reported missing. In the meantime, the body was put in a coffin and buried in an unmarked grave in the churchyard. Time passed and weeks became months, but no report of a missing lady or foundered vessel reached Teignmouth. The identity of the lady remained a mystery.

Perhaps this is why her phantom came back to haunt the stretch of beach where she was found. Walking disconsolately along the shoreline, the richly dressed lady in a long gown will pause occasionally to stare out to sea. Perhaps she is waiting for somebody who never arrives.

*　*　*

Equally disconsolate are the shades that lurk near the old burial ground at Princetown, high on Dartmoor. These ghostly men are never seen very clearly, but are glimpsed moving silently amongst the gravestones and pausing to stare out across the wastes of the moor. Locally it is said that these are the phantoms of the dozens of French prisoners of war who died in captivity here during the Napoleonic Wars. Far from home and no doubt miserable in captivity, they lie buried in unmarked graves. No wonder their spectres wander here.

Dorset

As befits a county with so ancient an appellation, Dorset manages to retain much of its historic character, while yet moving happily into the 21st century.

The thundering traffic of the modern A303 clips the northern edge of Dorset, but the county is otherwise untroubled by through traffic and travellers. This is still a region that is seen only by those who go there, not by those passing through. And there is much to see. The coastline is beautiful while the hills offer some splendid walking and the towns are as charming and historic as any in England. The ghosts, on the other hand, are a more dramatic lot.

The spectacular ruins of Corfe Castle are perhaps the most magnificent in England. The castle was built on a steep hillock where it could dominate the road leading inland from the great natural port of Swanage. The present ruins are generally 12th to 14th century in date, lying much as they were left by the military engineers of Oliver Cromwell. But the site has been fortified for much longer than that, and one of the ghosts dates from the earlier days of Corfe.

In AD 978 this was a fortified manor belonging to Queen Elfrida, widow of King Edgar, who had largely reunited England after the devastations of the Viking wars. In that year she was visited at Corfe by the new monarch, her stepson King Edward. Only a teenager, Edward was dashing, handsome and

THE RUINS OF THE MUCH-HAUNTED CORFE CASTLE TOWER OVER THE
SURROUNDING COUNTRYSIDE.

astonishingly tactless. He was loved by some, and detested by
others in equal measure. Among those who loved him was the
Archbishop of Canterbury – largely because the young king had
lavished gifts on the Church to buy himself out of the trouble
with God that his constant womanising and drinking was likely
to be storing up. Among those who detested the young king was
Queen Elfrida. She had a son by old King Edgar who was heir to
the throne, but only so long as the new king did not father a
legitimate son.

Young Edward seems to have been quite unaware of any likely
trouble when he rode in through the gates of Corfe on a summer's
afternoon. He had been out hunting and, on the spur of the
moment, had decided to stop off to see his stepmother and half-
brother. An outwardly jovial meal was enjoyed, after which King
Edward mounted his horse to leave. As he did so, Queen Elfrida
sent forward a servant carrying a last goblet of wine, but also
carrying a hidden dagger.

As the king leant forward to take the wine, the treacherous servant stabbed him in the chest. The king sprang back and spurred off at high speed. But he had been badly wounded. His galloping steed got no further than the village square just outside the castle when Edward fell from his horse to lie dead on the cobbles. Queen Elfrida gloated over the corpse, and hurriedly had her own son crowned king. The new king did not do well out of the crime that put him on the throne. Although he swore consistently and on the holiest relics in the kingdom that he was entirely innocent of his mother's crime, nobody really believed him. Nor did the nobles of England ever trust this new king. When he called on them for taxes, they avoided paying. When he called on them to march to war, they found reasons to stay at home. And so the new king became known to history as King Ethelred the Unready.

The unfortunate King Edward, meanwhile, was buried at Shaftesbury, where the Church declared him to be a martyr. It is generally reckoned to be the ghost of this murdered young man who gallops out of the castle, across the bridge and into the village square where he abruptly vanishes. This particular ghost is heard

A PHANTOM HORSEMAN GALLOPS OUT OF THE MAIN GATEWAY OF CORFE CASTLE, ONLY TO VANISH SECONDS LATER.

more often than he is seen. And when a witness does glimpse the galloping ghost, he passes by so quickly that no clear description can be given. He is a man on a large, black horse who dashes by at full gallop, and not much more can be said.

Seven centuries after the death of King Edward, violence returned to Corfe Castle and again the trouble gave rise to a haunting. When the English Civil War broke out in 1642, the castle was home to Sir John Bankes, Chief Justice to King Charles I. Unsurprisingly, Sir John declared for the king and began fortifying his home. Corfe was in a strategic position. The nearby ports of Swanage and Poole had both declared for Parliament, but Corfe blocked the road inland from one and raids from Corfe could be launched on the other. If Parliament were to use either port, its armies would have to capture Corfe.

After a few abortive attacks and raids, the siege of Corfe began in earnest in 1645. By this time Sir John was dead and the king's cause in serious trouble. But Lady Bankes was undeterred. Her husband's dying wish was that she should hold the castle for the king, and that is what she was determined to do. The mighty stone walls of the medieval fortress were vulnerable to the then new artillery, but only if the enemy brought up their heaviest guns. Even then, the hastily constructed earthworks on the lower slope of the hill could hold out.

The Parliamentarian army tried artillery, then mines and finally an armoured wagon carrying a cannon that they dubbed 'The Boar'. Nothing worked and the fortifications of Corfe remained impregnable. Conditions inside the castle were not, however, pleasant. Food was short, disease was rife and morale was battered by the news of Royalist defeats elsewhere. Finally, in February 1646, a man named Pitman opened the gates and allowed in the enemy. Lady Bankes was dragged down to the little bridge below the walls of her fortress, where she was forced to hand over ownership of the castle to Parliament.

The castle was then systematically ruined by the vengeful Parliamentarians. Determined that it should never again be used against them, they blew down the fortifications with gunpowder.

Angered by the long siege, they went beyond their orders and rendered the domestic chambers uninhabitable by setting them on fire. Lady Bankes was taken from the area, though Parliament soon released her and allowed her to return to her estates outside Corfe. When King Charles II came to the throne in 1660, he restored property confiscated by Parliament to its previous owners. But it was too late for Corfe. The castle was a roofless, derelict ruin and the gallant Lady Bankes had passed away.

She was not quite gone, however. Her ghost returns to walk the castle. She is seen most often down by the bridge where she was forced to surrender, but has been glimpsed walking about most parts of the castle. Those who have spotted her describe a lady in a long, pale coloured dress who walks with firm and determined stride. This is appropriate, for Lady Bankes was clearly a firm and determined lady.

* * *

West along the coast from Corfe stands the small town of Lyme Regis. The town is famous for its scenic harbour, protected from the crashing waves by the stone breakwater known as the Cobb. The port was busy throughout the medieval period, and by the later 18th century was a fashionable seaside resort for gentry from as far afield as Bath – it features in the writings of Jane Austen.

It was, however, politics that led to the best known haunting at Lyme Regis. In June 1685 a handsome young man landed here, accompanied by a body of armed men. This was the Duke of Monmouth, the illegitimate son of the recently deceased King Charles II. He brought with him a number of documents that, he said, proved that he was not illegitimate at all but was both legal and the heir to the thrones of England and Scotland. The young man's uncle, King James II, was unimpressed and began mustering a royal army to send against him.

Monmouth was counting on the fact that he was both Protestant and popular, while James was Catholic and unpopular. As he strode from the Cobb up the main street of Lyme, Monmouth was loudly

A HANDSOME GHOST RIDES DOWN THIS LANE OUT OF LYME REGIS, MOUNTED ON
A FINE WHITE CHARGER.

cheered. After pausing just long enough to send out messages announcing his arrival and calling for support, Monmouth mounted a fine white charger and rode north towards his destiny. Unfortunately for Monmouth the few West Country men who joined him were no match for the royal army. The rebels lost the Battle of Sedgemoor; Monmouth was captured and executed.

The ghost of the handsome young duke mounted on his white charger has been seen quite often riding north from Lyme Regis along the road to Taunton. His shade previously rode up from the Cobb, but in recent years he has not been seen in the town itself. A woman who saw the ghost one evening in the 1990s reported that he seemed to be waving, as if acknowledging the cheers of an invisible crowd. Perhaps the ghost comes back to Lyme to relive happier days.

After the defeat of Monmouth, King James ordered his most loyal and trusted lawyer, Judge George Jeffreys, to take charge of the trials of the rebels. He began his grim work at Lyme. Twelve men from the town had been captured in arms, and Jeffreys was determined that they would all hang to set an example. On 11 September, Jeffreys took up residence in the grand town house near the top of the high street, now occupied by Boots the Chemist. In the trial that followed, Jeffreys bullied witnesses mercilessly, quashed any evidence he did not like and gleefully sentenced all the men to death.

Jeffreys then retired to his lodgings for a dinner and selection of wines, the cost of which is still recorded in the town council's accounts. As dinner ended he was approached by a pretty young woman who begged him to spare her brother's life. Jeffreys agreed, but only if the girl would stay the night with him. The distraught woman did as she was asked, but Jeffreys then hanged the man anyway.

It is appropriate that the heartless judge has not rested easy in his grave. He returns here in spectral form. When the building was a house, he was seen with disturbing regularity in the suite of rooms that he had occupied while staying in Lyme. The ghost appeared most often at night, walking restlessly about and muttering. The ghost has not been spotted much recently, but then the shop is closed and locked at night. Perhaps he walks here still, but there is simply nobody to see him.

GRIM DEEDS FROM THE LATER 17TH CENTURY LED TO THE HAUNTING OF THIS BUILDING IN LYME REGIS.

* * *

Standing close to the centre of the county is Dorchester. Some 5,000 years ago this was the site of a great ceremonial henge, equal in size to Stonehenge. That was swept away by the Romans, who chose this location for their new city after capturing the fortified tribal capital of the Durotiges a few miles to the south at Maiden Castle.

The oldest of Dorchester's ghosts dates from Roman times. The steep hill to the north of the town centre was the site of the Roman fortress built to house soldiers who kept an eye on the local tribesmen. One of those legionaries remains here still. He paces steadily along the old fortress ramparts, now the West Walks, marching with his shield on his arm and armour clinking gently. He is seen often, but never for very long. No sooner does a witness glimpse this ancient spirit, than he is gone.

St Peter's church and its tall tower dominate the centre of the town. It is the site of one of the best authenticated ghosts in the county. The haunting began in 1813 when the vicar, Rev Nathaniel Templeman, passed away and was buried in the church. Over the following months there were sightings of the dead man in and near the church, but these were dismissed as the imaginings of simple rustics by the local gentry.

Then, on Christmas Eve 1814, the sextons Ambrose Hunt and Clerk Hardy were at work in the church decorating the building for the Christmas services. It was hard work and, by the time they had finished, both men were thirsty. There was some communion wine temptingly close to hand in the vestry, so the cork was popped and soon the men were seated on a pew in the nave admiring their handiwork while slaking their thirsts.

Suddenly they were not alone. The unmistakable figure of Rev Templeman was walking towards them. He had his arms raised and was shaking his fist violently at them. The mouth of the spectre was opening and closing as if he was shouting, but no sound came forth. The two sextons were shocked and aghast. Hardy made to stand up, but fainted into a heap on the floor. Hunt threw himself to his knees, closed his eyes and said the Lord's Prayer with all the fervour he could manage. Opening his eyes, Hunt saw the ghostly vicar drifting off towards the altar, where he vanished. By this point Hardy was coming round, so Hunt dragged him out of the church and the two men fled into the chilly night.

THE PHANTOM LADY OF THIS FINE DORCHESTER HOTEL SEEMS TO BE WAITING FOR SOMEBODY.

The ghostly vicar has returned several times since and has become one of the most seen ghosts of Dorchester.

Also frequently visible is the dark lady of the Wessex Royal Hotel. Strangely this ghost is never seen from inside the building, only by people passing by outside. She is dressed in a long, dark dress of early Victorian style and wears a tight bonnet. She seems to be quite young, but is clearly anxious about something. She appears to be watching the passing crowds of shoppers as if looking for somebody in particular. Whoever it is, he or she never arrives. It must be almost two centuries since the lady sat in the window in real life, so whoever her ghost awaits has long passed from this earth.

Perhaps his ghost will arrive one day, and the hauntings will cease.

Durham

County Durham has one of the most distinguished and distinctive histories of all the English counties. For almost 800 years the Prince Bishop of Durham wielded huge power. He minted his own coins, ran his own justice system and led his men to battle. Not until 1836, some 90 years after the last Scottish army crossed the border to loot England, did the bishops lose the last of their powers.

These days a chunk of County Durham has been carved out to form part of the county of Tyne and Wear, but many locals – and certainly those of a spectral persuasion – prefer to cling to the old boundaries. This is a place where towns are solidly urban islands set in a sea of rural countryside, and it is possible to be in a street of Victorian terraces, turn a corner and walk into a field. Each town and village has its own character and fiercely guarded local pride. The 'Mackums' of Sunderland know they are different from the 'Monkeyhangers' of Hartlepool; neither would welcome being mistaken for the other. And the people can be as proud of their ghosts as of anything else.

In Durham Castle, there is a troublesome staircase, ominously named the Black Staircase. The castle itself was built by the Normans to keep a grip on northern England in the wake of the conquest of 1066, though the oldest surviving part is a mere 800 years old. The Black Staircase is three or so centuries younger still. After the Reformation, the Prince Bishops who ruled this area on behalf of the king of England were permitted to marry and it is the phantom of one such wife who haunts the staircase.

The figure of a lady in a long dark dress is thought to date from the 17th century, but if so there is some mystery here. The ghost is said to be that of a bishop's wife who died on the staircase – though whether from a fall or a heart attack is unclear. There are, however, no records of a lady dying in this place. Perhaps the records were amended to show the lady in question meeting her maker in more genteel circumstances. We shall never know.

* * *

Across the broad green that fronts the castle stands the mighty Norman structure of Durham cathedral, which was begun in 1093 to replace an earlier and much smaller English minster. At the west end of the cathedral is the tomb of a man named Hobb of Pelaw, though

it is more popularly known as Huppabella's tomb. Hobb was the steward who oversaw the accounts while the cathedral was being built. It is said that his pay chest was miraculously refilled by unseen hands whenever the workmen needed paying. This same tomb covers the entrance to an underground passage that is now blocked off, but once ran down through the centre of the hill on which Durham is built and headed off towards Finchale priory. The

THE MIGHTY CATHEDRAL AT DURHAM HAS A MUCH-HAUNTED SECRET PASSAGE. (PHOTO COURTESY OF STEPHANIE LILLEY)

tunnel was blocked off in the 18th century after it gained a reputation for being haunted.

* * *

To the west of the city, now hemmed in by modern suburbs, lies the battlefield of Neville's Cross. It was here, on 17th October 1346, that an English army met and utterly defeated an invading army of Scottish. So total was the victory for the English that they captured the Scots King David II. The English army was led by the powerful local landowner Ralph de Neville, who placed his army on a ridge beside a wayside cross erected by a member of his family some generations earlier and known as Neville's Cross.

The stump of Neville's Cross itself still stands, and it is said that if a person runs backwards around it nine times he will conjure up Sir Ralph himself, armed and ready to face any fresh invasion from across the northern borders of England. It has been many centuries since England and Scotland faced each other in war, so nobody has had much call to summon the phantom of Neville's Cross.

A FAMOUSLY BELLIGERENT MEDIEVAL KNIGHT CAN BE SUMMONED BY RUNNING AROUND NEVILLE'S CROSS, JUST OUTSIDE DURHAM. *(PHOTO COURTESY OF STEPHANIE LILLEY)*

Essex

The county of Essex has been treated rather unfairly in recent years. Pundits and journalists have sneered at Essex Man and Essex Girl and ridiculed the area as a nouveau riche extension of London's East End. But the ancient kingdom of Essex has a character and a vibrancy all its own. Powerful kings ruled here when London was a tumbled Roman ruin with weeds growing in its streets. And the rolling countryside of Essex hides many a gem to tempt the visitor.

Many of England's finest foods hail from Essex. Jams come from Tiptree and sea salt from Maldon, saffron from Saffron Walden and shellfish from the myriad inlets along the coast. Colchester was the first British city to enter the written record, when Tacitus described its destruction by Queen Boadicea of the Iceni, and its castle still stands on the foundations of the temple she burned down. This is a thrilling county to visit, and its ghosts are among the most famous, not just in England, but in the world.

Borley is a name that resonates through the annals of the paranormal. What happened here was inexplicable, mysterious and very controversial. The area around the church had long had a reputation, and still does, for being haunted by a nun. The story goes that Borley church and rectory were built on the site of a medieval monastery. One of the monks at this monastery fell in love with a nun from the convent at Bures, some 8 miles away. The couple planned to renounce their vows and elope, but their plans were betrayed so that when the nun came to collect her lover she was met only by the implacable abbot of the monastery. The monk was promptly hanged, while the luckless nun was bricked up in a cellar of the monastery and left to die. Of the monk no more was heard, but the nun returned in spectral form. She followed a set route from the church, through the rectory grounds and down to a stream.

The ghostly tale was well known locally, but was not unusual in itself. Then in 1940 this tiny village shot to fame when a book was published with the title *The Most Haunted House in England*. It was written by Harry Price, the most highly respected psychic investigator of his day.

The book summed up the results of a series of investigations carried out at Borley by Price in the 1920s and 1930s. He claimed to have unearthed the truth behind the ghostly nun, to have found new restless spirits and to have encountered one of the most active poltergeists in existence.

Between 1892 and 1927 the rectory was inhabited by the Rev Harry Bull and his large family. The house lay empty for a year before the living was given to the Rev Eric Smith, who arrived with his family in October 1928. He found the locals telling tales of not just the ghostly nun, but also of the phantom coach in which she had failed to elope and of various unspecified, but decidedly unnerving ghostly activities in the rectory itself. Rev Smith did not believe a word of it and to prove to the locals that their stories were nonsense, he sent for Harry Price.

When Price arrived, he duly noted the local stories and collected eyewitness accounts of the ghostly nun. He then began recording events typical of poltergeist activity. Coins were thrown around, loud bangs sounded from empty rooms and invisible hands knocked on doors.

After less than a year of this the Smiths moved out to be replaced by the Rev Lionel Foyster, who had a younger wife and adopted daughter. The hauntings quickly began again and Price returned to investigate further. This time the poltergeist activity was more violent. A new aspect was the appearance of messages scribbled, apparently in pencil, on walls of the rectory. These were addressed to 'Marianne', Mrs Foyster, and appeared to come from a long dead spirit who was demanding candles and prayers for the good of his or her soul. The disturbances reached a peak, then trailed off and by 1935 seemed to have ceased.

The parish of Borley was then amalgamated with those of two neighbouring villages. Borley Rectory was suddenly surplus to the requirements of the Church of England. Harry Price leapt at the opportunity to rent it and moved in with a team of researchers and assistants.

The ghostly goings-on returned with redoubled ferocity. Newspaper reporters were invited in to document what was happening, and most left to write astonishing pieces about what was rapidly becoming known as the most haunted house in England. Price turned up some documentary evidence to support the tale of the nun, though no trace of a monastery at Borley could be found.

The interest in Borley was at fever pitch, when it was brought to a sudden end by the outbreak of the Second World War and the mysterious fire that reduced the rectory to ashes. Price then published his book, making the now ruined rectory world famous.

Well documented as the haunting was, it was not without its critics. Several of the reporters who visited the rectory during the time Price rented it were convinced that they had witnessed only clever conjuring tricks. One even caught Price faking ghostly activity and was hurriedly ushered out of the house. His editor refused to run the story for fear of libel.

After Price's death his private papers were studied. Remarkably, it was revealed that, while he had been convinced of the tale of the phantom nun, he had been dubious of the other manifestations. He had found out that no monastery had ever stood at Borley. In particular he thought that Mrs Foyster had faked many incidents as a bit of a lark to relieve the tedium of a rural parish. Price had never made these doubts public, but instead had embarked on a series of money-making lectures and radio shows based on the Borley mystery.

By the 1950s, Price's reputation as a serious psychic investigator was in tatters. It had become clear that much of his most famous work had been undertaken mostly for profit and may have been exaggerated to grab headlines and secure lucrative sales for his books. It was even suspected that he had, at times, fooled himself into believing things for which there was no credible evidence. On the other hand, there were no research grants available at the time. If Price wanted to devote his life to studying the paranormal he had to earn a living and pay his expenses somehow. Much of his work was of a high quality and beyond reproach, so perhaps he can be forgiven for making money from a high profile case when he could.

Similarly, the reputation of Borley for being haunted had likewise collapsed.

And yet the stories simply would not go away. The ghostly nun continued to be seen and strange noises were heard in the church – most noticeably the sound of doors opening and closing when none moved. A new investigation in 1974 produced credible evidence that the nun, at least, was a genuine ghost. As for the rest, it will probably never be clear if Price or Mrs Foyster faked the ghostly activities – or if Borley Rectory really was 'the most haunted house in England'.

* * *

The haunting of Layer Marney, on the other hand, is rather more typical of the ways of English ghosts. The hamlet is dominated by the magnificent castle gatehouse, the building of which marked the ending of one of Essex's premier families. The Marney family, who gave their name to the village, first acquired their estates hereabouts in the 1160s. Over the generations that followed they steadily built up their holdings to become perhaps the richest non-noble family in the county.

In 1520 the lands were inherited by Sir Henry Marney. He decided that the great wealth and prestige of his family should be reflected in their home. He pulled down the old, cramped medieval fortified manor that stood here and ordered the erection of a truly grand house. He had been impressed by the gatehouses built to guard the entrances to the Cambridge colleges and, on a visit to court, saw that the youthful King Henry VIII was following the fashion. So Sir Henry decreed that the gatehouse to his new mansion must be the finest in the land.

THE GHOST OF SIR HENRY MARNEY WANDERS IN AND OUT OF THE GATEHOUSE
AT LAYER MARNEY.

Building work was still under way when Sir Henry died after a short illness in 1523. His son Sir John inherited but, never healthy, he too died. The titles passed through the female line to another family. Already owning a house suitable for their needs, the new owners of the Marney estates halted the building at Layer Marney. Only the gatehouse and west wing had been completed. They were retained as a house, but no other work was undertaken.

The beautiful Layer Marney tower, together with its adjacent wing and a church, were all built in red brick and remain standing today pretty much as they were when building stopped in 1525.

It is a shame that the initial grand project was never completed. Certainly Sir Henry Marney would seem to think so. His ghost has walked in and around his tower ever since building work came to a halt. Some think he comes to admire what was completed, others that he mourns that which was left undone.

Gloucestershire

One of the most famous ghosts of Gloucestershire would seem to be rather elusive these days. This is the phantom of King Edward II, who met a grisly and tragic fate at Berkeley Castle. The unfortunate Edward II managed to combine weakness with stubbornness and breathtaking tactlessness. None of this made for good government or for popularity, while his habit of lavishing wealth, titles and power on his favourites and lovers made things even worse. The fact that he was openly homosexual alienated the tough barons who might have supported him and angered his queen, Isabella, daughter of King Philip IV of France.

After nineteen years of botched government, personal quarrels and endless incompetence the English had had enough of their charming but unfortunate monarch. Queen Isabella raised a rebellion in the name of her infant son, later to be King Edward III. Nobody stood by King Edward when Isabella had him arrested and forced him to abdicate at swordpoint. At first

BERKELEY CASTLE WAS FOR CENTURIES HAUNTED BY TERRIFYING SCREAMS, BUT THE GHOST SEEMS TO HAVE BEEN QUIET OF LATE. (*WWW.BERKELEY-CASTLE.COM*)

Edward was kept prisoner in royal comfort, but once Isabella and her lover Roger Mortimer, Earl of March, had their hands securely on the levers of power, the former king was packed off to Berkeley Castle in Gloucestershire.

At Berkeley he was in the cruel care of John Maltravers, brother-in-law of the Earl of March. Isabella ordered that Edward must die quickly, but that violence should not be used. Maltravers therefore refused to let Edward have fuel for a fire, or any warm clothes and fed him a starvation diet. But Edward was a strong man and would not die. In the end Maltravers had his royal prisoner pinned on the floor of his chamber under a wooden door so that he could not struggle, then a red hot spit was pushed up his back passage. The thrust caused massive internal injuries, but no external wounds.

Isabella announced that her husband had died of sickness and he was hurriedly buried in Gloucester Cathedral.

But the brutal killing did not remain a secret for long. In his hideous death agony poor Edward had screamed with terrific volume. Everyone in the castle and even nearby houses realised what must be happening to the former king. Those same terrifying shouts of pain continued to echo around the castle and up and down the river in ghostly fashion late at night. As late as the mid-20th century the phantom screams were being reported by those out and about during the hours of darkness.

* * *

IT WAS THE BRUTAL MURDER OF KING EDWARD II THAT LED TO THE HAUNTINGS AT BERKELEY CASTLE.

The Burgage in Prestbury is a quiet side street now that the A435 swoops round in a loop to the west, but there was a time when this was the main road north from Cheltenham and it is to those days that the most active of the ghosts in this little village belongs.

On 15 September 1643 the English Civil War was getting under way in earnest. The main Parliamentarian army had been in Gloucester, and then set out heading north up the Severn Valley. King Charles was marching with an even larger army in an attempt to intercept the Roundheads. He managed to overtake his enemies by making a forced march up through the Cotswolds to reach Evesham on 14 September. That same day, the Earl of Essex, who commanded the Parliamentarian army, doubled back. He crossed the river at Tewkesbury and marched south to Cheltenham.

King Charles had left scouts strung out along the Cotswolds to watch for exactly such a move. One of them spotted the Parliamentarians as they entered Cheltenham. He leapt to his horse and galloped north to warn the king. But Essex was no fool. He had scouts of his own on duty and a party of these tough troopers were in Prestbury. They were unsaddling for the night when they heard the desperate hoofbeats of the Cavalier approaching from the south.

The Roundheads quickly strung a wire across the street, just at the height of a man on horseback. The luckless Cavalier did not see the wire in the gathering gloom of that September evening. He galloped straight into the wire, which neatly sliced off his head.

Not until Essex and his men were south of the Thames did King Charles learn of his enemies' movements. He at once set off on another forced march, but by the time he caught the Roundhead army at Newbury, the London militia had marched out to oppose him. Faced by two enemy armies, Charles was able to achieve only a stalemate. If he had succeeded in defeating Essex in September 1643 it is very likely that Parliament would have caved in. But he did not and they did not, and King Charles ended his life on the executioner's block. And all because a messenger was lost at Prestbury.

Perhaps this is why the unfortunate man's spirit cannot rest, but forever tries to complete his journey. The landlord of Prestbury's

THE QUIET LANE IN PRESTBURY WHERE A ROYAL MESSENGER WAS KILLED IN GRUESOME FASHION MORE THAN THREE CENTURIES AGO AND RETURNS IN PHANTOM FORM TO THE PRESENT DAY.

Royal Oak in the 1990s was twice made aware of the ghost. Late at night he heard a horseman galloping up the lane, but when he looked out there was nobody there.

Rather more dramatic was the event that occurred in the mid-1980s, as recalled by a local man some years later. 'I was walking home up the road after midnight – a pal had dropped me in the High Street after a do. I heard the sound of a horse coming up from behind me. Well, it was dark, of course, so I thought the horse would soon come into sight. But it didn't. The hooves got louder and louder, like they were getting real close, but when I turned round there was nobody in sight. I was just beginning to get worried – I mean we all know about the headless horseman – when the noise just stopped. It was sudden like. And then I realised I was outside this pub, where the Cavalier had been killed. Yes, that was the galloping Cavalier all right. But I did not see him, only heard him.'

Rather less dramatic, but seen more frequently, is the Black Abbot who haunts the churchyard of St Mary's, Prestbury. He is

THE ROYAL OAK, A FORMER LANDLORD OF WHICH ENCOUNTERED THE GHOSTLY HORSEMAN OF PRESTBURY TWICE DURING HIS TIME HERE.

spotted in the churchyard quite a lot. And once or twice in the church itself. A churchwarden reported: 'He's no bother to us, of course. He just turns up now and then, has a little wander about and then vanishes. Sometimes we just hear his footsteps, but usually he is seen as well. He is dressed in a long black cassock thing and walks quite slowly with his arms folded. No clanking chains or running around shouting "Boo" at people. Like I say. He's no bother.'

Altogether more charming is the phantom girl of the Prestbury House Hotel. The house was built in the 1700s as the home of the wealthy Capel family, one of whose number was mayor of Gloucester as far back as 1484. As was then the fashion, a folly was erected in the house grounds, taking the shape of a grotto in the northern end of the formal garden, close to which stood a Chinese temple. King George III visited Gloucestershire in 1788 to learn more about farming practices – in his less mad periods the king promoted good farming practice to boost the prosperity of his people. He stopped at Prestbury House and took afternoon tea in the grotto.

Times changed and by the mid-19th century follies fell out of fashion with the gentry. But the nearby Cheltenham racecourse was doing booming business and attracting thousands of people from far and near. One inventive Prestbury man thought the crowds might welcome a nice hot cup of tea served in the same grotto where old King George had drunk his tea. He rented the grotto and temple from the Capels and ran a thriving business.

Among the staff he hired was a local teenage girl named Lizzie. She was a pretty youngster and popular with the racegoers – at least with the men. It was with sadness that the village and racing crowd greeted the news that Lizzie had died of a wasting disease. But only a few days later, she was back. Her ghost was seen drifting quietly through the grounds around the tearooms, strolling with evident enjoyment among the gardens.

These days, the grotto and temple are long gone and the house has been converted to an hotel, but Lizzie remains. She is often mistaken for a guest by staff, or for a member of staff by guests. She walks as quietly as ever through the charming wooded grounds. It is to be hoped that she is happy.

* * *

In the centre of Gloucester city stand the half-ruined remains of the Blackfriars. Once a priory, this building served as housing and workshops for centuries before being converted into a public hall and venue for the arts. One of the workmen who undertook the renovations saw the notorious Black Monk at close hand.

'I saw it a few years back when I was working on the restoration and such,' the man remembered. 'My mate and I were having a cup of tea before getting on with re-laying some of the stones when we saw this figure walk past us into one of the side rooms. Well, there wasn't meant to be anyone else

THE ANCIENT GATE WHICH LEADS TO THE BLACKFRIARS IN CENTRAL GLOUCESTER HIDES A SUPERNATURAL VISITOR.

there, so we went to tell whoever it was to clear out. He had walked into a room with no other exit, but he was gone. There was no way out except the one we could see. What did he look like? Well I only saw him for a second, but I'd say he was quite short and wore what I thought was a long coat. I suppose it was a monk's cloak thing really. But we didn't think it was a ghost, you see. He just looked solid and normal, like someone who had wandered in off the street. It was only after he vanished we thought there might be something odd.'

According to the account of the haunting that is most widely reported, the ghost is of a monk dressed in a long black robe and with a hood pulled up over his head. He is said to kneel in prayer in front of what used to be the high altar of the priory church. Having stayed silent and still for some moments, the spectral figure jumps abruptly to his feet and flees the church with his hands clasped to his head.

WHAT WAS ONCE THE MAIN PRIORY CHURCH OF GLOUCESTER'S BLACKFRIARS WAS CONVERTED INTO A PRIVATE HOUSE, THEN A SERIES OF TENEMENTS, BEFORE ITS RECENT RESTORATION. IT IS HERE THAT THE GHOSTLY MONK IS SEEN MOST OFTEN.

Whoever this phantom monk might be, he is most definitely a member of the Dominican order of friars, who built and manned this priory. The Dominicans were founded by St Dominic in 1239 with the specific aim of preaching Christianity to the poor and underprivileged. Gloucester was one of the first cities in England to become a centre for the Dominicans, though whether this was a reflection on the city's poverty or need for spiritual guidance is unclear. The friars were given a patch of land and quickly built a church and a series of buildings to act as an administrative centre for their work.

Hampshire

Hampshire was for centuries an essentially agricultural county. The valleys of the Itchen and Test provided lush watermeadows on which livestock could graze in the balmy summer months, while the drier land between was ideal for the cultivation of crops and fodder. At the heart of the county was always the beautiful cathedral city of Winchester. This was the home of the warrior-king Cerdic in the early 6th century. His family ruled first Wessex, then England and now a distant descendant sits upon the combined throne of the United Kingdom.

These days the county has changed greatly as Portsmouth, Southampton, Bournemouth and Winchester have all spread out to engulf the surrounding countryside. What was once a county of rural hideaways has become a place of suburbs and bustling modernity. It is none the worse for that, but the phantoms hark back to earlier times.

One of the oldest and least active of the ghosts is found at the Brushmaker's Arms in Upham. This pub is exactly the sort of friendly, jovial local hostelry that everyone would want to have at the end of their road. Apart from the murders, that is. Of course, both killings happened many years ago. Nobody has been murdered here for simply ages.

The less said about the gruesome events down in the cellar the better. They do not make for family reading and, in any case, have nothing to do with the haunting. It is the murder in the upstairs

THE BRUSHMAKERS' ARMS IN THE CHARMING VILLAGE OF UPHAM. THE HAUNTED
BEDROOM IS ON THE FIRST FLOOR, BEHIND THE LEFT-HAND WINDOW.

front bedroom that causes the supernatural activity. The ghost is
that of a 16th century man named Mr Chickett. It was he who had
the building constructed as part house, part brush factory – hence
the pub's unique name. As the man grew older, his fortune grew
greater. He would sit upstairs in his bedroom, counting out his gold
and silver coins before stashing them away safely in a hidden
compartment. It was not, however, hidden well enough. One
morning his workers arrived to find old Mr Chickett battered to
death, his room ransacked and his money stolen.

Ever since then, the ghost has walked. The most usual
manifestation is the sound of footsteps, which are heard in the bar
directly underneath the room where the murder was done. Less
often the sound of chinking coins is heard from the same small
room. Objects being moved around in the bar are a regular
occurrence, though they are not actually seen to move very often.
More usually an object is found in one place when it had been put
in another.

The ghost himself is seen only rarely. Jill, the landlady, spoke of a recent incident: 'I was upstairs doing some paperwork in the office. Suddenly I heard the door to the front bedroom (where the murder was committed) slam shut, very hard and loud. I looked round and there was the outline of a man, like a shadow on the wall, moving off. Only it couldn't be a shadow as the sun was not out. It was definitely a man moving down the corridor.' Jill smiled. 'Mind you, we haven't seen him since. People hear him of course. But I think he must like us. We get no trouble.'

* * *

Also not much bother to any mortal is the Phantom Copper of Romsey. 'He was stood there as clear as day,' said Mrs M (she would rather not have her name in print). 'Just like you. Solid. In books and on films you see ghosts floating above the ground or

THE ROAD JUNCTION IN ROMSEY WHERE THE PHANTOM COPPER IS SEEN MOST OFTEN.

going all see-through. He was not like that at all. He was solid and real. He was really there. Well, until he vanished, that is.'

This ghost is not so well known as the Roundhead Trooper who lurks in the Market Place outside the Conservative Club, nor does he seem to be seen so often. He is, however, rather more mobile. He has been spotted in at least two places, and there may be more, for other accounts do not pinpoint the location of the sighting.

Another person to see the ghost, Mrs Perry, saw the Phantom Copper on Winchester Road and gave a more detailed description. Judging by these accounts, the ghost dates from the period between the wars. He wears a wool serge uniform with what appears to be a cape slung back off his shoulder and a good solid helmet tops his head. Whenever he is seen the Phantom Copper just stands there. He does not walk as if on patrol, nor does he seem to be taking much notice of what goes on around him. He just stands and stares.

Given that he is a policeman of the 1920s or 1930s, there is only one incident on record that put the Romsey constabulary in the national press. In 1923 there had been a series of attacks on children by a dog running loose. One of Romsey's finest found an untethered dog that matched the description and promptly grabbed its collar. The policeman slipped a length of string through the collar and set off back to the police station in The Hundred, leading the dog behind him.

THE EMBARRASSING INCIDENT OF 1923 THAT MAY HAVE LED TO THE ROMSEY HAUNTING, AS REPORTED IN A LOCAL NEWSPAPER OF THE TIME.

DRAGGING AN UNOCCUPIED DOG-COLLAR behind him, this constable strode majestically to the lock-up unaware that the arrested dog had " sloped."

A contemporary newspaper takes up the tale. 'Then the dog began to follow the policeman as he led the way towards the station-house. The small crowd which had gathered to witness the occurrence grew, as small crowds will, into a fairly large one. Despite the smiles of the populace, the dignity of the law had to be upheld; but when the smiles of the crowd which followed became audible in the form of tittering, the constable looked round to see the cause. The cause was plain. The dog had become tired of the policeman's company and had broken arrest. He had slipped his head out of the collar and the policeman was merely dragging the empty collar along the ground by the string. The tittering grew into a laugh when the crowd found the policeman had discovered the situation, but the law had a card up its sleeve. The policeman solemnly conveyed the collar to the police station in lieu of its wearer as evidence of arrest.'

Embarrassing, no doubt, but enough to cause the poor policeman to return in spectral form? Only the Phantom Copper knows, and he isn't telling.

＊　＊　＊

Rather more bothersome, at least at times, is the phantom lady who frequents the Original White Hart Hotel at Ringwood. Dee Wade,

THE ORIGINAL WHITE HART IN RINGWOOD, A PUB WHOSE NAME HAS BEEN BORROWED BY MANY OTHERS, HAS A PHANTOM CHAMBERMAID.

the landlady, was cautious about her resident phantom. 'I've not seen her myself,' Dee said. 'And the only thing that I've experienced myself is the bother with the back door. In the summer we prop it open, but it keeps closing itself. Could be the wind, I suppose, but it never does it when you are here to see it. But turn your back and it shuts. Doesn't matter what you prop it open with – a chair, a brick, whatever. It just keeps shutting.

'Anyway, they tell me that our ghost is of an old chambermaid or something. She hangs about towards the back of the hotel, near the little flight of stairs that goes up to the kitchens. A lady in a grey dress, I'm told. And in the function room beyond. Well, we had all sorts of trouble back there. Before my time, mind.

'Well it was being all refurbished, to be a restaurant or function room. Anyway, our phantom chambermaid was obsessed with keeping things tidy. She does that, you see. Tidies things up. So she kept putting tools back in boxes when the workmen weren't looking. Like she shuts the back door when you are not looking. It got so bad that the men refused to work in there alone. There always had to be three of them at a time.

THE STAIRS IN THE WHITE HART WHERE THE PHANTOM MAID IS SEEN MOST OFTEN.

'She is also very active in the kitchen itself. Moving stuff about and so on. They do tell me, anyway. Odd, really. This is one of the newest parts of the building. I can understand those stairs, they are very old. Part of the original inn. But out here?

'I'm told we had an exorcism here back in the 1960s. You can see the cross they carved in the wall by the stairs. Can't say it did much

EBENEZER LANE, A NARROW CUL-DE-SAC IN CENTRAL RINGWOOD, WHERE OLD PHANTOMS HAVE RECENTLY BECOME MORE ACTIVE.

good. Maybe she was more active before, but she is still about. Well, so I am told.'

Elsewhere in Ringwood are other ghostly visitors. Tiny Ebenezer Lane became quite famous in the 1960s when a phantom lady and gentleman dating from the time the houses were built, in the 1750s, suddenly became a lot more active. The ghosts had been around for some time, but for an unexplained reason they were seen quite often during the summer months of 1967.

Then the ghosts became quiet again, until autumn 2003, that is. A lady who lives nearby saw the ghost of a man in 18th century dress one day. At the time she thought little of it. After all, she reasoned, he might be someone in fancy dress. Though even then she did think there was something odd about the man. A few weeks later she saw him again. This time she took more interest and watched as the man walked into Ebenezer Lane. She followed quickly, turning the corner only seconds after the man. But he was gone.

The other ghost is a grey lady, said to haunt the Market Place. This unfortunate lady was run down and killed by a truck in the Market Place some time before the Second World War.

* * *

Home to even more ghosts than Ringwood is the county town of Winchester. The mighty cathedral dominates the city and its ghostly entourage are among the most active in the neighbourhood. The first cathedral phantom is that of a monk. He seems to feel the attractions of the building more strongly at some times than at others. He was seen frequently in the post-war years and again in the 1970s, but previously and since has rationed his appearances to about once every twelve months.

He slowly materialises out of nothingness in the southern end of the Close, near to house No 11. Having become solid, the phantom moves towards the arch that marks a roadway to gardens near the south transept.

But this ghost does not glide in the approved fashion of ghosts. He limps. And he limps quite badly. No footsteps are heard, but those who have seen the ghostly monk notice that he almost drags his right foot as he moves across the Close. Continuing his painful progress, the monk approaches the arch and then fades from sight. Some claim he passes through the arch, others that he shimmers and slips away into a misty form that fades from sight.

WINCHESTER'S CATHEDRAL GREEN, WHERE A GHOST WITH A LIMP IS OFTEN SEEN.

Quite how old the phantom might be is rather unclear. But there is one clue. During one of the periods of alterations that take place around the cathedral from time to time a number of burials were unearthed in what is now a private garden, but was evidently then part of the cathedral precincts. The bodies were all male and date to about the 14th century. They were probably monks. What does this have to do with our phantom? Well, one of the bodies had a grossly deformed arthritic right knee. It would have given him a very bad limp.

Other phantom monks have been seen processing up St George Street to the corner of what is now Royal Oak Passage. This patch of land housed a small chapel in medieval days and was the site for the burial of the less exalted monks, who did not warrant a burial at the cathedral.

THIS NARROW ALLEY BESIDE THE ROYAL OAK PUB IN WINCHESTER IS HOME TO A GHOST FAR OLDER THAN THE PUB HE PASSES.

There are scattered accounts of processions being recreated in spectral form in several old histories of Winchester. One, from about 1640, talks of the procession marching sombrely with chanting monks, clanging handbells and flapping sacred banners. Later accounts are less dramatic. A Victorian writes of shadowy figures lurking around what was once the burial ground. These days there seems to be just one lone monk left of this grand procession.

One witness saw the ghost in the mid-1990s. 'That's right, the monk ghost chap,' said Stuart. 'It was one summer evening. I'd finished work and was walking back to my car when I cut down that alley by the pub. Nobody else around at the time. The shoppers had all gone home and the nightlife hadn't got going. Then I saw this figure coming towards me dressed in a long cloak and hood. I thought it was a bit odd 'cos it was a warm evening. Nobody would need to wrap up like that. Then, when we were passing each other, I felt suddenly cold. Like if you stand under the air conditioning unit in a shop. There was this cold draught. I looked round to see what could have caused it, then realised the figure had gone. There was nowhere he could have gone, you see. He was only a couple of feet away from me. Then he was gone.'

Rather more dramatic, in more than one sense of the word, are the ghosts at Winchester's Theatre Royal. It seems that the most active ghost at the theatre is the Man in Black, who haunts the circle. He is usually seen after the evening show is over and most of the public have gone home. He appears quite solid and normal. More than one usher, clearing up after the public, has mistaken him for a loitering theatregoer. Until he walks through a wall, that is.

The Man in Black is the ghost of John Simpkins, brother of James Simpkins who opened the Theatre Royal back in 1914. It seems that James was the artistic one who put on the shows and hobnobbed with the greats of the early 20th century stage. John was the brother with business sense. He left running the shows to James, but would visit regularly after the performance to go through the books and count the money. He had a small, private office located just off the circle where he would do his work. The room is now used for storage and the door that led into the circle has long since been blocked up. John died in the early 1920s, but James continued to run the theatre until the mid-1930s.

When John lay dying he asked his brother one last favour. Over the stage at the Theatre Royal was a scrolled ornament with the initials 'J S'. These could be taken to mean John Simpkins or James Simpkins, but now John wanted the letters altered to read 'J & J S', to make it clear that there had been two brothers. James agreed, but after John died he either forgot his promise or found the work would have been too pricey. The lettering was never changed.

Perhaps it is this broken promise that brings the ghostly John Simpkins back to the theatre.

The spectral John Simpkins lurks about the circle and his old office. He does not know the doorway between the two has gone, which is why he still walks through it, appearing and disappearing through the solid wall. He also likes to walk along the rear of the circle from the entrance stairs to what was his office. So often is the figure in black seen here, that the route is known to staff as 'the Ghost Walk'.

The second ghost has a more tragic story. Young Jim worked in the theatre as a lime boy, meaning that he operated the limelights that then functioned as modern spotlights do today. In 1915 this young chap joined up to serve in the Great War and marched off to the trenches in France. He left behind him not only his widowed mother, but also his sweetheart, Lucy, who worked as one of the chorus girls at the theatre.

THE MOST ACTIVE OF THE PHANTOMS AT WINCHESTER'S THEATRE ROYAL APPEARS IN THE CIRCLE SO OFTEN THAT HIS ROUTE IS KNOWN AS 'THE GHOST WALK'.

One night in 1916 the music hall show was playing to a full house. The chorus line came on, then suddenly collapsed into confusion when Lucy stopped stock still instead of dancing. The girl turned as white as a sheet, then ran off the stage. The manager found her sobbing uncontrollably in the wings.

'I've seen Jim,' the girl gasped. 'He was standing by the limelight, just like he always used to.'

'But you can't have,' said James Simpkins. 'He's in France and not due home on leave for weeks yet.'

'I know,' sobbed Lucy. 'Then he waved goodbye to me and just faded away.'

A few days later Jim's mother received a telegram from the War Office telling her that her son had been killed in the trenches. He had been shot at almost the precise moment he had appeared at the Theatre Royal.

Which brings us to the third ghost. A vague female wraith has been seen on the stage from time to time. Is it Lucy, the chorus girl? We don't know. The ghost always appears only vaguely and soon drifts off to nothingness.

Then there is the old lady who was sensed by the entertainer Michael Bentine when he performed at the Theatre Royal some years ago. She was dressed in very old-fashioned clothes and gave the impression of being from a house nearby and walking in the garden when, in fact, she was in the stalls bar. The theatre was built in the gardens of Tower House, a fine pile, which was erected in the 1700s and survived until about 1985. Perhaps the lady is the ghost of some long dead inhabitant of the Tower House who still wanders through, what are for her, lovely flowerbeds and lawns.

* * *

Across the water from Hampshire lies the Isle of Wight. This is a charming microcosm of rural England, which retains a rather old-fashioned atmosphere despite catering with very modern efficiency to the holiday trade. Among the welcoming establishments that look after visitors to the island is the Wheatsheaf Hotel in Newport. During the Napoleonic Wars there was a real fear that the Isle of Wight might be seized by the French as a springboard from which to invade England. To guard against this the island was garrisoned by the Duke of York's Regiment, an infantry unit raised in Munster, Ireland.

The Irish lads were popular on the island and in June 1813 one of the officers, Lieutenant John Blundell, married a local girl from Newport, named Anne. They set up temporary home at the

Wheatsheaf until more secure lodgings could be found. Sadly, however, their happiness was not to last long. A drunken squabble over a coat led to a dawn duel between Blundell and another officer, Lieutenant Maguire. Blundell was wounded by a pistol ball, and the wound turned septic.

For day after day he lingered in pain, with his young wife sitting beside him in their rooms at the Wheatsheaf. After more than a week, the unfortunate Blundell died. Young Anne went back to her family and lived a long life, marrying again in due course. And yet, her ghost returns still to the room where her beloved, dashing soldier husband died in her arms. Did she never get over the death? Or did the emotions of those awful days imprint themselves so strongly on the room that her image remains?

* * *

Another tragic young lady haunts the road outside the Blacksmith Arms on Calbourne Road, which runs out of Newport towards Carisbrooke. Young Betty lived here in the late 18th century, a time when smugglers were active on the island. Betty's brother was one of the smugglers, and she too was a member of the gang. Her role was to wear an elaborately low cut dress on the nights that the gang were bringing contraband ashore and to be most friendly and attentive to the customs men who called at the inn.

Alas for this cunning plan, Betty fell in love with one of the officers. She told him about the gang, though taking care to inform him of a landing on a night she knew her brother would not be involved. It was a grim night's work with gunfire and bloodshed. And later one of the gang lurked outside the inn to murder poor Betty. It is her troubled spirit that hovers still along the lane outside the pub, appearing as a young lady in a long dress who seems to be upset about something. She is usually about to accost passers-by or flag down passing cars when she abruptly vanishes.

Herefordshire

Herefordshire is dominated by the beautiful River Wye and its equally scenic tributaries, the Monnow and the Dore. So lovely is the land around the Dore that the stretch between Dorstone and Abbey Dore is widely known as the Golden Valley. This is rich, productive land where the hills are ideal for the vast orchards of fruit trees. Apples were once the staple crop and Herefordshire cider is justly famous.

But for many centuries this was not a peaceful county. The Welsh princes and lords to the west would make raids into Hereford when they got the chance, looting property and burning houses. When it wasn't the Welsh attacking it, it was the English armies marching the other way. Herefordshire was rarely quiet.

These days, of course, this is the most tranquil of counties. However, several of the ghosts hark back to more violent days. Among them are the tragic phantoms of Goodrich Castle. This magnificent fortress was first built by the eponymous Godric before the Norman invasion, though the ruins seen today date from the 12th century rebuilding by William Marshall, perhaps the most chivalrous knight of his day. The castle was later held by the Talbots and, when the Civil War broke out in England in 1642, the castle was held for King Charles against Parliament.

The ebb and flow of war did not reach staunchly Royalist Herefordshire until late in the conflict, when Parliament was in the ascendancy. This had given the garrison commander at Goodrich plenty of time to modernise his defences, constructing earthworks and bastions to withstand even the most modern of cannon. So, when a Roundhead army led by Colonel Birch eventually approached in 1646, Sir Henry Lingen was confident that he could hold out for quite some time.

Among the dashing Royalist cavaliers manning the defences at Goodrich was young Charles Clifford. Some days before the enemy arrived, Clifford had brought to the castle a pretty young lady, whom he declared was his fiancée, named Alice. What he did not tell his commander was that young Alice was the daughter of none other than the Colonel Birch, who was now coming to destroy Goodrich Castle. Nor was the worthy colonel aware that his daughter was within the walls, thinking she was safely at home.

Eyeing up the defences of Goodrich, Birch decided he could not storm them with success, so he set about starving the garrison into surrender. The weeks passed and nothing much happened, Sir Henry having piled high his supplies before the siege began. Realising that he was running short of time, Birch took a bold and dramatic step. He sent for a metal-founder of fame from the nearby Forest of Dean and ordered him to build a cannon able to smash the defences of Goodrich.

The ironmaster rubbed his chin, declaring it would be a savage gun of mighty proportions. Birch assured him money was no object and the man went to work. After several days he produced a true monster. Dubbed 'Roaring Meg', the mighty cannon swallowed vast quantities of gunpowder at each firing and was so cumbersome it could be fired only twice each hour. But it did belch forth cannonballs weighing 200 pounds.

No sooner was the monster in place, than the Royalists knew they did not have long to wait until their defences were breached. Alice and Clifford decided they could not await her father's wrath, and instead fled in the dark of night, mounted on Clifford's great black charger. They were spotted as they galloped through the Roundhead lines, and men mounted to ride in pursuit.

Exactly what happened next is unclear. But in the darkness something went terribly wrong. The fleeing lovers plunged into the

THE MIGHTY GOODRICH CASTLE OVERLOOKS THE RIVER WYE, WHICH PROVED
FATAL TO TWO LOVERS WHO NOW RETURN IN SPECTRAL FORM.

Wye, which was in flood after several days of rain. They were washed away and drowned.

But they have not gone. The ghosts of the young couple return frequently to Goodrich. They have been spotted walking quietly around the castle on many occasions. Less frequently, they are glimpsed riding on a black horse in the direction of the Wye. They are seen on horseback on or about 14 June, the anniversary of their death.

The fatal Roaring Meg, incidentally, was floated up the Wye to Hereford, where it remains, together with the few unused cannonballs.

* * *

Violence of a different kind led to the haunting of Avenbury church, near Bromyard. For a period during the 17th century the duties of playing the organ here were divided between two talented brothers. For some unknown reason, one brother stabbed the other to death during a practice session on the church organ. The man fled and killed himself the following day.

Ever since that tragic double death, the sound of organ music has occasionally drifted out of the church. Even today, when the place stands as a gaunt ruin at the end of an eerie and overgrown path off a quiet country lane, with no sign of an organ, the phantom music can sometimes be plainly heard. There is a certain sadness about the music, it is reported, so perhaps the long dead brothers return to mourn their loss of life.

* * *

For a city as ancient as Hereford, there are remarkably few ghosts to be found. Although people have lived here for many years, the crossing point over the Wye having long been of commercial importance, the city's climb to greatness began with a murder. King Offa of Mercia, who ruled the English midlands at the time, murdered King Ethelbert of East Anglia in AD 792. The Church, to which Ethelbert had been a great benefactor, reacted strongly and made the dead man a saint. The crime caused consternation among the nobility as well. Ethelbert had been Offa's son-in-law. If he was not safe from the Mercian king's violence, who was?

To expiate his sins, Offa moved the body of the saint, martyr and king to rest in a costly shrine within a stone church at Hereford. That church was destroyed by the Welsh raiders in 1056 and replaced by the magnificent cathedral that stands today. It is the ghost of one of the monks dedicated to serving the shrine who haunts the site. He is traditionally said to have been killed during the great raid of 1056. Seeing the Welsh pouring over the frontier, the monk tried to gather up the relics of the saint to carry them away to safety. The Welsh thought he was making off with gold or jewels and slew him to get them.

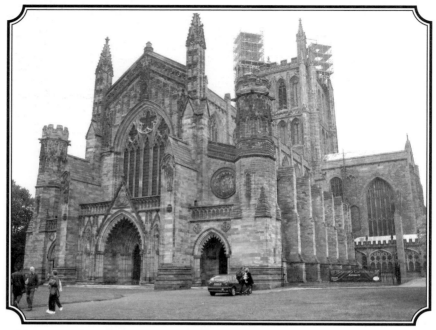

HEREFORD CATHEDRAL, WHERE THE GHOST OF A WHITE MONK HAS BEEN SEEN.

Whether such a romantic tale is true or not, the white monk is a frequent visitor to the area north-east of the present cathedral. He was famously seen by over a hundred people attending the Three Choirs Festival just before the Second World War. While waiting to enter the cathedral, the members of the crowd watched a man in a white robe approach and assumed he was a performer making a late entrance. Only when he vanished did they realise their mistake.

Hertfordshire

The M25 drives brutally through southern Hertfordshire, cutting ancient towns off from the bulk of the county to the north. Even beyond the circular motorway, the county is heavily influenced by London. Welwyn Garden City was built as a commuter overflow for the capital, while other towns have expanded enormously to meet the demands of the thousands who work in the city, but prefer a more suburban home.

And yet there are many ways in which the county has not changed so very much. Hertford itself has remained not much larger than it was a century ago, though there are some striking modern additions, and the River Beane meanders through unspoilt meadows as it always did. And the county was a major transport centre long before the M25 was built. The Great North Road, now the A1(M), cut straight up from London to carry merchants, bureaucrats and travellers of all kinds north from the capital. Nor was the Norwich road, now the A10, much less busy.

Those key transport links have carried not only peaceful folk but also armies, and it was the din of war that led to the first haunting of this bustling county. In May 1455 the Duke of York was marching towards London at the head of an army. He was not, York was careful to point out, a rebel, but a loyal subject who wanted only the best for his monarch, Henry VI, and the kingdom of England. Not everyone saw it like that.

The trouble had begun three years earlier when King Henry went temporarily mad. York was Henry's cousin and was heir to the throne, unless Henry should produce a son. He naturally stepped in to take over while the king was unwell. York proved to be honest, capable and skilled in the practice of kingship, but had the unfortunate gift of rubbing up almost everyone he met the wrong way. The common people loved the way he governed; the nobles and bureaucrats detested the man himself.

When Henry regained his senses, he promptly sacked York and sent him back to his estates. In his place, Henry put the Duke of Somerset, who was everything York was not: charming, handsome and utterly incompetent. And so York mustered an army and marched south in an attempt to persuade the king to reinstate honest, competent government.

Henry saw York's move as rebellion and gathered an army of his own. He set out towards Leicester and had got as far as St Albans when York learned where he was and turned off the Great North Road to approach the king. On 22 May York's army reached St Albans just after dawn. They sat down to wait while a message was sent to the king. Henry refused to read a note from a rebel and dispatched the elderly Duke of Buckingham, York's father-in-law, to offer surrender terms. York refused the terms, so the king condemned him to death as a rebel. The fight was on.

York led his men along the two roads into the town, but the routes were blocked by barricades thrown up between the houses. While the king's men had their attention fixed on the barricades, York's young friend the Earl of Warwick ordered his men to whip out their axes and hack their way into the wooden houses themselves. The tactic worked. After some minutes of furious chopping, the men were surging through the houses and into St Albans. Fanning out, Warwick's troops raced to attack the king's men from the rear. The street fighting that followed was savage, but short. In less than 20 minutes Somerset was killed and Henry was captured. The battle was over.

York promptly went down on one knee to his terrified monarch and pledged his loyalty and obedience, even handing over his sword. The king made York head of government and all the participants left the little Hertfordshire town behind them. The fight had triggered the Wars of the Roses, which would drag on for over 30 years.

But the ghosts remain. One of the houses through which Warwick's men fought their way is still standing. It is now known as Battlefield House on Hollywell Street. In and around this house are sometimes heard the sounds of clashing steel and hacking weapons. There has even been seen the figure of a man dressed in a grubby tunic and carrying a large axe. He is, presumably, one of Warwick's men who was killed here on the very threshold of victory.

Whether or not the five monks who process quietly across the lawns to the abbey, which stands at the heart of St Albans, are linked to the battle or not is unknown. They seem rather too serene to have been mixed up in violence, but nobody can be certain.

* * *

A rather more anonymous and mysterious phantom lurks in the centre of Ware, a small town noted for its large and imposing parish church. The ghost here is seen infrequently and then only for a few seconds at most. It takes the form of a motor car variously described as being 'old-fashioned', 'ancient' or 'vintage'. It certainly has great sweeping mudguards and running boards and is a dark colour, but beyond that it is impossible to be sure of much. It lurches into view as if driven by a person caring little for speed limits or other road users. More than one passing motorist has been forced to slam on his brakes with alarming suddenness as a crash appears unavoidable, only to be faced by an empty road.

Who the driver of this dangerous vehicle might be is unknown. There are no records of a car crash from the right period that might account for the phantom car of Ware.

* * *

Another spectral vehicle that is rather more clearly identified is the dramatic ghost coach of Hatfield. This takes the form of an early

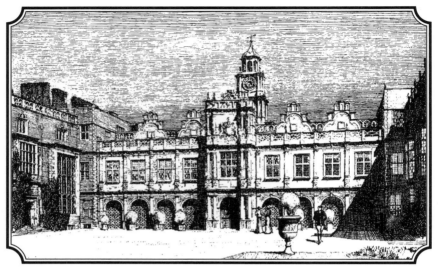

THE MAIN COURTYARD OF HATFIELD HOUSE, INTO WHICH A PHANTOM COACH
HURTLES AT HIGH SPEED, ONLY TO VANISH WITHOUT TRACE.

19th century coach pulled by four horses, which hurtles through the gates of Hatfield House and tears up the drive at a breakneck speed. Usually the coach will vanish abruptly as it approaches the doors of the house, but on one famous occasion in the 1920s it appeared to crash through the front doors and vanished only as it reached the foot of the stairs.

There can be little doubt that this is the phantom coach of the 1st Marchioness of Salisbury, a lady who had a character usually described tactfully as 'colourful'. She was widowed in 1804 at the age of 51, but saw no reason to curtail her social life. Her son, now the 2nd Marquis, gave her apartments in Hatfield House and rooms at his London home. She used both to the full. She entertained friends magnificently in Hatfield, then travelled up to London to gamble and visit shows with the best of them.

Everything this lady did, she did in a hurry. She was especially fond of fast horses, and of men who knew how to drive them. If she heard of a driver able to get that extra bit of speed out of a team of horses, she offered him fine wages to get him into her employ. The speeding coach of the Lady Salisbury became a well known, and best avoided, feature of the roads around Hatfield. It is unsurprising that after her death the coach has returned in spectral form.

In 1835 the lady, by now 82 years old, was enjoying life as much as ever. Then a fire broke out in her private rooms one night. Before any servants could reach her, the flames had not only taken the life of the Marchioness, but had also reduced the West Wing of the house to ashes. And it is not only the ghostly carriage that returns. The phantom of this Lady Salisbury has been seen herself, walking sedately along the Long Gallery of the house.

* * *

A few years after the death of Queen Victoria, Hatfield became famous for a quite different supernatural event. The last northbound express of the day thundered through the station at Hatfield in total darkness, as it did every day of the year. But on this particular occasion things were not going well in the driver's cabin. As the train had hurtled past, a wraith-like figure had materialised on the platform – or so the driver said. This was odd, for the station was not open so late at night, all the stopping trains having left.

Feeling an overwhelming sense of dread and fear, the driver had slammed on the brakes of the engine. Amid billowing steam and screaming wheels, the engine came to a shuddering halt. The driver cowered in his cabin, drenched in sweat and refusing either to get out or to explain why he had stopped the express.

Puzzled, the other crew members explored – to find a tree had fallen over the rails, blocking them completely. If the driver had not stopped, disaster would have followed. It was some days before the driver was induced to tell his story, and it was never really explained what had happened.

* * *

The romantic ruins of Minsden chapel, near Hitchin, have two ghosts if one can believe the stories. The original phantom of this lonely, eerie spot is that of a monk. This hooded spectre has been quietly haunting his ruined chapel for as long as anyone can remember. He drifts silently among the tumbled stones, seemingly unaware of, or at least uninterested in, the passing mortals who glimpse him.

In 1907 a visitor took a photo of the chapel, which, when developed, showed a startlingly clear figure of a monk walking out of the ruins. The picture caused quite a sensation at the time and was widely reproduced, though many photographic experts found it unconvincing.

The second ghost to lurk at the Minsden chapel is more of an enigma. The author Reginald Hine lived near the ruins and loved to visit them. In fact he enjoyed the place so much that he predicted a short while before his death in 1949 that he would return to haunt them as a phantom. A few people claim to have seen this local genealogist and historian mooching about the place in his customary tweeds, but it is the monk who appears more regularly.

* * *

Rather more shadowy is the ghost that frequents the Boar's Head pub in Bishop's Stortford. This tall, slim man is said to be a former churchwarden of nearby St Michael's church who favoured the Boar's Head as a place to relax and drink the odd pint or two. After his burial in his beloved church, it is said, he returned in spectral form to walk his old accustomed route from church to pub before vanishing. He is said to have been seen repeating his ghostly journey again more recently.

In 2003, after closing one night, Patrick, the landlord, was sitting with a friend and they both heard a stool being pulled away from the bar on the other side of the fireplace. They then heard it being pulled back into position, as if someone were sitting at the bar. It was a very distinctive, loud sound, as the floor here is of York flagstones and could not be explained away. Another time, a few

CUSTOMERS AT THE BOAR'S HEAD AT BISHOP STORTFORD WERE STARTLED TO SEE THE APPARITION OF A REGULAR DRINKER WALK INTO THE PUB JUST HOURS AFTER HIS FUNERAL.

months later – again after closing – Patrick was sitting on a bar stool talking to a friend when the poker from the fire jumped off its hook and, instead of falling, went sideways and hit the legs of the stool Patrick was sitting on. This was a yard or more away.

The pub itself dates back over 600 years and was originally owned by the Church, but was sold off at the Reformation. The heavy wooden beam over the fireplace has been dated to the 1400s. Only slightly more recently, this pub was a favourite watering hole of Samuel Pepys when he journeyed out of London, and crops up more than once in his famous *Diary*.

Kent

Popularly known as the Garden of England, Kent has lived up to its name for centuries past, with orchards, hopfields, flowerbeds and market gardening in plenty. With a warm, wet climate, Kent can produce the finest fruits and vegetables in England without too much to worry about in the way of frost or snow.

And Kent has long been famous for its oasthouses, where hops are dried ready for the brewing industry. Today most hops come from abroad, but oasthouses are retained even if they are put to use as bedrooms or bathrooms as farm after farm is converted to domestic use. To the inhabitants of this county, there is a clear divide between Kentish Men and Men of Kent, between those who live west or east of the River Medway. To the east is a land that was long one of swamps, marshes and islands where the Jutes settled after the fall of Rome, while to the west lie the dry farmlands that the Jutes owned and taxed, but did not colonise.

But Kent has not always been a land of plenty and of peace. This has long been the route by which invaders have sought to dominate Britain. The Romans came this way, and in more recent years the Germans under Hitler planned to invade along the fine roads inland from Dover and Folkestone.

But the ghosts do not seem to care. For them this is a county that does not alter, that exists as it did when they lived. But for some of them their localities have changed massively. Take the shades of Ebbsfleet, for instance.

These insubstantial phantoms haunt the Isle of Thanet fields that lie between the A256 and Ebbsfleet Lane. They tend to be vague and shapeless, but they were not always thus. Accounts dating back two centuries or more describe the ghosts of big men armed with spears, swords and shields. It has been surmised that these are the phantoms of Hengist, Horsa and other Jutish warriors, wading ashore in Britain for the first time. It may be so, for Ebbsfleet is the traditional site of their landing.

Interestingly, it has for some years been assumed that the first people to invade post-Roman Britain landed at the far end of the great bay of Ebbsfleet, at what is now Cliffsend. In 1949 a group of enthusiastic historical experts rebuilt an ancient Saxon ship and rowed it over the sea to Ebbsfleet to celebrate the 1,500th anniversary of the landings of Hengist and Horsa.

THE HUGIN SHIP WAS ROWED OVER THE SEA TO EBBSFLEET IN 1949 ON THE 1,500TH ANNIVERSARY OF HENGIST AND HORSA'S ORIGINAL VOYAGE.

The design of this Hugin Ship, as it is known, is based largely on archaeological finds and written accounts, but these are incomplete and vague. And nobody is entirely certain that the ship is preserved in the exact spot of the first landing. Perhaps the ghosts know best, but their wispy nature makes it unlikely that they will tell.

Only a few years after arriving, the English faced their sternest test as they faced a huge army of Romano-Britons blocking the route towards London. After some threats and parleys, it was decided that rather than risk a major battle, the issue should be decided by single combat. Horsa stepped forward for the English, while

HORSA DIED AT KITS COTY OVER 1,500 YEARS AGO, BUT HIS GHOST STILL RETURNS TO THE SCENE OF HIS DEATH.

the Britons put up their king, named Vortigern. The prize was Kent, the venue the hillside south of Chatham where a Roman road crosses the River Medway.

The rival armies sat on the slopes above, which form a natural theatre here. The champions strode forth. The duel proved to be long and violent, with wounds inflicted and received by both. Eventually Horsa fell dead and Vortigern claimed victory. True to his word, Hengist led his men out of Kent, but they went only as far as the Isle of Sheppey, where they established a stronghold. The English would be back.

Meanwhile, the scene of the combat, now known as Kit Coty House, became the site of a grim haunting. The ghosts of both Horsa and Vortigern returned to re-fight the battle that had, temporarily at least, decided the fate of Kent. They can be seen here still, from time to time. They appear most often on calm, hot days, perhaps reflecting the scene when they fought as mortals. They are visible for a few seconds only before they vanish.

Not far away from this scene of combat is the upright stone known as the White Horse Stone. Traditionally, this marks the burial site of Horsa. His brother Hengist is said to have painted on it a white horse prancing on a red field, which is still the emblem of Kent.

* * *

Some centuries later Duke William of Normandy invaded England, killed King Harold at the Battle of Hastings and seized power.

When preparing his invasion, William had put about a story condemning Harold as a man who had broken a sacred oath taken on the most holy of Christian relics. Whether or not the story was true, the Pope gave William his blessing for the invasion. In return, Pope Alexander II had extracted two promises from William. The first was that Alexander's old schoolmaster, Lanfranc of Bec, should be appointed Archbishop of Canterbury. The second was that Lanfranc should be given a free hand to impose papal authority on the Church in England, which was notoriously idiosyncratic in its observation of papal instructions.

One of these instructions was that priests should be celibate. When Lanfranc arrived he found that six priests in Canterbury were married. Although this was perfectly legal in pre-Norman England, the new Archbishop arrested the hapless men and had them thrown into prison inside the newly completed Norman fortress of Lympne Castle. A few days later the priests were conveniently dead. Lanfranc announced that this was due to divine disfavour, rather than Norman swords, and instructed all English priests to be celibate henceforth.

THE KILLING OF SIX PRIESTS AT LYMPNE CASTLE IN THE WAKE OF THE NORMAN CONQUEST LEFT A PHANTOM REMINDER BEHIND.

The ghosts of these unfortunate priests remain in Lympne. They are seen lurking mournfully around the stone walls that had held them prisoner, walking quietly as if in conversation with each other.

* * *

Another spectre with religious connections haunts the gate leading from the church at Penshurst to the vicarage. The ghost is a young man dressed in the smock that for centuries marked out the farm labourers in Kent, as elsewhere in southern England. He strolls across the churchyard to the vicarage gate, then stops as if in thought and vanishes.

Local talk has it that this ghost is that of a local farmer who was in love with the daughter of the vicar. The farmer was honest and hardworking, but did not work a particularly good set of acres. The vicar, on the other hand, was an educated man who hoped his daughter would make a good match. Three times the farmer approached the vicarage to ask the vicar for the hand of his daughter in marriage and three times he lost his nerve at the gate.

The heartache and anguish of the local yokel was clearly enough to leave its spectral mark here. But the story has a happy ending. On the fourth attempt the young man summoned up the courage to get through the gate and approach his prospective father-in-law.

THE PATH LEADING TO THE VICARAGE AT PENSHURST, ALONG WHICH A GHOST WALKS MANY YEARS AFTER HE CAME THIS WAY IN LIFE.

The vicar was, as predicted, hostile, but his daughter was hopelessly in love and talked him round. The wedding was held a few weeks later.

Just north of the church stands the magnificent pile of Penshurst Place, a beautiful Tudor mansion as large as any royal palace. This is home to two ghosts. The mysterious lady spectre, thought to be an early member of the Sidney family, is dressed in typically late Tudor fashion and is seen the garden, but only in the parts that date to that time.

More famous is the phantom of the elegant young man seen inside the house, dressed in colourful doublet and hose. This is Sir Philip

Sidney, who was born here in 1554 and went on to find fame as poet, soldier and courtier. After a short, but adventurous life, Sir Philip happened to be in the Dutch town of Zutphen in 1586, as the Dutch were fighting to throw off the yoke of Spanish imperialism. On 22 September a Spanish army appeared and Sidney, liking the Catholic extremists no better than did his Dutch hosts, volunteered to join the Dutch cavalry. Sidney led a successful charge, but was mortally wounded. As he lay dying Sidney achieved enormous fame by refusing his servant's offer of a drink of water. Instead, he gave the precious liquid to a wounded Dutchman saying, 'Your need is greater than my own.' Sidney's ghost has been glimpsed strolling about Penshurst Place ever since. He is thought to return to the house that he loved so well and where he was most happy.

* * *

A very different sort of kindness led to the haunting at Minster. The phantom here is that of a lady who was married to the owner of Cleve Court, a private house in the northern part of the village. She lived in the mid-18th century and, although she loved children, never had any of her own. She made up for this by lavishing affection and gifts on the young people of the village. She always welcomed the local toddlers to her home, passing them sweets and toys to keep them amused.

Unfortunately her husband did not appreciate the expense of these trifles, or the constant chattering of mothers and the cheerful squealing of children about his house when he was trying to work. Angrily he banished the villagers from his home and forbade his wife to spend any money without his approval. It was too much for her, and she died soon after of what was generally recognised as a broken heart.

This gentle lady haunts the streets and lanes of the village. Not that she is seen by adults, but children will often report a kindly woman who watches them as they play. Even when they point her out to their parents, the grown ups see nothing. Presumably the caring lady from so long ago still cares for the local youngsters.

Lancashire

Lancashire has a mixed aspect. There are the great industrial cities of Manchester and Liverpool, both now separated from the county for the purposes of local government. There is the county town of Lancaster, still dominated by its ancient castle, and a scattering of prosperous market towns. This has long been an important region nationally – the Queen of England still draws much of her income from the estates she holds as the Duke of Lancaster and the county is the only one that has a seat in the national government, for the Chancellor of the Duchy of Lancaster is a member of the cabinet.

But it is the landscape that defines the county. Lying between the great natural boundaries of the Mersey to the south, the Pennines to the east and the Cumbrian mountains to the north, Lancashire has long looked out across the wild waters of the Irish Sea to the west, and beyond them to the Atlantic. And with over a hundred miles of coastline, the county has a lot of looking to do.

Nowhere have the good folk of Lancashire looked out across the waves more often than from Blackpool, playground of the north. Some of those who have gazed across the sparkling waters have witnessed a very odd sight indeed. Somewhere, out among the haze between sea and sky, have been seen the spires of churches. And those who have taken pleasure boats out onto the sea have heard the distant sound of church bells. This is the ghostly lost city of the west. Centuries ago, Lancashire stretched out much further to the west than it does now. Sadly a great flood poured in from the Irish Sea, drowning the land and driving out the inhabitants. The ruins still lie beneath the sea and the bells can be heard in rough weather, while on calm days the phantoms of the lost parishes rise above the waves.

Nor is there any respite at Blackpool for those who turn their eyes inland. In the early hours of the morning, when all is quiet and still, a lone tram will trundle down the Promenade. Its lights are lit, but it never stops to collect passengers, nor does its driver slow down for any reason. This is the ghost tram that has been running this route for the past century.

* * *

Startling as these ghostly apparitions may be, they are at least less terrifying than old Peg O'Nell who lurks on the banks of the Ribble. This gruesome old hag lives along the river and may be seen at almost any time. But it is when she appears to be searching for something that she adopts her most terrible appearance. She is looking for a victim.

This vicious old lady will be content with anything, so long as it can assuage her macabre tastes. She will drag cattle, foxes or sheep into the watery embrace of the Ribble to snuff out their life and drink deeply of their blood. But if seven years pass by without her managing to take an animal life, she will come looking for a human. And then the good folk of Lancashire walk warily around the Ribble, for the old hag will not be happy until she has made a victim of one of them.

Old Peg O'Nell is an ancient spirit. When the Romans came here, they identified her with their own goddess Minerva. This specialist in trade and commerce was notoriously touchy and, armed with a spear and helmet, more than capable of striking down a mere mortal. Over the centuries the spirit has lost her status as a god, such was the victory of Christianity in these islands, but she still walks the lands around the Ribble. And she still claims her blood sacrifice.

* * *

A very modern spectral intrusion into the realm of old Peg O'Nell is to be found above Gisburn, near Barnoldswick. During the grim days of 1940, when Luftwaffe bombers cruised the night skies of Britain to pound these islands into surrender, industrial dispersal was popular. This meant moving machinery from central factories to a number of smaller plants that were more difficult for the Germans to find and so bomb. At Barnoldswick was a factory producing Rolls Royce aero engines.

On clear evenings, as the dusk begins to settle over the Ribble Valley, some people have reported seeing a broad winged aircraft with four engines coming in low over the landscape. There are few four-engined propeller aircraft around these days, so it attracts attention even from those who do not recognise the distinctive throb of Rolls Royce Merlin engines. When a man who was something of a specialist in military history saw and heard the aircraft, he identified it as a Lancaster.

One person who witnessed the ghost plane said that it dived down out of low cloud, as if about to hit the ground, but then

A LANCASTER BOMBER, PHOTOGRAPHED DURING THE SECOND WORLD WAR, WHICH RETURNS IN PHANTOM FORM OVER LANCASTER.

vanished without trace. 'It was so low I fully expected it to hit us, or at least hit the houses near the Bankfield site. We both fully expected to at least hear the impact of a crash, but there was nothing. And when we both looked back there was nothing. Whatever it was had vanished.'

The workhorse of the British bombing campaign against Germany in the later years of the war, the Lancaster was the aircraft chosen for such specialist raids as the Dambusters attack and the bombing of the *Tirpitz* battleship. In all some 7,400 Lancasters were built during the war, but only a handful remain airworthy today. And none of them is to be found flying low over the Ribble Valley on calm, clear evenings. Why a phantom aircraft should be seen here is unknown. Perhaps it is flying home a spectral crew from Lancashire who perished in the war-torn skies over Germany.

* * *

Where the A6068 runs up towards the Pennines it crosses bleak open country, goes over a tributary of the Ribble at Laneshaw Bridge, then climbs up to the forbidding hills beyond. It was at this lonely spot that a woman was murdered more than two centuries ago. When the battered body was found it was at first thought that footpads had committed a random act of savagery while intent on robbery. Later it was discovered that the unmarried woman had been pregnant. Suspicion began to focus on her notoriously bad-tempered boyfriend, who could not account for his movements on the day the woman went missing day. No real evidence could be found to send the man to the gallows, but he had to leave the district, as nobody would deal with him.

Clearly the poor murdered woman could not rest without her killer being brought to justice. She lurks in the area still. Seen most often by the roadside where she died, her tall, thin figure can give motorists a bit of a shock when it suddenly vanishes from view.

* * *

The most famous ghost of Lancashire is the wicked squire of Wycoller Hall. Built by the Hartley family at the end of the 16th century as a comfortable and impressive, but by no means grand, manor house, this property subsequently passed to members of the Cunliffe family, who seem to have been a thoroughly bad lot.

Simon Cunliffe was squire here in the early 18th century and a very active and outgoing man he was too. He did not spend much time looking after his estates, and even less looking after his wife and children. But he did enjoy riding, drinking, chasing women and – a particular favourite of his – chasing foxes. It was this last activity that led to tragedy and to the haunting.

Squire Simon Cunliffe was out riding to hounds over the bleak hills around Wycoller one wild day as the winds whipped across the landscape and glowering storm clouds above the Pennines threatened to come down to the lowlands. A fox was found and soon the hunt was on its trail. Down from the hills the chase swept into the little valley where Wycoller stands. The terrified fox raced through the front door of Wycoller Hall, up the stairs and into a bedroom. Behind it stormed Squire Cunliffe, whip in hand and hounds at his feet.

THE DOORWAY AT WYCOLLER THROUGH WHICH THE GHOST STORMS AS IF IN A TERRIBLE TEMPER.

What happened next has become the stuff of legend. According to Squire Cunliffe, he and the hounds burst into the room, cornered the fox and killed it in seconds. Only then did he realise that his wife was resting in the bed. The poor lady, Squire Cunliffe said, died of fright. According to the servants, the bored and ignored mistress of the house had been entertaining one of the more handsome servants in her bedroom at the time. The servant leapt from a window as the squire stormed in, but for Mrs Cunliffe there was no escape. Her furious husband lashed her to death with his horsewhip.

Whatever the truth, Mrs Cunliffe was most certainly dead. She was laid out in the main hall of Wycoller and buried next day. The squire did not much care for Wycoller Hall after that terrible day and spent most of his life away from the locals who knew too much about him. He died abroad, leaving the estates to a young son.

It would seem that he also left his ghost. When the wind whips over the hills and storm clouds gather over the Pennines, the dread phantom of Squire Cunliffe rides once more. He gallops over the bleak uplands, then rides down into the valley and up to the front door of his old home. Bursting in as if in a fury, the spectre races up the stairs. The sounds of a woman's screams follow, rising to a

THE RUINS OF WYCOLLER HALL STAND GAUNT AND MAJESTIC IN THE NARROW VALLEY OF THE SAME NAME.

terrifying pitch of anguished intensity. Then all is quiet. Silence descends once more on grim Wycoller Hall.

The house was later enlarged and improved in the 1780s by Squire Henry Owen Cunliffe as part of his campaign to attract a wealthy wife. The plan, one must assume, was to appear to be so wealthy that nobody would think he was in desperate need of money. None of the heiresses that he approached would suspect he was after only their money rather than themselves. The one small flaw in Squire Cunliffe's plan was that he was such an unappealing character that no respectable or self-respecting young lady would have married him anyway. He was a notorious gambler with a quick temper, who consorted with various disreputable hoodlums.

Nevertheless, he made a good job of Wycoller Hall. The work took more than a year and saw the installation of a grand porch, fine windows and the most impressive fireplace in the county. This particular bad squire died in 1818 leaving a mountain of debts. Charlotte Brontë is thought to have visited Wycoller village frequently in her many walks around the area. She based Ferndean Manor in her novel *Jane Eyre* on Wycoller Hall.

The house is now in ruins, but the ghost of Squire Cunliffe remains. There is a second ghost, though this is never seen in the house, preferring the fields and hills nearby. Going by the name of Guytrash Lightfoot, this spectre is a large dog of fearsome appearance that roams the countryside. He is best avoided, they say, for his master is the Devil and he brings bad luck whenever he patrols the hills.

Leicestershire

Most would agree that Leicestershire is a delightful county. The ancient county town of Leicester was old before the Romans came, but it was they who defined the centre with walls and ensured the town's prosperity by building roads that link it with the rest of the country. In modern times, it has spread extensively, engulfing what were once the separate villages of Aylestone, Eyres Monsell and Evington. It is even sprawling beyond its own ring road, the A563.

Today's large city of Leicester is home to the county's most active ghost. The imposing house of Belgrave Hall was first built by Edmund Cradock between 1709 and 1713. He died soon afterwards and the next owners were John and Helen Simons. Not much was ever recorded about the Simons but they resided within until the Vanns took over in 1767. The Vanns ran an extremely successful hosiery business, using the outbuildings as warehouses. They were decent, kind people, who gave generously to charity and employed many of the locals as knitters. They did much work to the house, before selling up to the Ellis family.

It is generally thought that the ghostly lady who haunts this house was one of the Ellis family. The genteel spectre is seen quite often, though only fleetingly, upstairs, on the stairs and in the gardens. She wears a terracotta coloured dress that reaches to the floor and walks with a quick, determined stride. Her footsteps are heard clipping across the wooden floors as often as the ghost itself is seen. And there are the occasional scents of baking bread or pies drifting through the premises.

In December 1998 the ghost hit the national headlines when it was caught on a security camera walking along a path outside the hall. The lady was dressed in a paler colour than usual and seemed to glow with an unworldly interior light. It was seen clearly on a photo taken at 5 am, but was absent from all other shots.

Photographic experts were called in, and were puzzled. The figure did, indeed, seem to emit its own light rather than being lit by any external source. It is usually said that the phantom is that of Charlotte Ellis, who lived at the hall with her seven sisters after John Ellis brought the property in 1845. There is also said to be a ghostly child at the hall, but she is not seen very often.

Though the lady at Belgrave Hall may be the most active ghost in Leicester, she is not alone. Nor is Belgrave the most haunted building that the city can boast. The Guildhall claims no fewer than four phantoms. As at Belgrave Hall, the most frequent visitor is a lady ghost. This entity appears in a flowing gown, variously described as being cream or pale pink by those who see her. She seems to centre her activities around the library, and particularly an ancient Bible that is kept there. Not only is she seen often hovering around the book, but it can be found open on mornings when it is known to have been firmly shut the evening before.

* * *

Beyond the embrace of Leicester, the county remains a charming vista of rolling hills dotted with woods and patched by agricultural fields. The underlying soil is a rich clay, producing fertile soil above for arable crops. This landscape was created by hunting as much as by farming. The woods provide coverts for fox dens, the hedgerows give foxes cover and test the jumping skills of man and horse. With foxhunting having been banned it remains to be seen if the owners of Leicestershire's broad acres will continue to maintain the woods and hedges, or replace them with more productive crops and cheaper barbed wire.

It is unlikely that whatever changes come to Leicestershire will much bother the White Lady of Thringstone. She has been walking the area north of the village for some centuries now, so she will probably continue to roam for some time yet. She haunts the ruins of Grace Dieu Priory, that lie just off the A512.

The ghost is seen quite often. Once, in 2002, a bus driver stopped to pick her up, as she was standing beside the road just a short distance from the bus stop. As soon as he stopped, she vanished. The bus stop is not her usual stomping ground, however. Most sightings put her walking to the ruins from the prehistoric stone in the field on the other side of the brook that runs by the ruins. This standing stone is the sole survivor of what had once been a henge of fourteen standing stones. The others were destroyed centuries ago by local Puritans fearful of these reminders of pagan days. The ghost moves off to cross the stream by a little ford that goes by the name of White Lady Ford. It is the only place where the stream can be crossed without the water being so deep it runs over one's shoes.

THE RUINS OF GRACE DIEU PRIORY AT THRINGSTONE AS SEEN FROM THE FOOTPATH LEADING UP FROM WHITE LADY FORD.

THE PREHISTORIC STANDING STONE
WHICH MARKS THE SPOT WHERE THE
WHITE LADY OF GRACE DIEU PRIORY
STARTS HER WALK.

Close by the ford stands a charming statue of a seated nun. She looks across a stream straight at the tumbled ruins of Grace Dieu Priory, which stand in broad open fields fringed by woodland. The old priory is now fenced off, as the remaining structures are in danger of collapse, but the local Grace Dieu Trust is caring for the ruins, and work to make them safe is under way.

Grace Dieu was founded in 1239 by Roesia de Verdun for fourteen Augustinian nuns and their prioress. In thanks for her worldly generosity, the nuns buried Roesia in the priory church when she died in 1247. Over the following centuries Grace Dieu – the name means 'By the gift of God' – flourished. The original complement of nuns increased as the wealth of the establishment grew through exploiting local lime deposits and glass-making, and it became not so much a priory as a convent.

All seemed to be going well until 1536, when King Henry VIII ordered an investigation into alleged scandals and improprieties at the many religious houses in England. A large number were deemed to be debauched institutions and were closed down, the king seizing their wealth and lands. Grace Dieu, however, was one of those found to be beyond reproach. King Henry promised the then prioress, Agnes Litherland, that Grace Dieu would be left alone. Three years later he needed more money, so Grace Dieu was closed down anyway.

The site and lands were bought by a local gentleman, John Beaumont of Thringstone, who converted the buildings to a comfortable house. In 1690 the Beaumonts sold the lands to Sir Ambrose Phillips of Garendon. Already having a home of his own, Phillips pulled down most of the old buildings to sell the materials. He left only the ruins to be seen today. It was a sad end to over four centuries of Grace Dieu.

The remains of Grace Dieu's founder, Roesia de Verdun, were moved to nearby Belton church. And there she rests to this day in her fine alabaster tomb.

But who is the White Lady? Probably just some gentle soul from the days of Grace Dieu's greatness who could not bear to leave her old home. And who can blame her?

* * *

Considerably less peaceful is the ghost that roams the fields and lanes near Market Bosworth. On 22 August 1485 this area saw the Battle of Bosworth, at which the crown of England changed hands in battle for the last time. King Richard III, the capable but personally unpopular Yorkist ruler, faced the rebel army of Henry Tudor, who was backed by disaffected nobles from the Lancastrian faction. It was to be the last major battle in the Wars of the Roses, that had racked England for a generation.

The royal army stood on the hilltop, with the rebels in the valley below. But there was a third army, that of the powerful Stanley family, which belonged to neither York nor Lancaster faction. As the fighting reached its height, the Stanleys threw their men into the battle on the side of Henry Tudor. Richard was killed and much of his army slain. Henry Tudor became king as Henry VII, the crown of England having been found under a bush where it had fallen when Richard was killed.

It is to this bloody battle that the ghostly soldiers belong. They have been seen staggering across the old battlefield, or lying slumped down as if wounded. One unfortunate spectre has lost his head, presumably hacked off by the brutally simple weapons of the time. Who these armoured knights may be, or which side they fought for, is quite unknown.

Lincolnshire

If any county in England suffers a split personality, it must be Lincolnshire. In the south are the Lincolnshire fens. Once a vast expanse of marsh and swamp that stretched deep into Norfolk and Cambridgeshire, the fens have been drained over the centuries to produce rich, black soil that is among the most productive in the kingdom. Then there are the Lincoln wolds, a range of rolling chalk hills that run north to south providing well-drained soils for arable farming. And finally there are the wet grasslands that fringe the North Sea coast to provide grazing for cattle such as the famous Lincoln Red.

But the one thing that unifies all of Lincolnshire is its sense of otherworldiness. No major through routes run across the county. The A1 and M1, together with the main line railway, lie to the west. Only the road and rail links serving the docks at Grimsby intrude across the north of Lincolnshire. People travel to Lincolnshire only if they are going there, not if they are heading elsewhere. And, by and large, that is how the good people of Lincolnshire like it.

The ghosts too, seem to like the company of their fellow Lincolnshire citizens. None more so that the ghostly squire of Digby. For if there's one thing to be said for Robert Cooke of the village of Digby it's that he knows how to throw a jolly good party.

This is a welcome ability in anyone, but in this case it is most impressive, for Squire Cooke has been dead these past two centuries. It is his ghost that throws the parties for his fellow phantoms. And it is no wonder, for Squire Cooke has the largest and most impressive tomb in the churchyard of Digby.

Squire Cooke was born in 1746 as the Georgian period was getting into its stride. Like many other gentlemen of his period, he enjoyed a booming prosperity based on the gathering pace of the industrial and agricultural revolutions that ensured ready markets for the food he was growing on his broad acres around Digby.

By all accounts, Robert Cooke was not one to hoard his gold. His house became famous for its hospitality and for the good time to be had there. Local families vied for invitations to the Cooke home and the matrons eyed up the squire's growing son as a good marriage prospect for their daughters.

The merry life obviously agreed with Robert Cooke, for he lived to be 72 years old, a most respectable age for the 18th century. In spite of being a big spender, Cooke must have left considerable wealth, for his heirs had enough money to pay for a large stone

THE TOMB OF SQUIRE COOKE AT DIGBY IS THE VENUE FOR SPECTRAL JOLLIFICATIONS.

table tomb in the churchyard. On the tomb they proudly described the deceased squire as 'Robert Cooke, Gentleman' and gave the dates of his birth and his death.

It was not long before the stories began to circulate. Squire Cooke had been preceded to the tomb by most of his boyhood friends. Now, it was said, the old squire was inviting his pals to visit just as he had done when alive. And the parties, folk related, were every bit as impressive.

All you had to do to hear the venerable old squire and his friends was run backwards around the tomb twelve times, then listen. If Squire Cooke was partying you could clearly hear the clink of glasses and the sound of merrymaking.

One man who tried this a year or two back reported: 'It was not easy as the ground is uneven and the other tombs crowd in around those of the Cooke family. I tripped twice, but managed to keep going. Eventually, I had completed the required twelve circuits and, a spot out of breath, leant on the tomb to see if I could hear anything. Amazingly I could. The sound of laughing and rattling glasses was clear enough. But it was coming from the Red Lion just down the road, so I went there for a pint and a ploughman's. Lovely grub.'

* * *

As one of the oldest buildings in Grantham, it is hardly surprising to learn that the Angel and Royal Hotel is haunted. But what is unusual is the frequency with which the ghost is noticed and the fact that she is seen by many who do not know she exists – until she disturbs their sleep.

Typical is the experience of the American visitor who recently came down to breakfast and asked the manageress, 'Why didn't you tell me the place was haunted?' It seems that the guest had awoken in the early hours of the morning to find a lady dressed all in white standing at the foot of her bed. The lady had stood still for a few seconds, then turned to walk off, and gently faded from view.

THE HAUNTED CORRIDOR AT THE ANGEL AND ROYAL, WHERE AN AMERICAN LADY HAD A BIT OF A FRIGHT.

The description given by the guest was exactly the same as that provided by the many other people who have encountered the ghostly white lady. She is of average height and rather slim with long hair tied into a plait or bun. The phantom is dressed in a full-length white or cream dress, which is fitted over the bodice, but very full in the skirt. It appears to be stiff when the lady moves, rather than soft and flowing.

Nobody is entirely certain who the white lady is, but the fashions she wears would seem to put her in the 18th century and she has certainly been seen off and on for as long as anyone can remember.

The white lady is usually encountered in the second floor corridor and the bedrooms off it. As well as waking the American visitor last year, the white lady gave an English guest such a fright that she fled her room and spent the rest of the night with a friend on a different floor. That was in 1999, but the ghost has not let up on her appearances. Several staff at the hotel are wary of the corridor and report a strong feeling of being followed or watched, even if they do not see the white lady herself.

Not so long ago she flitted through the reception area late one night, to the surprise of the porter, who was usually careful to keep away from the second floor in order to avoid just such an encounter.

One of the clearest sightings was in 2000 in the restaurant, which occupies a magnificent chamber on the first floor overlooking the High Street. In one corner there is a tiny spiral

THE RESTAURANT AT THE ANGEL AND ROYAL; THE NARROW SPIRAL STAIRCASE IS BEHIND THE SUIT OF ARMOUR TO THE RIGHT OF THE PICTURE.

staircase that runs up to the second floor but was blocked off many years ago. The then manager, Mr Tony Chang, was clearing the room after the last dinner guest had gone when he saw the white lady stride across the restaurant, pause at the foot of the staircase and then climb up out of sight. Presumably the stone wall at the top of the stairs would not have been a problem for her.

Ghosts apart, the Angel and Royal is a fine town hotel. It was built about 850 years ago as a lodging for the Knights Templar and transferred to the Church after that militant order was disbanded in the later medieval period. It was at this time that visiting kings held their court in the building, which was one of the finest and most comfortable in the town. King Richard III was one of those who stayed here. The hotel still possesses a framed copy of the execution warrant which was drawn up in the hotel by King Richard in his own hand and which sent the then Duke of Buckingham to his death. After the Reformation, the building went through a number of owners before becoming a hotel serving visitors to Grantham.

* * *

As befits its ancient role as county town, fortress city and sacred hill, Lincoln itself has more than its fair share of ghosts. And nowhere has greater spectral activity than the White Hart Hotel in Bailgate. This comfortable and welcoming hotel has been receiving guests ever since the 1380s, when it was a hostelry catering for clerical visitors to the cathedral. Of course, it has been renovated, altered and improved many times since and the oldest part of the building standing above ground today dates back about 300 years.

The most persistent of the phantoms is the highwayman who haunts the Orangery restaurant. This spacious room was formed by putting a glass roof over what had been the courtyard where coaches had their horses changed and where the animals were led off to stabling. No longer needed in this age of the motor car, the courtyard was converted. But the ghost remains.

THE WHITE HART IN LINCOLN PLAYS HOST TO A NUMBER OF PHANTOMS.

This particular highwayman came to a nasty end. He had tried to hold up a coach travelling north from London to Lincoln a couple of miles south of the city. The occupants of the coach, however, had no intention of handing over their valuables. One of them had a lantern by which he had been reading. Flinging open the door he thrust the burning flame into the highwayman's face. This inflicted hideous burns on the robber, who was then bundled into the coach and taken to Lincoln to face the law. The coach pulled into the courtyard at the White Hart, but when the staff unloaded the criminal they found he was dead. His ghost has never left. Clad in a long, dark cloak and with a tricorn hat pulled firmly down over his brow, this badly scarred man lurks in the shadows. Perhaps he still looks for revenge on the man who killed him.

Just as active is the young girl who haunts the corridor on the first floor. Dressed in a smock and mob-cap, she appears to be about seven or eight years old. This girl was the daughter of the local rat-catcher and she earned some extra pennies as a cleaning maid at the hotel. Everyone knew she was treated appallingly by her drunkard father, and staff at the hotel often gave her little treats and found excuses why she could not go home. Then one sad day she was found dead of neglect and ill treatment. Her ghost returns, perhaps to the only place where she found happiness and peace.

Just as content to remain at the White Hart is the gentleman in a suite on the third floor. This was formerly the flat occupied by the manager, and it is frequented today by the ghost of the manager who died in harness here in the 1920s. He appears dressed in a caramel-coloured smoking jacket of deep velvet with a cream satin cravat and black trousers. He appears, wringing his hands, and asks 'Please help me find my ginger jar,' before abruptly vanishing. Presumably he had been looking for the jar when he died.

Two more ghosts lurk in the private part of the hotel. These are the phantoms of a young man in dashing military uniform of early 19th century date, and a young lady whose clothes place her in a similar period. The lady is seen more frequently, often in a bathroom used by staff and in the corridor outside. In the 1990s one member of staff stayed here for a few weeks while looking for accommodation in the city. She had a young son, who one day asked about 'that nice lady who tucks me in at night'. Given a pencil and paper, the boy produced a childlike image of a lady identical to that described by others who had seen the ghost.

Just around the corner from the White Hart is the majestic cathedral. The first stone church here was built in the very earliest days of Christianity in England, apparently on the foundations of a large Roman building that may have been a temple. This small church was replaced by a larger cathedral by the Normans, but in

LINCOLN CATHEDRAL IS SURROUNDED BY A SPACIOUS GREEN WHERE A GHOSTLY NUN HAS BEEN SEEN.

THE LAMP-POST ON GREESTONE STEPS, WHERE ONE OF LINCOLN'S GHOSTS PUTS IN REGULAR APPEARANCES.

1141 that burned down and was replaced by the fine Gothic structure that stands today. This is the third largest cathedral in England, and it was completed in magnificent style.

The mighty church is surrounded by a pleasant green to the north and east, and by a cobbled courtyard to the west and south. It is the green that is haunted. A nun clad in long dark vestments has been seen walking quietly across the grass. Who she is and how long this phantom has been walking is unknown.

Equally obscure, but seen more often, is the ghostly vicar of Greestone Steps. The narrow alley that runs south from the far eastern end of the green goes between houses, then grows steeper, passes under an arch and becomes a flight of steps that drops down to the lower part of the city. It is up these steps that the ghostly cleric toils his way.

Jane, who lives just 100 yards away in a house with views to the cathedral, knows the phantom well. 'People are seeing him all the time. He even features in that Ghost Walk the tourist people organise round here. Of course, they tell an awful lot of nonsense about him, you know. Saying he glows with an inner luminescence, interferes with cameras and jumps about shouting boo, I shouldn't wonder. But he is real enough. I saw him once, some years back now. It was mid-winter and dark, though it was not yet five o'clock. I was walking up the steps, and a stiff climb it is too, when I just happened to glance ahead of me. Now I was all alone, see. I knew that, as you can see right up those steps from the bottom. But suddenly there was this man there. I saw him as he walked into the light cast by that lamp-post that is up near the top. He walked into the light and I saw him. Tall he was, but bent forward a bit so I could not see his head properly. And dressed in a long, dark coat of some kind. Then he walked on out of the light and was gone. There were no footsteps like you should hear on the stones and, though you can see the arch by the light beyond it, he never went through it. So there was me and a vanishing ghost in a coat. What did I do? Well just carried on walking up the hill. I had to get home to cook tea for the children, didn't I?'

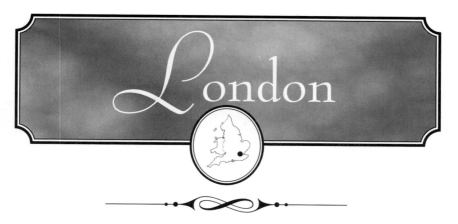

London

There is no city quite like London. It sprawls across many square miles of England, embracing dozens of villages and towns in its arms. It throbs with a never-ending vitality and presents a face to the world that is both grubby and lovely. It has been the capital of England, of Britain and of Empire, and boasts the monuments and memorials of all three.

The original London was a Celtic village that stood where firm gravel beds hemmed the sprawling, marshy Thames in on both banks. Here the river could be crossed with some ease. When the Romans invaded, they built a bridge here and made the settlement the administrative capital of the province of Britannia. That bridge, and its successors, guaranteed London's prosperity for centuries. It was the lowest point on the Thames that allowed for secure crossing and was a key focus of the nation's trade. Soon the city was the centre for the kingdom's commerce, politics and government.

It is scarcely surprising, therefore, that the greatest names in English history feature among the ghosts of London. The Tower of London was begun in 1066 by William the Conqueror to keep his newly acquired capital in subjugation, later serving as the bulwark of London against foreign invaders, as a royal palace and as a prison.

One of the most famous of the ghosts at the Tower is that of Anne Boleyn, second queen to King Henry VIII and the first of his wives that he sent to the executioner's block. Beheaded in 1536 on

THE TOWER OF LONDON, ONE OF ENGLAND'S MOST FAMOUS HAUNTED BUILDINGS.

charges of adultery, which was treason in a queen, Anne was almost certainly innocent. But King Henry wanted her out of the way so that he could marry another woman who he thought had more chance of giving him a son and heir. Anne died with dignity.

Her ghost has returned frequently ever since. She walks with stately step around the small church within the walls of the Tower where she lies buried. One of the most celebrated sightings came in 1864 when a detachment of the 60th Rifle Regiment formed the guard at the Tower. One sentry was found slumped unconscious outside the King's House, where Anne had been lodged. His officer hauled him off to face court-martial for sleeping on duty.

One the day of the trial, the soldier claimed to have fainted after seeing a woman approach him. When he challenged her, she made no reply and did not stop advancing. Presenting his bayonet, the man saw her walk straight through his rifle. At which point he fainted and remembered nothing more until his officer shook him awake. The man was acquitted when two other soldiers came forward to back up his story of the night-time spectre. Another guard saw the ghost in 1933, but this soldier did not waste time challenging the apparition. He fled to the guardroom, arriving in a sweat.

Another victim of execution to return in spectral form is Lady Jane Grey. When Protestant King Edward VI died in 1553 there was a succession problem. The obvious heir was his elder sister Mary, but the Protestants did not want her, as she was a Catholic. Next came another sister, Elizabeth, but the Catholics did not want her, as she was a Protestant. Third in line was a cousin, Lady Jane Grey, whom nobody wanted very much as monarch, but to whom nobody would much object.

Lady Jane's father-in-law, the Duke of Northumberland, hatched a scheme to put her on the throne. However, Princess Mary moved too quickly for him and secured the throne for herself. Northumberland and Lady Jane both went to the block, Lady Jane being only 17 years old. The sad phantom of this lady has been seen on Tower Green.

The Tower is home to other ghosts, including Sir Walter Raleigh, the Princes in the Tower and an assortment of unidentified grey ladies, dark men and others. The final word should go to an officer of the Welsh Guards, one of whose men reported seeing a ghost in 1957. 'Speaking for the regiment, our attitude is this: All right, so you say you saw a ghost. This is the Tower of London. Let's leave it at that.'

* * *

Just yards from the main gate of the Tower stands All Hallows by the Tower. This charming church had one of London's most active and inoffensive ghosts until 29 December 1940. Between 1840 and 1880 the organist here was one Miss Liscette Rist, who resided in the small apartment over the porch. She lived alone apart from a succession of pets, the last of which was a white Persian cat. When this cat died at an advanced age, Miss Rist asked if it could be buried in consecrated ground. The Bishop of London refused, but

ALL HALLOWS BY THE TOWER WAS
FORMERLY THE HOME OF LONDON'S
FRIENDLIEST GHOST.

GREYFRIARS IS NOW A CITY PARK, BUT
IT WAS ONCE A CHURCHYARD,
HAUNTED BY THE MOST BEAUTIFUL
GHOST IN LONDON.

nonetheless she interred it secretly within the church premises. Miss Rist herself died soon after.

It was the ghost of the cat, not of Miss Rist, that frequented the church. It was seen often in her old chambers and almost as often in the organ loft, but could be caught sight of almost anywhere at any time of day.

But on that fateful night in 1940, Hitler's Luftwaffe bombed London and destroyed the old church apart from the tower and the north wall. It was rebuilt to the original plans by 1957, but the ghostly cat returns here no more.

* * *

Another phantom that seems to have been driven away is that of the beautiful Lady Alice Hungerford, wife of Sir Edward

Hungerford. The lady was not as virtuous as she was lovely, for she poisoned her husband and was hanged at Tyburn in 1523. She was buried at Greyfriars and her ghost regularly walked the churchyard. Until the bombs came to destroy the church, that is – and now she too is seen no more.

* * *

Rather older and still active is the ghost belonging to St Bartholomew the Great, the ancient church that lies just off Smithfield. This mighty Norman church was built in 1123 on the orders of Rahere, a courtier of King Henry I. Rahere had a vision one night in which Christ ordered him to found a monastery and become a monk. Without delay he poured his worldly wealth into the foundation and took holy vows to become its first abbot. The church he constructed was large enough to be a cathedral, and, although the nave was demolished in the Reformation, it is still able to impress the visitor with its sombre, dimly lit bulk.

THE OLDEST GHOST IN LONDON WALKS THE ANCIENT STONES OF ST BARTHOLOMEW THE GREAT.

The monastery became famous for its work with the sick of London and in time gave rise to Bartholomew's Hospital, which is today one of the largest in London. The monastery itself was dissolved by King Henry VIII, but Rahere remains. Or at least his ghost does.

The tall man in a cloak is often mistaken for a visitor. The Rev F.G. Sandwith was rector here in the early 20th century when he met Rahere. He entered the church on an errand, to see a man staring at the carved decoration on one of the massive pillars. Thinking to help a tourist with a short history lesson, Rev Sandwith approached and was only some five feet away when the man suddenly vanished. The ghost is seen more often near the altar or close to his tomb, standing quietly as if in contemplation.

* * *

THE SMITHFIELD MONUMENT MARKS THE LAST RESTING PLACE OF DOZENS OF RELIGIOUS MARTYRS.

Just outside St Bartholomew's is Smithfield. This open space was once much larger and housed the great livestock markets of medieval London. These days the meat markets are under cover and housing has encroached on the open fields. But one corner has remained undeveloped. This is the area where Catholic Queen Mary I burned the Protestant heretics who refused to go along with her plans to return England to the Catholic fold. It is thought that 277 men were burned at the stake here over a four-year period.

For years it was said that at the dead of night the dim echoes of the screams and shrieks of the dying martyrs chilled the air. In these modern days of 24-hour traffic, there is never really a quiet moment for the ghosts to make themselves heard. In the 1860s workmen digging a sewer across this area found a heap of charred bones and wood ash that had been shovelled into a pit and covered over. Today a memorial marks the spot.

* * *

The area south of the Strand and Fleet Street is known as the Temple. This was once the London home of the Knights Templar, those stern warrior monks who carried the sword of the crusader to the Moslems in the Holy Land. Later the old Temple property was taken over by the legal fraternity and it is now the unofficial centre of the law in England. This is a quiet, pedestrian only retreat, where narrow alleys link elegant squares lined with trees and ancient buildings.

This area is the haunt of the spectral Lord Brampton, otherwise known as Sir Henry Hawkins, one of the greatest lawyers of the later Victorian period. He was a noted prosecutor who secured the conviction of the Tichbourne claimant after what was at that date the longest trial in English history. Sinisterly, he was known as Hanging Hawkins for the relentless manner in which he hounded defendants in trials where the crime carried the death penalty.

THE DUKE OF YORK'S THEATRE HAD AN UNUSUAL 'HAUNTED JACKET' IN ITS COSTUME DEPARTMENT.

His ghost is seen scurrying along with an armful of papers bound up with ribbon and string. For all the world he looks as if he is rushing to get to a trial at the nearby Old Bailey, or is trotting back to his office after a successful appearance. His wig and gown are of an old-fashioned cut, though only a lawyer would notice such details. For most, this ghost might be mistaken for any present-day lawyer.

* * *

One of the most bizarre ghost stories of London is linked to the Duke of York's Theatre in St Martin's Lane. For some years the costume department there had what was jokingly referred to as 'the haunted jacket', a bolero-style garment of rich velvet. It was used whenever an actress had to play a Victorian lady of quality, but several found it uncomfortable in an odd way, and a few refused to put it on.

In 1949 the actress Thora Hird wore it for a show and became convinced it was, indeed, haunted. She insisted on calling in a medium. This lady held a séance, after which she announced that the jacket had been worn by a woman when she was killed during an attempted rape by somebody she knew well. She advised Miss Hird never to wear it again. It later transpired that the jacket had been owned by a Miss Edith Merryweather, who worked at the theatre and who allegedly died of a fall while out walking with her boyfriend.

* * *

A phantom keeping to more usual ghostly behaviour is the Man in Grey of the Theatre Royal, Drury Lane. Tall, slim and handsome, this ghost is of a man dressed in a long grey riding cloak and black tricorn hat. He appears in the upper circle, seeming to prefer a seat in the fourth row towards the right side of the auditorium. He attends for rehearsals and for matinees, but is never seen in the evenings. This Man in Grey is generally reckoned to be a good omen, as he is present only during the run of a successful show, avoiding flops with great skill.

* * *

Father Benedictus is the name given to the ecclesiastical ghost of Westminster Abbey. He is usually said to walk the cloisters in the later afternoon with a quiet, determined tread. However, the two most famous sightings took place in the church itself. In 1900 a young lady was attending Evensong, sitting in the south transept, when suddenly 'I became aware of someone staring at me very intently. I turned

A SPIRITUALIST ONCE CONTACTED THE MORE ACTIVE OF THE GHOSTS AT WESTMINSTER ABBEY.

round and looked into the eyes of a monk. He was standing with his hands hidden in the sleeves of his habit and his cowl half back from his head. He swept the assembly with a very contemptuous glance, then looked at me again. Slowly he walked backwards, pausing at intervals to scornfully look at the people in the transept. Finally he disappeared at the wall to the south. The whole appearance lasted 25 minutes.'

Some 34 years later a well known spiritualist was visiting the abbey when he was suddenly contacted by the spirit of a monk. This spirit claimed to have been killed here in the reign of King Henry VIII by robbers who had come to steal the royal treasure, stored on the premises for security. Unfortunately, the abbey archives record no such death, nor any such burglary – though there was an almost identical crime in the reign of King Edward I.

The other ghost seen here with some regularity is that of a soldier dressed in uniform of World War I vintage. He lurks near the Tomb of the Unknown Warrior, which commemorates the war dead of Britain. Clearly he is one of the men who laid down their lives for king and country, but quite who he is remains obscure.

Norfolk

Those who don't know Norfolk dismiss this county as 'cold, flat and windy' – which is most unfair but not altogether untrue. The landscape does have its valleys and its hills, but there is no denying that they are far gentler than their counterparts elsewhere in England. And only those who have not come wearing a sensible outfit would find the easterly wind cold rather than bracing.

That said, this is a county that counts its true glories among its man-made wonders. Norwich is a beautiful city crowded round its soaring medieval cathedral. The great writer on English architecture Sir Nicolas Pevsner wrote 'Norwich has everything', and from his point of view he was right. Nor are the villages to be neglected. Amid the timbered houses are magnificent churches that rival the cathedrals of less favoured lands for their size and ostentation.

When it comes to the world of the supernatural, Norfolk is famous for the Brown Lady at Raynham Hall. This phantom appears with some regularity and is thought to be a former resident of the Hall, Lady Dorothy. This lady was sister to Sir Robert Walpole, who effectively established the office of Prime Minister in Britain and governed the country from 1721 to 1741. The ghost leapt into the national headlines in 1936 when a team from *Country Life* magazine came to Raynham Hall to do a piece on the house and managed to take a photograph of the phantom.

Although many tests have been made of the photo, no evidence of trickery has ever been found.

* * *

Considerably more dramatic is the ghost coach of Potter Heigham. The story behind this haunting is an object lesson in making sure that the small print on any contract is carefully read and understood. In 1741 the beautiful but penniless Lady Evelyn Carew decided that she did not want to spend her entire life as the poor relation of her various wealthy cousins – and she hatched a plot to capture the heart of the enormously wealthy Sir Godfrey Haslitt of Bastwick. She made a pact with the Devil that she would sell him her soul in return for winning the affections of Sir Godfrey and getting him to walk her up the aisle.

The Devil duly obliged Lady Evelyn with a love potion of great potency, which she administered to the unsuspecting Sir Godfrey. It worked even better than the Devil had promised. Sir Godfrey could not take his eyes off his impoverished neighbour and proposed marriage, setting the date for the ceremony as 31 May – only a few days away. Excitedly Lady Evelyn bought a dress, got married and set off back to her new home to enjoy married life to a rich man.

But she had not been careful enough when making her pact. The Devil is notorious for sticking to his deals, but finding a way to turn them to his advantage. So it was with foolish Lady Evelyn. She had forgotten to specify for how long she was to be left alone as Lady Haslitt of Bastwick before surrendering her soul.

And so the night after the wedding, the Devil came calling. He loaded the hapless woman into a black coach pulled by black horses, leapt into the driving seat and whipped the steeds into a frenzy. Hurtling down the road at high speed, the coach careered dangerously from side to side as it approached the arched bridge over the River Thurne. On reaching the bridge, it lurched to one side, smashed through the parapet and exploded into a thousand flaming fragments of glittering fire. And then the coach vanished, taking the Devil and Lady Evelyn with it.

This dramatic scene is replayed time after time in spectral form. Usually seen on or about the night of 31 May, the ghost coach of Potter Heigham is a terrible and terrifying vision to behold.

* * *

Beautiful Blickling Hall is one of the premier Stuart country houses of England. Building of the current house began in 1616 by Sir Henry Hobart, then the Lord Chief Justice. He employed as architect Robert Lyminge, one of the most fashionable builders of his day. The house has been remodelled several times since, though the exterior is pretty much as Lyminge left it in 1624.

It is the earlier inhabitants of the place who return in spectral form. Sir John Fastolf, on whom William Shakespeare modelled Sir John Falstaff, lived in the old manor in the 15th century. He is generally identified with the phantom knight seen in the grounds.

ANNE BOLEYN MAKES A DRAMATIC ENTRANCE TO BLICKLING HALL ONCE A YEAR.

Rather more famous is the ghost which makes a spectacular entrance on or about 19 May each year. This is the ghost of Anne Boleyn, the unfortunate second wife of King Henry VIII, who ended her life on the scaffold after being accused of adultery, though in truth her crime was to fail to provide a male heir at the very time that Henry's roving eye was moving on to a new conquest. Anne's spectre is said to arrive at Blickling in a coach pulled by four horses. She comes down the road, turns into the driveway, and trots up to the front door, then vanishes. Perhaps Anne is returning to the house where she spent much of her childhood in the hope of recapturing some of the happiness that she knew there.

* * *

There is a haunted bridge at Acle, which is between Norwich and Great Yarmouth. Back in the 17th century a man named Josiah Burge murdered his wife, but was acquitted at his trial through lack of evidence. He was released from gaol in Norwich on 7 April and set off home, but he got only as far as Acle. Here he was waylaid by the murdered woman's brother, who manhandled him to the bridge parapet, then slit his throat with a razor-sharp blade. Most locals were convinced of Burge's guilt so nobody did much to bring his killer to justice.

Then Burge himself took a hand from beyond the grave. On the anniversary of the killing, the perpetrator happened to be walking over the bridge at Acle when a phantom skeleton suddenly appeared, hurled him against the parapet with enormous force, slit his throat and threw the body into the river below. The story goes that these gruesome incidents are played out in phantom fashion on their anniversary, or thereabouts.

* * *

But the most characteristic supernatural inhabitant of Norfolk is the great black dog that goes by the name of Black Shuck. This terrible spectral beast stands as tall as a pony and as broad as a bull.

Its shaggy fur is pure black, so dark that light seems to fall into it as into a bottomless pit. The eyes of this hound glow red as if lit by an inner fire, and its gaze is frightful enough to root brave men to the spot like rabbits in headlights.

Some believe that Black Shuck is a hound of hell, sent up to earth by its master the Devil to do evil among mankind. Others think that it is a left over from the pagan past of England and link it to the forgotten deities brushed aside by Christianity. But all agree that it is a powerful and dangerous beast and best avoided if at all possible.

One of Shuck's favourite haunts is the stretch of hills and lanes around Cromer. Here he patrols his best loved paths with regularity. When Cromer was expanding from a remote fishing village to a bustling seaside resort in Victorian days, one young boy was foolish enough to try to befriend Shuck. Thinking the huge hound he met in the pleasure gardens to be a friendly labrador, the boy – a stranger to Cromer – threw it a stick and pulled its tail. Shuck clearly did not enjoy being treated as a mere pet. He lured the boy down to the beach, then frolicked in the surf until the lad stripped off and joined him for a swim. Once in the sea, the black dog showed its true nature. With savagely bared fangs and lashing claws it stopped the youngster getting back to the beach, and drove him further and further from shore.

A small fishing smack happened to be putting into Cromer with a catch of crabs and saw the commotion in the water. The crew dragged the exhausted boy on board, at which point Shuck turned into a ball of flame and vanished in a cloud of steam.

Rather more prosaic is the ghostly lifeboat crew that haunts the pier at Cromer. The town's lifeboat is launched from here, making this a unique station for the RNLI. Today the craft is named the *Henry Blogg* after the man who coxed the lifeboat here from 1909 to 1947 and who is credited with saving almost 100 lives. He won the George Cross, the British Empire Medal and six awards from the RNLI in his career. It is presumed that they are the ghosts of Blogg and his crew that pace the pier restlessly in bad weather, scanning the distant horizon in search of craft in trouble. They are still on watch in case they are needed.

Northamptonshire

The gently rural county of Northamptonshire is, according to the old saying, the county of spires and squires. The squires have drawn their wealth from the richly fertile soil of the county and their standing from their sense of duty to their tenants. The landed gentry here were among the most respected and highly regarded in England.

The spires have grown from the belt of limestone that runs across the county. Easily worked and durable, the stone here has a light touch of iron that adds a russet hue of attractive quality. Few of the county's towns have made better use of this stone than Oundle, which stands on top of the subterranean belt. The old town centre is built exclusively of this charming stone, with the Collyweston roof tiles and steep gables that make the most of the material.

One of the finest buildings in Oundle is the Talbot Hotel, which stands back off the High Street in the little market place. This is a magnificent 17th century edifice with gables and mullioned windows. It also has a ghost. The Lady in Black is seen most often on or near the staircase. She will appear for only a few seconds at a time, standing quietly as if in thought, then she fades from view.

The locals believe that it is the staircase, not the hotel in which it stands, that is haunted. The staircase was brought here from the much-haunted Fotheringhay Castle when it was demolished at the time the Talbot Hotel was being built – many of the stones came

THE TALBOT HOTEL IN OUNDLE IS HAUNTED BY A GHOST THAT MAY HAVE COME
WITH A SECOND-HAND STAIRCASE.

from the castle as well. It was at the top of this staircase that Mary, Queen of Scots was standing when she learned that she was to be executed the following day.

* * *

Fotheringhay lies just three miles to the north on the banks of the River Nene. The castle was demolished most thoroughly, but the moat, mound and other earthworks remain beside the river where the lane from Oundle crosses the river over an ancient bridge. The site is overgrown with thistles, the originals of which are said to have been planted here by Mary, Queen of Scots, to remind herself of her homeland.

Mary had a colourful life filled with adventure and romance, but it ended in sadness and execution. It has been said that much of her good luck was the result of her skills, but her misfortunes were just as surely the results of her foolishness. She was born in 1542, inheriting the crown of Scotland at the age of just eight days old. At the age of six she was engaged to Francis, heir to the throne of France. The marriage effectively united the thrones of Scotland and France, and so was treated as a hostile move by King Edward VI of England. Edward would have been angrier still if he had known that the marriage arrangement contained a secret clause handing Mary's claim to the English throne – she was a granddaughter of England's King Henry VII – to Francis.

In the event, Francis died just a year after becoming King of France, so the treaty was void, but Mary was ever after distrusted by the English. Mary returned to Scotland as a staunch Catholic ruler of a Protestant kingdom. She was in the middle of negotiations with Queen Elizabeth of England to marry an English nobleman, the Earl of Leicester (Elizabeth's favourite), when she abruptly announced that she had married a Scottish nobleman, Lord Darnley. This annoyed both the English and a large number of Scottish lords who disliked Darnley's arrogance and ambition. Just two years later Darnley was murdered, apparently by men acting with Mary's encouragement. This upset the few Scottish nobles who had liked Darnley.

By now isolated and distrusted by just about all the nobles and churchmen of Scotland, Mary next married the Earl of Bothwell, a dashing, handsome and romantic Highland lord who had been involved in Darnley's murder. The Scottish lords and Parliament had now had enough of Mary's intrigues and double-dealing. They announced that they were ousting her from the throne in favour of her son, James VI, with the Earl of Mar as regent. An army was mustered to force the Queen to accept these plans. She signed her abdication at swordpoint, then fled to England.

Her arrival came as a severe embarrassment to England's Queen Elizabeth I. For complex dynastic and religious reasons, the Catholic Church regarded Elizabeth as illegitimate, which made Mary the rightful Queen of England. As a Catholic, Mary thought much the same, although she recognised that largely-Protestant England preferred Elizabeth to herself – at least at first. Elizabeth had no intention of using English money or soldiers to put Mary back on the Scottish throne, which might have led on to her gaining the English throne. Instead Elizabeth gave her comfortable quarters at Carlisle Castle in the hope that Mary could sort things out with the Scots nobles.

When it became clear that this would not happen, Elizabeth moved Mary to Coventry, then Tutbury. As the years passed by, the guards set to watch Mary became increasingly severe and hostile. Communications with foreign Catholic powers were forbidden in case they were conspiring against Elizabeth. Links to English Catholics suspected of traitorous intent were also banned. By 1571 Mary was effectively a prisoner. Naturally she resented this and began to plot with Catholics to gain her release. So long as the plots were aimed only at getting Mary out of prison, Elizabeth refused to take any punitive action against her fellow queen, except to move her to Fotheringhay, which was more secure.

Mary hated Fotheringhay, arguing that the damp riverside location affected her health. She now entered into a new plot, with a Catholic gentleman of wealth named Anthony Babington. This scheme aimed to murder Elizabeth and put Mary on the throne of England. Elizabeth could no longer ignore the threat posed by Mary and ordered her execution. The sentence was carried out on 8th February 1587 in the great hall of Fotheringhay Castle.

MARY, QUEEN OF SCOTS WHO WAS FIRST IMPRISONED AND LATER EXECUTED AT FOTHERINGHAY.

Ever since, Mary's ghost has been seen wandering the castle – or more recently the site where it once stood. It takes the form of a lady in a long pale dress, who walks with stately, slow step.

But the execution of Mary was not the first link to royalty

FOTHERINGHAY CASTLE, SCENE OF A ROYAL BIRTH, A ROYAL DEATH AND A ROYAL FUNERAL. THE MOUND BESIDE THE RIVER MARKS THE SITE OF THE DEMOLISHED CASTLE.

that Fotheringhay Castle and its great hall had known. Nor is she the only ghost. In 1452 a boy named Richard was born here to the Duke and Duchess of York. His father, also Richard, was Protector of England while the king, Henry VI, was going through a spell of weak-mindedness. However, York's stern and uncompromisingly honest rule did not suit Henry's wife, Queen Margaret, who preferred a free-spending court and was not too fussy where the money came from.

In 1460 Richard, Duke of York tried to solve the impasse with Queen Margaret by persuading the council of lords to appoint him Prince of Wales and successor to King Henry. Margaret refused to see her son disinherited in this fashion and gathered an army. She ambushed York and his eldest son, Edmund, at Wakefield in Yorkshire on 30 December. Both men were killed, and Margaret moved on, hoping to seize York's other three sons: Edward, George and the boy Richard.

Edward, a clever and notoriously charming youth, moved too quickly for them. He gathered his own army, then hired some lawyers who managed to prove to the satisfaction of Parliament that he was the true king of England. He raced north to crush his enemies at the Battle of Towton, although he was outnumbered by two to one. He was then crowned as King Edward IV.

Only then did Edward arrange the funeral of his father and brother. The bodies were taken to lie in state in the great hall of Fotheringhay Castle. Then, in solemn procession, the coffins were carried out of the castle and along the village street to the beautiful church of St Mary and All Saints. There they were buried, and there

FOTHERINGHAY CHURCH IS HAUNTED BY A PHANTOM FUNERAL.

they lie to this day. Edward lavished money on the church, installing one of the finest double-canopied pulpits in England and rebuilding the tower to include the impressive octagonal lantern tower that still stands.

The ghosts that lurk here are from the magnificent funeral that Edward held for his father and brother. The sound of trumpets, lyres and other instruments mingles with the gentle singing of mournful hymns. The sounds have been heard intermittently ever since that sad day in 1461.

* * *

Further upstream, the Nene flows past the little village of Ringstead. One night in the 1780s a local girl by the name of Lydia Atley went missing and was never seen again. Local gossip had it that her boyfriend, a farmer from Addington, had killed her after she told him that she was pregnant. There was, however, no evidence against the man and no body was ever found.

The ghost of poor Lydia, however, was soon seen out and about. It stands beside the gate to the church, dressed in the long frock and tight bonnet that she was wearing when she vanished. Usually she simply fades from view, but one or two witnesses say that they have seen the spectre turn and walk off along the lane to the east. Perhaps she is recreating her last walk on earth, or she may be trying to lead humans to the spot where her bones lie buried. If so, she has not succeeded. She vanishes too quickly for any mortal to learn where she is going.

Northumberland

Northumberland is a land apart from the rest of England. To the east lie the growling waters of the North Sea, to the north is Scotland, while to the west are the wild Cheviot Hills, crossed by only two roads in their entire 50 mile length. For many years the county formed the heartland of the independent English kingdom of Northumbria, which stretched from the Humber to the Forth. In medieval times this was the fortified border area with the troublesome Scots, who were always ready to go raiding in England if they scented easy loot.

Northumberland has never entirely lost its character as a borderland. There are fortresses, castles and walled towns scattered here and there, and the landscape is empty of humans for miles on end. It is a bleak county too, in places, with the wind whipping off the sea across the pastureland of the sheep and cattle that for so long were the mainstays of the local economy.

Standing on a rocky promontory jutting out into the North Sea is the imposing bulk of Bamburgh Castle, one of the most ancient in England. The site was the fortress of the first Germanic invaders to land in the old Roman province of Britannia. Ida, leader of the Bernicians, built a wooden stronghold here in AD 547, later handing it on to his granddaughter in law, Bebba, who gave her name to the place.

The castle was rebuilt by the Normans and alterations were made throughout the Middle Ages to ensure that it remained at the

BAMBURGH CASTLE STANDS ON A ROCKY CRAG OVERLOOKING THE NORTH SEA. THE OLDEST GHOST HERE DATES BACK OVER A THOUSAND YEARS, BUT THERE ARE MORE RECENT PHANTOMS AS WELL.

forefront of military technology. In the 18th century it was converted into a comfortable home by John Sharp, Lord Crewe, and in the 1890s it was again modernised by Lord Armstrong, to its current form.

David Campbell, who works at the castle, is just one member of staff who has seen its remarkably active ghosts. He says of the Pink Lady that she is the castle's 'official ghost' and records: 'Many centuries ago – in the seven hundreds or thereabouts – there lived in the royal residence that stood where the keep is now, the King of Northumbria and his family. The city of Bamburgh was the royal capital of the kingdom, which then stretched from the Humber to the Forth, and this particular king was not much of a father. He did not like his daughter's boyfriend. As he was the king, he was able to send the young man away for seven years. Naturally, the young people wrote to each other, but dad stopped the mail getting out and in.

'The years passed and shortly before her fellow was due home, the king told his daughter that his spies had told him that the young man had married while he was overseas. Of course, the princess burst into tears at this news, but her father said that, to ease the pain, he had asked the seamstress to make her a lovely new dress in her favourite colour – pink. The girl went away to try the dress on, then, tears streaming down her face, she threw herself off the roof, killing herself instantly.

'Needless to say, when the young chap got back, he was unmarried. If she had only waited, poor girl, but now she walks every seven years through the oldest part of the castle, through the gardens and down to the beach to look for her lover's ship.

'I am told by the housekeeper (now retired), who has seen her many times, that the Pink Lady is very beautiful. I would not mind meeting her!

'A few years ago, I was talking to the housekeeper by the open door to the backstairs and the subject was ghosts. All of a sudden, there was a rush of cold air up the stairs and between us, then the doorknob on the library door (which was behind her) was suddenly turned vigorously. She jumped forward, saying "It moved." I looked straight at the door and said, "Yes, we were talking about you." We both knew that the library was empty, and the door was locked on our side.

'Some years ago, a colleague was on duty at the entrance to the first room. It was very quiet, and nobody was about. He heard the wooden chair to his left being dragged along the floor. He looked and saw that it had been moved although there was nobody there. A few days later, I saw a young man wearing a soldier's uniform (English – 18th century) standing in the same spot with his hand on the back of the chair. Perhaps it was a case of "it was me". He was only visible for a few seconds, but was very clear.

'Other happenings include a piano played when no one was near except for the lady watching the keys moving; two people, on separate occasions, seeing the shadow of John Sharp; and the voices of men and women talking quietly in a locked room, but absolute silence when the door was opened. A gatekeeper a few years ago heard about 50 horses coming up the hill at three in the morning. He looked out of the door, and saw nothing, although he heard them ride past him – through the locked main gates.

'There is also a man in armour, who is said to be Lord Mowbray. He was very active in the early 20th century as he clanked around the battlements, but has not been seen recently.'

Another guide reported an odd event. 'I was standing, minding my own business in the King's Hall, when a lady came up to me and asked, "How do you get out of this place?" I told her that you follow the arrows through the rooms and then down the stairs. She said, "The stairs that turn left at the bottom?" I replied, "Yes." "I can't get down them," she said. "They are too narrow."

'I was puzzled at this, so I asked her to show me what she meant. We walked to the stairs. She took two steps down to the small landing, turned to face the staircase – and then fell against me in shock. "That isn't the staircase that I saw ten minutes ago. It was a spiral one!" She left pretty quickly.'

* * *

Another haunted castle is that of Haltwhistle, which guarded the road running over the southern shoulder of the Cheviots. There is not much left of the castle these days, except for the ghostly lady who walks from the ruined fortress to the still intact church in the town centre. She is dressed in white, as befits her status as a bride, but does not appear very happy. This is the phantom of Lady Abigail, who was forced into an unwelcome marriage by her father in the 15th century. The poor young lady was deeply in love with another man. She soon wasted away and died.

But this is not the usual tale of a heartless father and hapless young girl. The young man with whom Lady Abigail had fallen in love was a gentleman from southern England who had arrived at Haltwhistle one day with a letter of introduction from an old friend of Lord Haltwhistle. What nobody knew, apart from Lord Haltwhistle and the friend in the south, was that the young man was the illegitimate son of Haltwhistle, who had been brought up miles away to avoid scandal. It was to prevent a romance and marriage between his daughter and her half-brother than Lord Haltwhistle acted as he did, with such tragic results.

* * *

THE MONUMENT AT OTTERBURN, ERECTED BY A VICTORIAN DUKE OF NORTHUMBERLAND TO COMMEMORATE HIS FAMOUS ANCESTOR, HARRY 'HOTSPUR' PERCY.

Also in the foothills of the Cheviots is the village of Otterburn, on the A68 as it heads toward Scotland. In 1388 one of the most famous battles of medieval Europe was fought here – for possession of a small scrap of silk. The cloth in question was the lance pennant of Sir Henry Percy, known as 'Hotspur' because of his rash behaviour and great courage in battle.

In 1388 the Scots sent a raiding army into County Durham led by James, Earl of Douglas. The raid was successful in grabbing a huge amount of booty and even reached the gates of Newcastle, which managed to hold out. In a skirmish outside the North Gate of Newcastle, Harry Hotspur led a group of English knights against Douglas. In the fray, Douglas managed to snatch the pennant from the tip of Hotspur's lance. Douglas laughed long and hard, flaunting his trophy in front of the infuriated gaze of Hotspur. Watching from the battlements of Newcastle, Hotspur vowed that Douglas would never live to carry the piece of silk into Scotland.

As soon as the Scottish army moved on, Hotspur sent out urgent messages to all his tenants, friends and the gentry of Northumberland urging them to grab their weapons and join him. Douglas marched up Redesdale on his way back to Scotland and on 18 August camped at Otterburn.

The men of Northumberland had moved fast and Hotspur moved them even faster once they had joined him. By rapid marches he got to Otterburn early on the evening of 19 August. Without waiting to deploy his men, Percy led his 8,000 strong force in an assault on the Scottish camp with its 7,000 men. Under cover of the gathering dusk, Douglas led part of his army on a flank attack that tore into the English army. Hotspur was, however, an inspirational leader and rallied his men to his banner.

The battle went on beyond sunset, but the fall of night brought no end to the fighting, for there was a bright full moon in the sky. Hotspur's brother was wounded, rather unfortunately in the buttocks, and Hotspur himself was knocked unconscious and captured. The surviving English fled back to Newcastle. Douglas himself was killed at the moment of his triumph, struck down by some unknown hand wielding a heavy sword.

It is this grim moonlit battle that the ghosts of Otterburn recreate. Appearing when the pale, silvery light of the moon bathes the hills west of Otterburn, the ghostly figures seem to come up out of the earth, clutching their weapons and following their banners as they did so long ago. They strike each other in phantom combat for a while, then sink back beneath the ground. All this in the most unearthly and disturbing silence. It is, they say, quite a spectacle.

THE FIELD JUST WEST OF OTTERBURN WHERE GHOSTLY KNIGHTS RECREATE A BATTLE FOUGHT IN 1388.

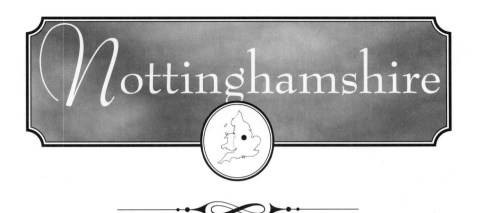

Nottinghamshire

N ottingham aside, Nottinghamshire is not an urban county. The villages tend to be smaller than elsewhere, but more closely scattered over the countryside. And it is a countryside that is as varied as its geology. To the east are limestone hills that roll to the horizon, while Ollerton stands on a belt of wet clay and the centre of the county enjoys a free-draining sandy subsoil.

This is, of course, the county of Sherwood Forest and Robin Hood. Of the vast forests that once blanketed so much of the county, some extensive stretches remain, but they are now tamed by the Forestry Commission and private owners, so that wolves, bears and bandits are but distant memories.

At least the living variety are gone, but spectral bandits are still to be found. Just outside the village of Edwinstowe looms the Major Oak, the largest oak tree in England. The area of forest around the tree is one of the more untouched in Nottinghamshire. It is also haunted by a certain 'something'. Quite what this something might be depends on whom you talk to. One witness described the phantom as being a man standing some seven feet tall and dressed all in green. Another likened it to a shambling bear. Whatever it is, it is very big, very heavy and absolutely terrifying.

Back at Edwinstowe, the church is reputedly haunted. The ghostly figure is said to lurk at the rear of the building, but who this man might have been in his human life is obscure.

* * *

THE ENTRANCE PASSAGE TO THE LION HOTEL IN WORKSOP IS IN THE OLDER PART OF THE HOTEL, WHERE THE GHOST IS SEEN MOST OFTEN.

Rather more solid is the ghostly maid of the Lion Hotel in Worksop. This sad spectre is the ghost of a servant girl who worked here some 250 years ago and who had the misfortune to experience unrequited love. The object of her affections was the owner of the hotel, a good-looking man who was clearly something of a heartless brute. He was happy enough to toy with the girl's affections to pass the time, but had every intention of marrying for wealth. The girl was distraught when she discovered her supposed beloved was paying court to another woman. She hanged herself upstairs at the hotel.

Ever since, she has walked the scene of her sorrows. Understandably, she prefers that part of the building that was standing when she lived there, so she is seen most often at the front of the building on or around the stairs and also on the landing on the first floor – perhaps it was here that she took her own life.

* * *

Another young girl haunts the White Hart at Retford. Her history, though just as sad, is quite different. She was a perfectly happy and contented girl, but she had the bad luck one day not to pay attention to what was going on. It was during the stagecoach era, and she got behind a mailcoach that was being manoeuvred in the back yard of the hotel and died when she was crushed against one of the walls.

Her ghost does not seem to hold a grudge against the hotel for this unfortunate accident. She seems just as happy and contented in phantom form as she was in life. She is seen most often in the courtyard where she died. These days the mailcoach trade has long gone and the area is no longer needed for the changing of horses and storing of tackle. Instead it is a pleasant seating area with wooden tables and chairs, where those enjoying the excellent fare on offer here can relax on summer days. The ghost will walk across the yard, appearing to be every bit as solid as the modern diners. More than one customer has remarked casually enough to the staff on the 'waitress in fancy dress', only to be surprised to learn what they have really seen.

Not quite so forgiving were those relatives of the girl who set up a memorial to her in the form of a small white bust that was placed in the front bar of the White Hart. This small statue is widely held to be cursed in some way. Certainly when some recent refurbishment work was under way it became the focus of some

THE MAGNIFICENT TOWN HALL AT RETFORD IS HOME TO A GHOST THAT
APPEARS IN TWO VERY DIFFERENT MOODS.

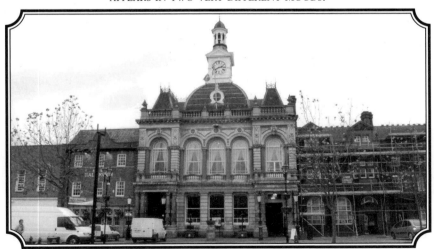

unease. A workman accidentally struck the statuette, whereupon a whole section of ceiling collapsed on top of him. The white bust was promptly boxed in so that no future accidents of the type would occur.

Elsewhere in Retford are other ghosts. The Town Hall is home to the phantom of a Victorian lawyer who appears on the staircase, and in the private chambers on the first floor. Dressed in wig and gown he seems to be in a perpetual bustle and hurry when seen upstairs. Confusingly, his appearances on the stairs are very different. There the phantom lawyer seems to be quite relaxed and in little hurry as he strolls down to leave by way of the imposing front door into the The Square.

* * *

Even more important than a bewigged lawyer was the man whose ghost lurks at the Saracen's Head in Southwell. This inn dates from the 1180s, though the current building probably dates back only so far as the 1540s. In August 1642 King Charles I stayed here on his way to Nottingham, where he raised the royal standard and called on all loyal subjects to arm themselves and join him in suppressing the pretensions of Parliament.

The ceremony was intended to be grand and impressive and no expense had been spared. A new king's standard had been produced, made of rich silks and heavy embroidery. Mounted on a towering pole, the long banner had the royal coat of arms embroidered next to the pole, followed by a portrait of the king, a crowned rose to symbolise England, a harp for Ireland, a thistle for Scotland and finally a fleur-de-lys, for Charles still maintained his notional right to be King of France. The heavily armed royal guard was present, but few volunteers turned up, if for no other reason than that the weather was awful. The rain and wind were so bad that the standard promptly blew over. This bad omen did not cause the king any concerns, but others would afterwards look back on it as being symbolic of the way King Charles fought the Civil War that followed. He was big on show and display, but light on substance.

THE PHANTOM OF THE SARACEN'S HEAD HAS BEEN SEEN LURKING NEAR THIS ANCIENT FOUR POSTER BED IN ONE OF THE OLDEST ROOMS AT THE HOTEL.

His Parliamentarian foes, in particular Oliver Cromwell, took the opposite line by having good, solid armies but not much in the way of display.

By 4 May 1646 King Charles was a beaten man. On that day he came to stay once again at the inn in Southwell, but he was on the run. He dared stay only a single night, and the following day he was seized by his enemies. Negotiation between King and Parliament dragged on for a while, but Charles proved to be a dishonest dealer and ended his life on the executioner's block in London.

Back at Southwell the rooms he occupied on both visits were dubbed King Charles' Suite and opened to the curious. These days they are among the most impressive in the hotel, complete with open fireplace and four poster bed. It is in and near this suite that the King's ghost is to be encountered. He does not look much like a regal monarch, more like the dispirited and broken man that he was on his second visit. He wears travel-stained clothes of coarse wool and boots splashed with mud.

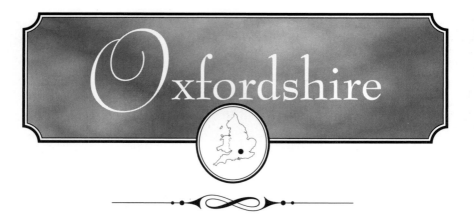

Oxfordshire

The rural parts of Oxfordshire are dominated by the upper Thames and its famous tributary, the Cherwell, as well as by the gentle hills that surround it. To the south-east is the great towering scarp of the chalky Chiltern Hills, from which magnificent views can be had over the lowlands.

The city of Oxford dominates the county, in terms of population, wealth, history and supernatural activity. The poet Matthew Arnold dubbed Oxford 'That sweet city with her dreaming spires', though it should be noted that he was viewing the city from some miles away at the time, not trying to sleep through the seemingly interminable ringing of the bells those spires contain. Nevertheless, the spires do dominate the city and many of them belong to haunted colleges.

One of the best known of the Oxford ghosts is that of the scholar John Crocker, which frequents Exeter College. Not well known these days, Crocker was a famous academic in late Tudor times, who was sufficiently important and wealthy to have his portrait painted by Nicholas Hilliard, one of Queen Elizabeth's favourite artists. He appears in phantom form dressed in a yellow jacket, brown breeches and long woollen cloak. This thick, warm clothing was much more suitable for the chilly corridors of Exeter College than the silk doublet that he wears in his portrait and may show him as he really looked in life.

Throughout the English Civil War of the 1640s, King Charles I had his headquarters in Oxford. The city was strategically positioned near the centre of the kingdom and within striking distance of staunchly Parliamentarian London, while the various colleges provided adequate accommodation for the court and the various army officers who came and went on the King's business.

The war left is spectral mark in the garden of Merton College. The King had appointed one Colonel Francis Windebank to defend Bletchingdon House as a northern outpost of the city. The house, some miles to the north along the River Cherwell, was surrounded by earthworks and equipped with cannon. So confident of his defences was Windebank that on 19 April 1645 he held a ball. He was surprised when a mass of uninvited guests turned up in the shape of Oliver Cromwell and a force of Roundhead troopers. Rather than risk the lives of his lady guests, Windebank promptly surrendered his fortress.

Hurrying to Oxford to break the news of the fall of Bletchingdon, Windebank chose an unfortunate time to arrive. The King had just learned of the surrender of his last intact army, that of Sir Ralph Hopton, in Cornwall, together with a number of West Country strongholds. Charles was angry and wanted to persuade other commanders not to surrender so easily. When Windebank arrived, the King made an example of him. Less than two hours after arriving, Windebank had been charged with dereliction of duty, tried, convicted, sentenced to death and shot in the gardens of Merton College. No wonder the poor man haunts the place.

* * *

Downstream of Oxford lies Henley, famous for its regatta. As one of the oldest buildings in the town it is not surprising that the Bull in Bell Street is haunted. A couple of years ago the pub was undergoing refurbishment under the watchful eye of landlord Nick, but nothing was changing about the ghost.

'She appears here,' said Nick as he waved his hand to indicate the welcoming front bar of the pub. 'First you get a strong whiff of

THE HAUNTED BULL INN AT HENLEY AS IT APPEARED IN THE 1890s.

candles being blown out. You know, the funny burnt smell. Then she comes sweeping past you and then vanishes. You only see her for a second or two. Usually you see her out the corner of your eye, not full on.'

It appears that crowds hold no fears for this ghost. She will appear when the pub is busy with customers as well as when a lone member of staff is clearing up the bar. Sometimes she walks past the bar itself; at other times she is seen near the far wall. This wall formerly had a door opening directly on to the street, though that has long since been bricked up. Perhaps the ghost is using the door that existed in her day.

Asked to describe the ghost, Nick paused. 'I've not seen her myself,' he said, 'but several other people have. She is young and dressed in white, like a long nightdress. Very pretty, too, I am told.' Some say that the ghost is not dressed in a nightdress at all, but in a funeral gown. The Bull used to share its yard with an undertaker and the ghost is thought to be that of lady who was laid out in the pub bar when the undertaker's premises were full to overflowing. This must have been back in Victorian days, for the undertakers ceased trading here about the time of the Great War.

* * *

Rather more active than the young girl at the Bull is the phantom lady of Rycote Chapel, south-west of Thame. Reckoned to be one of the most charming places in Oxfordshire, this was built in the

THE CHURCH AT MINSTER LOVELL SEEN THROUGH THE DOORWAY OF THE RUINED HALL, WHICH IS HAUNTED BY A PREVIOUS OWNER.

15th century as a domestic chapel, with a fine west tower, but is now used as a parish church and is dedicated to St Michael and All Angels. It contains an unusual two-storey pew, complete with organ, which was built for a family of local gentry.

The identity of the lady ghost here is unknown, though local villagers refer to her affectionately as Arabella. She wears a long dress of a dull grey or fawn colour and is seen frequently walking quietly around the elegant building.

Seen rather less often here is the ghost of a portly gentleman dressed in a long velvet cloak. Local opinion has it that this is Sir Thomas More, though More's only connection to the place seems to be that his daughter married Sir Giles Heron of Rycote.

Born in 1478 as the son of a judge, Sir Thomas More trained as a lawyer before entering government. By 1521 he was Treasurer of the Exchequer to King Henry VIII. In 1529 the King promoted him to Lord Chancellor, much against More's wishes for he did not want the awesome responsibility of running the government for a notoriously fickle ruler. More resigned in 1532 and retired to private life, but this did not save him. When Henry broke with the Pope and made himself head of the English Church, he demanded that More, as a senior lawyer, agree the move was legal. More refused and was beheaded for his reluctance.

* * *

Another ghost in Oxfordshire is that of a man who also fell foul of the Tudors. Minster Lovell Hall stands as a gaunt ruin in the village of the same name. It was home to the Lovell family from at least as early as the 1150s, and for most of that time both the Lovells and their hall led peaceful and blameless lives. Francis, 9th Baron Lovell, however, had a somewhat unfortunate career. He supported the Lancastrians in the 15th century Wars of the Roses. That faction did badly and Francis lost much of his wealth. In 1483 he decided to change sides to support the Yorkists, earning himself the derisive nickname of 'Dog' from the former colleagues he had betrayed.

Just two years later, the Yorkists were defeated at the Battle of Bosworth and Francis lost even more wealth and prestige as a result. Two years later again, Baron Lovell made his final and most disastrous choice. The new king, the Tudor Henry VII, surrounded himself with Lancastrian loyalists, putting Lovell in the shade. In 1487 a young man appeared who claimed to be Edward, the missing son of the Duke of Clarence. The missing boy had a better claim to the throne than did Henry VII, and Lovell joined his rebellion, anxious to regain his wealth and position.

Unfortunately for Lovell it soon became clear that the boy was not the missing heir to the Duke of Clarence, but a baker's boy who merely looked like him and was being used as a pawn by powerful noblemen. Support fell away from the youth, now known to be named Lambert Simnel. The remaining rebels were defeated at Stoke Field in Nottinghamshire. Lovell escaped the battle alive, and fled to Minster Lovell Hall. He was seen collecting up his treasures; then he vanished. It was widely believed he had fled abroad, but no evidence of this was ever forthcoming.

In 1708 the hall was in urgent need of repairs, so workmen were put to the task. They found a tiny chamber hidden in the thickness of a wall. Inside was 'the entire skeleton of a man, having been at a table which was before him with a book, paper and pen. Beneath his feet was the skeleton of a hound. All this much mouldered and decayed'. Was it the last mortal remains of the fugitive baron? It may have been so, for as soon as the skeleton was found the ghost of a man in 15th century dress began to be seen around the hall. He is seen still, though not very often.

* * *

In the far north-west of the county can be found the enigmatic group of megaliths that go by the name of the Rollright Stones. These take the form of a circle of standing stones, about 100 feet in diameter, set up by prehistoric farmers some 3,500 years ago, with a single towering monolith not far away and, down near the church, a group of smaller stones dubbed the Whispering Knights. It is the Whispering Knights that are haunted, by the Little People.

These folk like the stones just the way they are. When one vicar ordered the old pagan stones to be moved away from his church, a team of horses was hitched up and set to work. No matter how hard they strained, they could not shift the stones. More and stronger horses were brought until, after much effort, one of the stones was dragged a short distance away. Unnerved by events and by sightings of the Little People, the villagers persuaded the vicar to change his mind. A single pony was able to haul the stone back into position with ease.

THE ENIGMATIC ROLLRIGHT STONES, AROUND WHICH MANY LEGENDS SWIRL.

Rutland

A t just 60 square miles, Rutland is the smallest county in England. The 1974 reform of local government saw it abolished, just one of several much-resented alterations to the thousand year old face of England. Happily, it has been reinstated and once again is a county in its own right. The little county has always had its heart at Oakham, where the splendid great hall of Oakham Castle is one of the finest examples of late 12th century domestic architecture in England.

The ghosts, however, seem more at home on the periphery of the county. At Stoke Dry, near Uppingham in the south, the church of St Andrew plays host to an unquiet spirit. This is the ghost of an old lady who was thought by her neighbours in the later 17th century to be a witch. Not all the old women accused of witchcraft were as guiltless as some would have us believe. Not a few traded on their reputations by extorting food and clothing from neighbours with threats of sending disease to kill livestock or blight to destroy crops.

Whether the witch of Stoke Dry was one such or merely a harmless old crone we do not know. What we do know is that the vicar felt it incumbent on himself to put a stop to the nonsense. At this time witchfinders were patrolling the countryside, offering to distinguish between genuine agents of satan and the innocent. They charged the local courts a sum and then subjected the accused to a variety of tests. These varied, but most involved either testing the supposed witches for the invisible 'Devil's Mark', or imposing on them Christian duties that – it was thought – no agent of the devil would undertake.

It was this latter course that the vicar of Stoke Dry chose to follow. He locked the suspected witch up in the small room above the church porch with nothing but a Bible, a prayer book and a cross to keep her company. She was, it seems, set to learn the scripture by heart as a test of her devotion to God or devil. Whether by starvation or shock, the old lady died before she could perform her task. Taking this as a sure sign of divine anger, the vicar had her buried outside consecrated ground as a confirmed witch.

She returns to the churchyard to this day. Some say she comes to seek a burial place, others that she wants to vent her anger on the village that treated her so badly. We shall probably never know the truth, for this ghost says nothing and vanishes from sight after only a few seconds in view.

Shropshire

Shropshire can be a daunting county for those unfamiliar with it. There are the towering heights of the Long Mynd and the Wrekin, where bleak moorlands are whipped by gales and drifted by snows in winter or baked dry under a windy sun in summer. It was in this remote area that Edric the Wild kept alive resistance to William the Conqueror for a full decade after the Norman Conquest and here that he is said to ride still in spectral form.

From the heights, the lowlands of Shropshire can appear flat and featureless, but once the viewer is down on the plain it becomes a succession of rolling hills and wooded slopes. For generations these rich lowlands formed the fortified outpost of England, facing the wilds of Wales. Nobody was ever certain when the Welsh would come raiding over the border, so every man had to keep a weapon within reach to be ready to protect hearth and home.

In these more peaceful days the major threat to the fertile farmlands of Shropshire comes in the form of urban sprawl tipping over the county border from Birmingham and Wolverhampton. In 1968 town planners staring through rose-tinted glasses decided to turn over much Shropshire countryside to the bulldozers and build Telford, described as 'an exciting concept city'. Embraced within its modernity is one of the most historic estates of Shropshire. Fortunately, the old manor house was turned into a hotel and much of the surrounding parkland kept free of late 20th century concrete.

Perhaps it is because the building retains its rural setting that the ghost of Madeley Court remains as active as she does. The current house and gatehouse were built in 1553 on the site of a priory grange belonging to the Much Wenlock monastery. The house has had a chequered history, being at times the centre of an iron ore mining and smelting business, a farm, and council offices. It is now a luxurious hotel, which welcomes visitors.

Although it is not certain to which date the ghost belongs, it is generally thought that she must be at least 200 years old. The phantom form of the elderly lady has a degree of gentility and elegance that would indicate that she lived here before 1828, when the Brooke family sold up the estate for commercial use. She wears a long dress that sweeps with the distinctive rustle of heavy silk as she walks.

THE FIREPLACE IN THE RESTAURANT AT THE MADELEY COURT HOTEL IS A FAVOURED HAUNT OF THE GENTEEL LADY GHOST.

She is seen most often in the main house and has a particular affinity with the lower ground floor area, which is now used as a bar, and to the main hall, now a restaurant. From time to time she has been noticed walking up or down the spiral staircase that links the two rooms. Strangely, her head is usually turned away from the witness so that a clear view of her is impossible.

While the old lady causes no trouble upstairs in the restaurant, she is rather more bother downstairs. The glasses are often found pushed to one side of the bar when no human has been around to move them. More spectacularly, a table set by an old blocked-up window is often found cleared of its cutlery or even up-ended. Changing the table for some other item of furniture did nothing to solve the problems. Whatever is placed by this old window seems to come in for unwanted phantom attentions. Why the ghost should behave in such a fashion is unknown, though several members of staff will testify that they suddenly feel uneasy when in the bar alone, seeming to confirm that the ghost is there and up to no good.

* * *

A very different female ghost is the phantom that lurks at ground level at the Feathers Hotel in Ludlow. This young lady is dressed in fashions that are unmistakably those of the 1960s. She sports a very short mini skirt and a tight top that leaves little to the imagination. It may be for this reason that she is noticed, especially by the male clientele of this ancient and welcoming hotel. She trots along the pavement outside, then turns into the hotel foyer and vanishes. The young lady – some who have seen her think she is but a teenager – seems happy enough. Strangely, there is no known event from the 1960s that might account for her appearances here.

THE ANCIENT AND DOUBLY-HAUNTED FEATHERS HOTEL IN LUDLOW. THE MORE MODERN OF THE TWO GHOSTS APPEARS ON THE PAVEMENT JUST IN FRONT OF THE BUILDING.

Much older is the ghost that is seen upstairs on the second floor. Some think that this shadowy figure may be the phantom of Rees Jones, the man who was responsible for the splendid house that is the core of the Feathers Hotel. Born around 1580, Rees Jones was the younger son of a well-to-do farmer from Pembrokeshire. His father gave him a good education, but the family estates went to the eldest son, so Rees had to make his way in the world on his own. He set up as a lawyer in Ludlow and was soon doing remarkably well.

It was in 1619 that Rees Jones, by now approaching middle age and married to a local girl named Isabel, bought a house in the Bull Ring from a Ludlow clothier named Richard Blashfield. Rees ordered that the house be largely torn down and replaced by a then thoroughly modern structure. The front door of the Feathers is the original installed by Rees and it still has the handsome lock plate with an engraved RJ intertwined with IJ as the initials of the couple whose house this was.

The English Civil War saw Ludlow declare for the king, and Jones handed over his impressive new house to serve as the Royalist headquarters for the southern part of Shropshire. After the end of the war, Jones preferred to live on his country estate, so the Feathers began its new career as an impressive town house for rent. It became an inn in 1670 and a hotel in 1863, and now, with the acquisition of property on either side, boasts 40 bedrooms as well as banqueting and conference facilities.

Over all the years and changes of owner, the ghostly Mr Jones – if it is indeed he – has favoured a bedroom on the

THE FIRST FLOOR BEDROOM AT THE FEATHERS, WHERE THE OLDER OF THE TWO GHOSTS HERE IS TO BE ENCOUNTERED.

second floor that overlooks the Bull Ring. Perhaps he likes to keep an eye on what is going on in his old home and in the streets of the town where he made his fortune.

* * *

At the northern end of the county stands another haunted hotel: the Corbet Arms at Market Drayton. This magnificent establishment has been brought back to its former glory after some years as a mere pub. The ballroom is once again available for functions and grand events, and the upgrading of the facilities is following a phased programme.

The ghost here is traditionally said to be that of a young lady dressed in a long gown of fine silk in a pale cream or perhaps pink colour. Exactly who this lady might be is unclear, but she is blamed for the various paranormal events that take place in the building. The ghost herself is seen most often in the ballroom, at the back of the hotel. She walks with stately step across the dance floor, usually moving from the back of the room to the front and vanishing halfway across the floor.

The lady is seen also in the corridor leading to the kitchen, though here she seems to be in something of a hurry. She was also caught sight of – though apparently only once – down in the cellars. This gave the man delivering drinks such a start that he fled the premises and refused to return. These cellars are gloomy places, and it is not just the lack of light that lends them atmosphere. In past centuries, when police stations and their cells were not yet common, the Corbet Arms served as the local lock up. Trials were held in the hotel, as the largest public building for some miles around, while the cellars held the more dangerous local criminals. One chamber has a stout wooden door – much stronger than would usually be needed in a hotel cellar – and there are massive iron rings set deep into the walls. The miscreants were tied to the rings while they awaited trial.

It is generally thought to be this same lady phantom whose footsteps disturb the rest of those who sleep in Room 9, while

THE ENTRANCE TO THE IMPOSING CORBET ARMS IN MARKET DRAYTON, WHERE A SINGLE GHOST IS BLAMED FOR A HOST OF PHENOMENA.

Room 4 can also play host to her footsteps. Room 7 sees the ghost in more active mood. Here she will snatch bedclothes off the bed in the middle of the night. For some reason it is young men who are most often the victims of this prank.

The lady ghost is also blamed for the rather peculiar antics of the large, gilt-framed mirror that stands on the first floor landing. It has been here for as long as anyone can remember and for most of the time it is simply a mirror, reflecting the images of those that pass by. But just occasionally it will mist over and reveal to the passing guest a quite different view. The landing is shown decorated in another style, and sometimes people are seen dressed in long gowns and eveningwear, or in uniform. The vision lasts only a second or two, but can be most unnerving.

No wonder some hasten downstairs to settle their nerves with a glass of the well kept ale on offer at this most welcoming of hotels.

Somerset

Somerset takes its name from the summer settlers who drove their livestock down onto the marshlands during the dry summer months to graze on the rich grasses to be found there. Those same marshes gave sanctuary to King Alfred the Great when he was on the run from the Vikings and organising the great national resistance that would throw out those pagan invaders.

The marshes have long since been drained to provide fertile farmland, but the old names persist with 'isles' and 'marshes' being named where no such features now exist. Glastonbury is one of the better known islands, with its famous abbey and tor, and its links to the 'New Age' movement. But Somerset is not just the area of former wetlands and islands. There are the Quantock and Polden Hills as well and the Mendips further north, while the far west sees the bleak uplands of Exmoor rising over the salt waters of the Bristol Channel.

The old county town, and still one of the most important centres in the county, is Taunton. It originally based its wealth on the fertile farmlands around here, while the red sandstone of the nearby Quantocks provided good building stone. The town later drew wealth from wool, having gained a lucrative market charter from King Stephen in the 12th century, and in the Civil War it was one of the few West Country towns to declare for Parliament.

This decision brought trouble to Taunton, and ghosts. It was in 1644 that the Royalist armies moved against the town with siege artillery and vastly superior numbers of men. In command of the small garrison at Taunton was a young officer who would later be recognised as one of the few military geniuses produced by England at this time: Robert Blake. Before the Royalist cavaliers arrived in force, Blake had organised his men and the local people in the task of throwing up elaborate and stoutly constructed earthworks around the town. These provided platforms from which the cannon could sweep the surrounding land with their fire and make any attempt to gain access to Taunton itself fraught with difficulty. He also packed the town with food and military supplies.

When the siege of Taunton began, the Royalists looked to an easy victory, but they were to be disappointed. For week after week through the summer and autumn of 1644 the townsfolk drove off all attacks and resolutely refused to give in. The bad weather of autumn brought heavy rains to Somerset, flooding out the trenches of the besieging army and ending active attacks. The town continued to be surrounded, however, and neither food nor ammunition could get in. By spring the garrison desperately needed food, so a relief column under Oliver Cromwell was sent by Parliament. But before Cromwell arrived, Blake had got supplies of his own by raiding those laying siege. When Cromwell finally got through, in August, the Royalists had given up and left.

Blake went on to take command of the navy during the rule of Parliament. He defeated the Dutch twice at sea, crushed the Moslem pirates of the Barbary Coast and captured a Spanish treasure fleet off Tenerife. In 1657 he died on board his flagship while returning to Plymouth after yet another successful voyage. He was buried in Westminster Abbey.

Given that Taunton held out so successfully for Parliament, it might seem odd that the most active ghost from this period is that of a cavalier. He appears at the castle, dressed in the rich fashions of the mid-17th century, complete with thigh-length riding boots and feathered hat with a sweeping brim. He is seen most often on the staircase, looking rather pensive and thoughtful. Perhaps he was a prisoner who served his time in the castle, where the stout walls

TAUNTON CASTLE IS HOME TO A NUMBER OF GHOSTS, WHICH APPEAR WITH SOME REGULARITY.

meant he could be closely confined. Or he may date from earlier times before war came to Taunton.

The castle also plays host to the shade of a young lady in a long, dark coloured dress who seems to have lived at about the same time as the cavalier. She has long blonde hair, but her face is rarely seen for she usually walks away from witnesses. One resident of Taunton who saw her when visiting the museum that now occupies most of the castle reported: 'I had only just entered when I saw this woman in a long dress walk past and turn away down a corridor. She was in fancy dress – or so I thought – and I took her for a member of staff. Not knowing my way around, I thought I would ask her advice about what exhibits were where or which route to follow round the museum. I opened my mouth to speak, but she had gone. Now she had been there a second before and I could not see how she would have had time to duck into one of the rooms. Thinking that she must have moved quickly, I entered first one room, then another, but there was nobody there. It was only after I got home that my husband joked I must have seen the ghost. And looking back, I think he was right.'

Next door to the Castle is the Castle Hotel, which has been constructed from buildings that once formed the outer bailey of the castle. These ancient buildings are haunted by a most charming, if elusive, phantom. She is a young lady who plays a violin. She has been spotted sitting downstairs, but she is heard far more often than she is seen. The haunting, plaintive notes of her violin drift through the hotel convincing some that a musician is present, but she can never be found if the sounds of music are followed.

Not far away stands The Crescent, one of the finest Georgian streets in England. The imposing brick façades on the street are both elegant and stolid, contrasting bravely with the concrete and glass town hall that the local council has seen fit to throw up opposite. Walking down this street may be seen a lady dressed in black who has grey hair pulled back into a bun.

This phantom lady is identified as Maria Fitzherbert, who lived here for some years after her retirement from public life. Born in 1756 as the blameless daughter of a Hampshire squire, Maria married twice and was twice widowed before she was 30. She then met the Prince of Wales, later King George IV, and they fell in love. In 1785 they married, but because King George III withheld his permission the marriage was illegal. The couple remained devoted to each other until 1803, when George was forced to give her up for reasons of state, following his legal marriage to Princess Caroline of Brunswick.

Maria Fitzherbert retired on a generous pension of £6,000 per year. She shunned the fashionable set she had known when with the Prince of Wales and, after he became king in 1820, became almost a recluse. She died in 1837, and soon after her ghost began to walk along The Crescent in Taunton.

* * *

A few miles to the north-east of Taunton spreads one of the old, drained marshes of Somerset. This one goes by the name of

Sedgemoor and was the scene of one of the more tragic events in Somerset history. In 1685 the popular King Charles II died, leaving the crown to his arrogant and tactless brother James II. The new king was already unpopular, but was further handicapped by the fact that he was an ardent Catholic when most of his subjects were equally passionate Protestants. Fearing that the new king's religion might lead him to put the interests of the Pope above those of England, many people were restive.

Suddenly the country was agog with the news that Charles' illegitimate son, James, Duke of Monmouth, was declaring that he was not illegitimate at all. He had, he said, documents that proved Charles had married his mother, but had kept the union secret for state reasons. This would make the popular and charming Protestant Monmouth the rightful king.

In June 1685 Monmouth landed at Lyme Regis, unfurled a royal banner and called on all loyal Englishmen to come to his support. James denounced his nephew as a traitor and demanded that all loyal Englishmen support him. It was a tense time. Monmouth toured the West Country, rallying support. Many young men joined his cause, but many others hung back. On 6 July Monmouth reached Taunton and was declared king in front of a cheering crowd.

Then news was brought that some 2,500 regular army troops of James II were camped at Sedgemoor. Hoping to catch his enemies by surprise, Monmouth marched his army out at once, although there had been no time to train the raw recruits in modern tactics or formation marching. On the way to the enemy camp, Monmouth lost his way in the dark. Instead of approaching Sedgemoor from the south, he and his men came on it from the west and found their way blocked by a wide drainage ditch known locally as the Bussex Rine. Monmouth, it is said, blanched when told by a local man where he was, for years earlier a witch had told him he would meet his death on the banks of the Rhine, and he had carefully avoided that great river ever since.

The troops of King James, led by the Earl of Feversham, were roused and as dawn broke over Somerset the battle began. The professional soldiers of the royal army had more modern weaponry

THE MODERN MEMORIAL ERECTED TO MARK THE SITE OF THE BATTLE OF
SEDGEMOOR, FOUGHT IN 1685.

than the rebels. With a greater range to their guns, the men of King
James could hang back behind the impassable Bussex Rine and
shoot down their hapless opposition.

'Come across and fight,' shouted the supporters of Monmouth
at their enemies, but the men of King James did no such thing.
Monmouth's cavalry fled first, and though his infantry did their
best they were outclassed and outgunned. By mid-morning it was
all over. Monmouth himself was captured later that day by a
mounted patrol. He was dragged to London and thrown at the feet
of his royal uncle, who scornfully ordered his execution.
Monmouth was beheaded on 15 July. His followers were rounded
up; many were hanged but most were transported to work as
convict labour in the American colonies.

It is on that fateful field at Sedgemoor that the ghosts gather. The
marshland is much drier now, and the Bussex Rine, then an
impassably deep drainage channel, is little more than a wide ditch.
But it is still damp on the low-lying ground and mists gather on chill
dawns when rains have wet the land. On such mornings shadowy
figures have been seen moving across the meadows. And sometimes
a voice will call out from the fog: 'Come across and fight.'

For those who witness it, it can be a most unnerving experience.

Staffordshire

S taffordshire is a county of two halves. To the north are the bleak uplands of the Peak District, more usually thought of as being in Derbyshire, where sheep graze on windswept turf between dry stone walls. Just below the hills sprawl the industrial lands of the Potteries that have joined Stoke on Trent to Newcastle under Lyme and a dozen other towns and villages between. The south is more determinedly rural, though the Black Country intrudes as an outlier of the industrial mass of Birmingham. It is here that Cannock Chase spreads over some 16 square miles of forested wildlife preserve.

Tutbury stands at the far eastern edge of the county, overlooking the River Dove, that forms the border with Derbyshire. Tutbury Castle is a quiet place with tumbled ruins surrounding its still inhabited sections. It is owned by Her Majesty the Queen, though she does not visit often, and has long had close links to royalty, as it forms part of the Duchy of Lancaster. But the modern peace belies a furious and violent history, and it is these past events that the ghosts recall.

The castle was built by the Normans less than five years after William the Conqueror won the Battle of Hastings and it was intended to control the English people of this part of Staffordshire. This first castle was utterly destroyed in a siege in 1178, when its owner, the Earl of Derby, rather foolishly rebelled against King Henry II. The building was rebuilt almost immediately and it is this castle, though altered over the years, that still stands today.

THE ROUND TOWER OF TUTBURY
CASTLE, ONE OF THE MOST
HAUNTED CASTLES IN ENGLAND.

Conflict came to Tutbury again in the Civil War of the 1640s. As a possession of the Duke of Lancaster, who was also King Charles, the castle was defended by a Royalist garrison. In 1642 a force of Roundheads appeared outside the gates and demanded the surrender of Tutbury Castle. The garrison jeered, and, being without siege guns, the Parliamentarian force moved on a few weeks later. In 1645 King Charles himself stayed at Tutbury for a while with his dashing cavalry commander, Prince Rupert, before proceeding elsewhere.

The next year the Roundheads were back. This time they had guns and were serious. The following siege proved to be hard fought and violent. After some 300 of the garrison had been killed and the survivors were facing starvation, a surrender was agreed. The Royalists marched off to captivity and the vengeful Roundheads set about destroying the castle as a military installation. The mighty walls were blown up with gunpowder and most of the domestic buildings burned down. Only the south range remained and here a custodian was put to care for what was left. This state of affairs has remained ever since.

One of the more active ghosts is thought to date from the terrible siege of 1646. A boy was on duty at the north tower to watch for a surprise attack when he spotted a force of Roundheads creeping forward under cover of a dawn mist. He at once sprang to his drum and began to beat the alert, but almost immediately was shot dead. His ghost is heard more often than it is seen, the faint sound of drumming beating out around the north tower for a few seconds, then fading away. It is said that to hear the ghostly drummer is a sign of impending good luck.

Another ghost of a child has been seen from time to time running past visitors or guests to the castle and on odd occasions touching them.

One room is particularly haunted. The King's Bedchamber was where King Charles slept during his stay here. Many visitors report that they have seen orbs of light or strange spark effects, and a few claim that an invisible man has reached out and held their hands in this room.

Recently during a tour one gentleman told the guide that he had really enjoyed the ghost walk and what made it special was the little boy in costume sitting at the top of the stairs. This came as a surprise to the guide, as there are no little boys in costume on the tour!

Another ghost at Tutbury Castle is that of a little old woman. Many visitors have seen her outside the great hall and floating outside the hall's window. She has also been seen in other areas of the castle, including the cellar, where she has removed keys and moved furniture around.

Finally, there is some dispute as to whether the ghost of Mary, Queen of Scots lurks here or not. She was certainly held prisoner at Tutbury for some years in the 1570s before being moved to Fotheringhay Castle, where she was executed. Some claim to have seen a lady in 16th century costume wandering about the castle and believe it is the ghost of the doomed queen. She is not seen often, but gives the impression of a great force of personality when she does appear. The present custodian, Lesley Smith, cares greatly for the castle and its history. Among the many attractions she lays on to make

CUSTODIAN LESLEY SMITH DRESSES AS MARY, QUEEN OF SCOTS TO ENTERTAIN VISITORS TO TUTBURY CASTLE.

a visit by the public enjoyable are costumed pageants, in which she herself dresses as Mary, Queen of Scots, but this does not explain the sightings, which take place whether she is in costume or not.

* * *

Upstream from Tutbury is the little village of Checkley. This is an ancient place, with prehistoric earthworks showing it has been inhabited for three millennia. The church has a 14th century façade, but this masks a Norman structure. And beside the church stands the shaft of a cross that is at least 1,100 years old. Before the community could afford a church, the priest stood beside this cross to preach the good word of Christianity to his flock.

The ghost that walks here is, however, quite modern, dating back only a little over a century. In 1895 Mrs Hutchinson, the wife of the vicar of Checkley, passed away and was buried in the ancient churchyard. Parishioners attended the funeral and, no doubt, voiced their sadness at their vicar's loss. But there must have been at least a few who were not too sorry to see the back of the redoubtable Mrs Hutchinson.

THE HAUNTED LANE AT CHECKLEY RUNS BESIDE THE CHURCH.

She was not one to suffer fools gladly, nor one to keep a still tongue in her head when she had a view to express. Children who failed to attend her classes in the village school were hunted down mercilessly to be given a stern lecture on the value of a good education, as were their parents. Adults who were absent from the services given by the Rev Hutchinson were likewise sought out and treated to a verbal admonition on the charity of the Lord and the sins of humanity.

But if the villagers thought they had seen the last of Mrs Hutchinson, they were wrong. Within just a few days of her funeral, the good lady – or at least her phantom – was seen once again walking the streets of Checkley. She appears to this day, wearing her habitual plain grey dress and white blouse. Perhaps fortunately, this is a silent phantom. She merely walks quietly around her old home village, allowing modern day truants or those who fail to attend church to escape the lectures that their forebears had to endure.

*　*　*

The little village of Fradley stands on the A38, the old Roman Ryknild Street, outside Lichfield. These days many passing motorists know the place best for the motorway-style services that stand there, but in the early decades of the 20th century it was better known as the site of a large RAF training camp. The camp has long gone, replaced by a bustling industrial estate, but the ghost that haunted it remains as active as ever.

The spectre is that of an unfortunate man who was training to be a tailgunner here during the Second World War. The position of tailgunner on the bombers that took off nightly to fly into the dark skies over the Third Reich called for nerves of steel and keen eyesight. The German nightfighters would pounce from the darkness and only quick reactions gave the bomber crew much chance of survival. Unfortunately this man never made it to active service. He was killed at Fradley when run down by a training aircraft.

Ever since that fatal day, the figure of this trainee airman in his sky blue uniform has been seen skulking around the place. He is seen slipping behind buildings or disappearing through doorways and has given more than one worker here a sudden shock. The ghost seems to be harmless enough, however, and prefers to shun the company of humans, moving off as soon as he is seen and remaining visible for only a few seconds at a time.

Suffolk

The county of Suffolk has one of the more ancient names among English counties. This is the land of the South Folk of the kingdom of East Anglia, perhaps the second of the kingdoms that sprang up as the north-eastern invaders took over what had been Roman Britain. Domesday Book, compiled in the late 11th century, shows that Suffolk was then the most densely populated county in England, drawing its prosperity from its rich soil and good harbours.

These days, Suffolk is more sparsely populated than much of England, for this is a rural county with few major towns. It has, strangely, produced two of England's finest painters, as both Thomas Gainsborough and John Constable came from here. Both delighted in portraying the scenic beauties of their home area, as well they might, for this was and remains among the best looking of the counties in England.

However, beauty did not stop it attracting the paranormal at its most fiendish to Blythburgh on 4 August 1577. A church service was taking place in the village when a sudden storm blew up outside. Rain lashed down and winds whipped past. Then the church door was thrown open and a gigantic black hound paced silently into the sacred building. With fire flashing from its eyes and sparks glittering along its teeth, the dark dog glared malevolently at the startled congregation. Then, with a bound, the fearsome animal leapt up. The roof caved in as the spire came crashing down, causing injury and mayhem among the good folk who were present.

The roof of Holy Trinity was quickly repaired and a major renovation of the entire church took place in 1931, so there are few marks to show the devastation caused that day. The main door, however, remains the same. It still boasts the scorched wood caused by the claw marks of the hell hound as it forced open the entrance to the church.

Although the black dog has gone, a black ghost remains. This is the phantom of Toby Gill, a negro drummer in the local regiment. In 1754 he got horribly drunk and while in a towering rage raped and murdered a girl from nearby Westleton. He was tried, convicted and hanged near the scene of his crime, at what is now Toby's Walk. His unmistakable ghost in full dress uniform is still encountered occasionally, stalking the spot where he died.

* * *

The cathedral city and county town of Suffolk is Bury St Edmunds, which has more than its fair share of both history and ghosts. Nobody knows quite how old the place is, but as Beodricesworth it certainly existed around AD 750. In AD 869 the Christian King of East Anglia, Edmund, was murdered by the pagan Vikings. His bones were brought here for safekeeping and the town changed its name in his honour.

In 1215 history came again to this city, for it was here that the rebellious barons met to plot the uprising that would force King John to sign the Magna Carta, the foundation of the freedom of Englishmen to this day. Since then the city gradually slipped in importance as it was overtaken by larger towns. In Georgian times the wooden buildings were largely rebuilt in brick, and it is this Georgian face that the city presents to the visitor.

The more active ghosts of the city are, however, a good deal older than Georgian times. They are linked to the mighty abbey, which housed the bones of the eponymous St Edmund. In 1327 a dispute broke out between the abbey and the townsfolk. The monks tried to solve the disagreement by attacking their rivals with axes and knives during a church service, but they were driven back to the abbey, which was then destroyed. The rebuilding that followed lasted 200 years and ended only just in time for King Henry VIII to close down the abbey as part of his reformation of the Church in England.

These days the outline of the vast abbey buildings remains, as do some of the structures, but the mighty church itself is all but gone. It is around the Norman tower, originally a gatehouse to the abbey precincts, that the ghostly monks congregate. This is the oldest surviving part of the complex, dating back to the 1090s. Dressed in the obligatory cowls and walking with heads bowed, these phantom monks seem very different from the belligerent clerics who once fought with the townsfolk. Perhaps they are a later, more holy group of monks. They have also been seen in Abbeygate Street and around the Cathedral Cottage.

THE NORMAN TOWER AT BURY ST EDMUNDS IS THE CENTRE FOR THE HAUNTING OF THE OLD ABBEY.

In 1417 a rather unsavoury episode led to a double death and single haunting at St Mary's church nearby. At the time England was not a happy country. The glittering successes of the early years of the Hundred Years War with France were being frittered away. Town after town, fortress after fortress fell to the French. The source of the trouble, most people believed, was the weak-minded nature of King Henry VI and the graspingly corrupt greed of his queen, Margaret of Anjou – a Frenchwoman. Margaret and

THE DISCOVERY OF THE BODY OF GOOD DUKE HUMPHREY IN 1447, FROM A 19TH CENTURY PAINTING BY R. NORBURY. THE MURDER OF THIS NOBLEMAN HAS LEFT ITS SPECTRAL MARK ON BURY ST EDMUNDS.

her cronies were too busy helping themselves to lucrative government positions and contracts to bother pursuing the war in France.

The opposition to their rule came to be headed by Humphrey, Duke of Gloucester and uncle to the king. He had fought bravely at the Battle of Agincourt in 1415 and captured Cherbourg in 1417. With a track record as a heroic soldier and a reputation for honesty when serving in government, Duke Humphrey soon became known as 'The Good Duke' by the common people in contrast to 'The Bad Duke', Margaret's favourite, the Duke of Suffolk.

In 1417 Parliament was due to meet in Bury St Edmunds. Good Duke Humphrey, along with all other nobles and a number of elected commoners, made his way to the town. When he arrived at the town gates, he was met by armed men sent by the Queen. They escorted him under duress to a house next to St Mary's, where, he was told, he would lodge until sent for by the king. It was a form of imprisonment, but worse was to follow.

Next morning the servant sent to wake the Duke found him dead. The king and queen were sent for and ordered public mourning. But it was widely believed that the duke had been murdered on the orders of the queen. Why else, people asked, had his own servants been barred from the fatal house until dawn? Blame for the death was never proved, but none of the nobility ever again trusted King Henry

VI or Queen Margaret. Within a decade England would collapse into the civil war that is known in history as the Wars of the Roses.

Back in Bury St Edmunds, a ghost began to be seen on 24 February in St Mary's churchyard. It was not the phantom of Duke Humphrey, but of a woman. Gossip began to spread that a local monk had cursed the killers of the Good Duke, condemning them to wander forever without rest, and to return each year on the anniversary of the murder to the scene of the crime. Some swore the shade was that of Queen Margaret, others that it was the likeness of a servant girl who had gone missing soon after the death.

Whoever it was, the ghost walks still. These days she is as likely to be seen on almost any winter's evening as on 24 February. She is dressed in a long dress and walks slowly round the churchyard. It has been a great while since the death of Good Duke Humphrey, but it seems that the nameless monk was able to put a powerful curse on the person who killed him. It was, there is no doubt, a terrible crime. But forgiveness is a Christian virtue. Perhaps it is time this particular ghost walked no more.

Not far away, in Eastgate Street, can be seen the phantom of a military man in magnificent full dress uniform of the later 19th century. This is a soldier who came back from the Crimean War, fought against Russia in the 1850s, hoping to marry a local girl. The father disapproved of his daughter marrying the man – though why we do not know – and refused permission. The young couple tried to elope, but were caught by the girl's father and brother. In the scuffle that followed the soldier was stabbed, later dying of his wounds. He returns to the spot, apparently in search of his lost love.

*　*　*

Up the coast at Dunwich, a small village with a shingle beach and the crumbling ruins of a priory nearby are all that remain of a thriving medieval town. A terrible storm in 1326 that smashed the harbour and washed three churches and dozens of houses into the sea began the decline. It also dumped an estimated million tons of shingle onto the shoreline, almost completely blocking what was left of the port. Periodic floods and storms over the years have hastened the decline of the town until today there is only a handful of houses left. On still nights the phantom sound of church bells from the lost churches will drift up from beneath the waves to echo across the beach.

The ruins of the Greyfriars monastery on the clifftop are clearly doomed. Sooner or later the sea will reach them and wash them away. Until then, however, they remain the home to some very persistent ghostly monks. These ghosts process about the ruins in pairs, their heads bowed low and faces hidden beneath their cowls.

Just inland, where the bleak heath stretches to the horizon, a ghostly horseman may be seen on moonlit nights. This is Squire Miles Barnes of Sotterly Hall, who lived here in Victorian times. He was a keen horseman, spending a great deal of money on good bloodstock. He particularly loved to ride the open heath on his fastest horses and continues to do so more than a century after his death.

Surrey

The historic county of Surrey has long since been carved up and disjointed by the sprawling growth of the capital city to the north-east. Yet something of the old county remains amid the suburbs, dormitory towns and stock-broker belt that dominate. It originally ran all the way up to Southwark, but the more built up areas have been cut away to be incorporated into Greater London.

One relic of its rural past is the Silent Pool, a beauty spot that lies just off the busy A25 east of Guildford. It is here that Surrey's most beautiful ghost may be encountered.

Splashing about in the pure waters, entirely naked, the spirit washes herself and swims playfully before diving into the waters and disappearing from sight.

It is said this phantom girl was the daughter of a local farmer, who, many centuries ago, went to the Silent Pool to wash herself. But while she was bathing a nobleman rode by and saw her. Overcome with lust for the pretty farm girl, the nobleman splashed into the Silent Pool in an attempt to grab the girl and drag her ashore. Rather than give in to his decidedly improper advances, the girl waded into deeper water, slipped and drowned. The girl's cries attracted her father, who arrived too late to save his daughter, but in time to see the evil nobleman ride off.

Although this version of the girl's tragic fate seems to be widely believed in the area, it is sadly untrue. The evil nobleman and his unwelcome advances were invented by a local writer, Martin Tupper, in a short story he wrote in 1858. Which leaves us to wonder who the beautiful maiden of the Silent Pool actually is. She may indeed be a poor drowned local girl, but there is a more interesting theory. Water sources, such as the Silent Pool, were sacred to the beautiful water goddesses of the pagan past. It is clear that the more atmospheric the place – and this pool is nothing if not atmospheric – the more sacred the spring was considered. Could it be that the beautiful ghost of the Silent Pool is simply the half-forgotten memory of a powerful pagan goddess?

* * *

Two ghosts in one building might seem a bit excessive, but the Marquis of Granby, which stands beside the old Portsmouth Road, now the A307 at Thames Ditton, manages to cope. The modern extensions to this pub hide the fact that it dates back almost 400 years, and it is in the oldest part of the pub that the ghost – or ghosts – lurk.

Mark Nicholls, a former bar manager, reported: 'The lady upstairs. We all know her. I've only heard her once myself, but everyone knows all about her. You hear her footsteps behind you and some rustling – like a silk dress, they tell me. Then when you turn around there is nobody there. It's a really weird feeling to know that somebody is in the room with you, but there isn't really. Mind you, she's no bother really. It gives you a bit of a start, that's all.'

This ghost is said to be that of a servant girl. From the descriptions given by those who have heard the footsteps and skirts of the ghostly lady, she would seem to date back at least 150 years. The dainty steps and heavy silk rustling seem to indicate fashions from the early 19th century at least. And stories of the ghost have been circulating in the area since the later 19th century, when a local gentleman mentioned belief in the story as typical of the gullible nature of local farming folk.

But the ghostly goings-on at the Marquis of Granby are not entirely harmless. In one of the upstairs rooms a small cupboard is set into a wall. The door is nailed shut and an old Bible is kept pushed against it – to stop 'the Thing in the cupboard' from getting out.

This 'Thing' was a most dreadful phantom, much given to slamming doors, smashing crockery and hammering on the walls. The 'Thing' made life a misery at the Marquis in the middle of the 19th century. All that is a thing of the past since a passing clergyman banished the 'Thing' to the cupboard and left his Bible to secure the door with holy powers.

* * *

Another supernatural terror that now seems to be under control is the ferocious water monster of the small stream west of Reigate known as Shag Brook. Stories about the monster are common in old books about Surrey. One tells of a Reigate lad who joined a cavalry regiment to fight Napoleon's French armies in the early 19th century. By the time he returned home on leave the lad had grown into a strapping trooper with a wealth of tales about his courage. Late one evening after a particularly boastful tale over a mug of ale, the soldier's more timid friends, who had stayed at home to farm, laid a hefty wager that he would not have the courage to ride to Buckland and back, crossing the fateful stream. The soldier trotted out bravely enough, but came back at the gallop with a white face and trembling hands. He collected his wager, but never again dared to cross the Shag Brook after dark.

A few years later a farmer was returning to Reigate after delivering a load of corn to Dorking. On reaching the brook his horses halted and no amount of whipping or leading could persuade them to move forward. The horses were shaking with fear and finally backed off and stared with terrified eyes at the stream, seeing something the farmer could not.

But what was this monster? The soldier described the beast he saw as being like a large, hairy man with bulging muscles and an animal head equipped with razor sharp teeth. Other witnesses gave a similar description. On the other hand, the farmer saw nothing when his horses stopped.

So was there a dreadful water monster lurking west of Reigate, or were the stories just the dimly remembered echoes of a pre-Christian Anglo-Saxon demon story? The beast has not been seen since. Yet.

* * *

One final ghost of Surrey is a very modern phantom indeed. In December 2002 motorists on the A3 dual carriageway just east of Guildford saw a car go out of control, skid off the road and crash into a patch of undergrowth. Two called the police on their mobile phones and one stopped at the scene of the accident.

The police arrived with commendable swiftness, but at first were mystified. Like the passer-by who had stopped, they could not see any sign of a car having left the road. There were no skid marks, no areas of flattened undergrowth and no signs of any disturbance at all. The motorist was, however, adamant that he had seen a car crash, and the police had the two calls from mobile phones logged as well.

The officers decided to investigate the seemingly undisturbed patch of scrubby woodland. Sure enough, there was a crashed car upside down in a ditch. Its position and intervening greenery meant that it could not be seen from the road. But the police were in for a shock. The car had clearly been there for some time and contained a skeleton. It was later found that the car, and its occupant, had been reported missing five months earlier.

Had the motorists seen a phantom recreation of the fatal crash that took place so many weeks earlier? It seems they must have done, for there was not a more recent wreck to be found.

Sussex

T he county of Sussex is as diverse a stretch of countryside as could be expected in southern England, where the landscapes tend to be softer and more gentle than those of the north or west.

The high sweeping Downs stretch their bare grassy slopes beneath the sun of summer, the rain of autumn and the winds of winter. The lower forests of Ashdown offer green shade to the traveller, and comfortable living to those lucky enough to be residents of Sussex. And many would argue that the true glory of the county is its coastline. There are towering white cliffs, gentle combes and wide beaches.

It was on one of these beaches that an event took place that would change English history and lead to several of the hauntings in Sussex. In 1066 Duke William of Normandy landed with an army to enforce his claim to the crown of England. One of William's first actions was to build a castle at Hastings to act as his base. The castle is haunted, though it is not entirely certain who by. The most persistent reports are of the sounds of prisoners rattling chains and bemoaning their fate. Whether these are the phantoms of prisoners of William or not is unclear. Rather more exciting is the ghostly nun who potters about the castle. She was photographed some 30 years ago and is the spectre that is seen most often.

Having established his base, William moved inland. He met the English army, led by King Harold II, at a place then known as

PRISONERS RATTLING THEIR CHAINS ARE SOMETIMES HEARD AT
BATTLE CASTLE.

Sandlake – which the Normans pronounced Senlac – but which is now better known as Battle. It was here on 14 October 1066 that William defeated the English army, killed Harold and won the crown of England.

The ghosts here recreate the opening and closing actions of the battle. The struggle began as the two armies drew up to face each other. This took some time and William's favourite minstrel, Taillefer, decided to raise Norman morale. He rode his horse out across the open space between the armies to come close to the English. He then began juggling with his sword while singing songs of praise to Duke William. An Englishman stepped forward and killed him with a single blow, which did little to help Norman morale, but boosted that of the English.

This incident is played out in phantom form as a lone horseman trots down from Telham Hill, where the Normans formed up, and rides to Battle Hill, where the English stood. The man is not seen to fall, but vanishes as he reaches the crest of the slope.

Seen rather more often is the ghost of the English King Harold. The king was in his forties at the time of the battle and was a seasoned warrior. He was famously hit in the eye by an arrow, but the wound was not fatal. He was killed late in the day when a small group of Norman knights broke the English line and hacked down the wounded monarch with their swords. His ghost has been seen dressed in a long mail jacket and wearing a conical helmet. The phantom lurks most often around the ruins of the abbey that was built by William to mark the site of his victory. The fact that the ghost is seen near to the high altar would seem to confirm the tradition that the altar was put on the spot where Harold died.

* * *

The magnificent Michelham Priory at Upper Dicker was founded in 1229 by the Augustinians, but like all monasteries in England it was dissolved by King Henry VIII in the 16th century. This priory was

converted to a private home, and both the prior's house and refectory have survived the centuries. So too have the ghosts.

There is, perhaps inevitably, a ghostly monk. Unlike most such phantoms this one has a name. He is believed to be Prior John Leem, who carved himself a successful career in government service as well as running the priory. Seen more often is the lady wearing a grey gown, who sometimes appears with a small brown terrier. She appears very solid and on one

MICHELHAM PRIORY IS HOME TO SEVERAL GHOSTS.

occasion was turned away at the entrance, as no dogs are allowed. The daring member of staff did not realise he was dealing with a ghost until she abruptly vanished. This ghost too can be identified. She is Mrs Childs, whose five year-old-son was drowned when his clothes became trapped in the nearby watermill.

More ominous is the man in a black cloak who is chased by a woman wearing a Tudor gown. Rather unnervingly, the pair descend from the ceiling of a room in the Tudor wing as if descending invisible stairs. Investigation has proved that this particular chamber was originally a staircase, but the stairs were removed after a fire.

* * *

An old church ruin haunted by its former occupants can be found at Winchelsea. The church of St Thomas was built in the 14th century as a magnificent and impressive building more than fit for its role in what was then one of the busiest ports in England. Unfortunately the town, and most of the church, was burned by the French during the Hundred Years War and only the chancel now remains complete, with some ruins of the transepts.

The ruined church is haunted by a former cleric in a long dark cloak wearing a hood pulled up over his head. This inoffensive soul has been seen many times emerging from the south transept as if on his way to a service in the long-vanished nave.

He is very different from the ghost that hovers near the gate on the far side of the churchyard. This is the spectre of a man intent on murder. Back in the 1770s he hid here, for a rival in love who was in the habit of riding past the church on his way home from work. In the fight that followed, the ambusher got the worst of things and died of his wounds. He comes back repeatedly to recreate the minutes that led up to his death, and more than one modern pedestrian has been startled by the hiding man who is so obviously up to mischief.

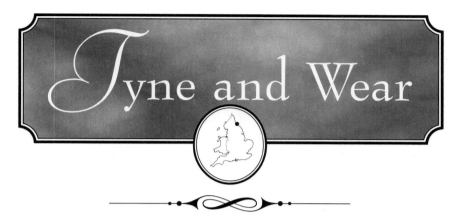

Tyne and Wear

The Empire theatre in Sunderland is famously haunted – its ghosts featuring with some regularity in the local press. The older of the phantoms goes by the name of 'Molly'. She was the stage manager before the Second World War and, one night after the show, she was walking home with a friend when she said she had to pop back to the theatre to pick up something she had forgotten. She never came back. The police found a witness who said he saw her in the Dun Cow pub drinking with a Russian sailor. Then she just vanished. No body was ever found nor any trace of her. Soon afterwards she returned in spectral form.

A woman who worked at the Empire as a barmaid in the circle bar in the 1990s was clearing up one night and heard the doors slam shut. She looked round, thinking it was the manager, and caught a glimpse of a lady in a white dress walking through the archway to the stairs that led to the top circle. She knew that no such person should be there, but bravely crept up to the top circle to check. It was empty.

Molly appeared again in 2002 . There was a musical show at the Empire and during the final rehearsal one young male singer happened to look up at the top circle. He saw a woman dressed in white watching the rehearsals. He did not think much of it at first, assuming it was a member of staff. Then the figure just vanished right in front of his eyes. Seconds later one of the canvas bits of scenery blew in a draught and touched him on the back. He fled the

SUNDERLAND'S EMPIRE THEATRE (LEFT),
WHICH IS HAUNTED BY A FORMER
EMPLOYEE WHO VANISHED AFTER A LATE
NIGHT DRINK IN THE DUN COW (RIGHT).

building and refused to go back at all. The company had to do the show without him.

The theatre staff treat Molly as quite a friend. 'We see her from time to time, mostly in the circle or top circle, but elsewhere in the theatre as well,' said one. 'She's a lady in a white dress walking around. Checking things out, I suppose. Making sure everything is just how she likes it. Must be, I think. She never gives any trouble and is a very friendly ghost.

'Of course, you get funny noises and such in theatres anyway. You know, a seat stays down when a person stands up and then gradually works its way loose until it snaps shut with a bang a couple of hours later. And there are all sorts of draughts in an old place like this. They can blow doors open and shut, move scenery and such. That might account for some of the stories. But I won't hang around after dark, not on my own. You never know.

'I won't go up to the top circle on my own,' he continued. 'It can be right spooky up there, you know. When you are by yourself. I wouldn't like our night watchman's job. Not my idea of fun at all.'

The more recent ghost is not so active, but his name is familiar far beyond Sunderland. In 1976 Sid James died on stage there during a performance. People at first thought it was all part of the show. But it wasn't. He had a heart attack and died. It is rumoured that when a member of the theatre staff phoned up his manager to tell him the news, he said: 'I've got something terrible to tell you,

Sid James has just died on stage in Sunderland.' The manager is said to have replied, 'Don't worry, son, every comic dies on stage in Sunderland at least once.' It took some time to convince him that Sid was really dead.

Ever since, strange things have gone on in Sid James's old dressing room. One cleaner claimed to have entered the room to tidy up, only to see Sid James's phantom sitting in front of the make-up mirror as if preparing for a show.

* * *

Marsden stands on the coast in a wide, sheltered bay, where a broad sandy beach attracts day-trippers in hot weather. At the foot of the cliff stands the Grotto pub and restaurant, beside the beach, built into a cave with various galleries hewn out of the living rock.

The ghost that is seen here most often goes by the name of 'John the Jibber'. He was a smuggler back when the pub was a just a cave, some 250 years ago. He gave information about his gang of smugglers to the revenue men. Understandably, the gang members were none too pleased when some were put in prison and one was hanged. But not every member of the gang was caught, and those that escaped wanted revenge. They got hold of John the Jibber and tied him up, then put him in a barrel that they hoisted up to the roof of the cave. They gave him just enough food to keep him alive, and left him there for months and months. When one of the smugglers got out of prison, he came to the cave and killed the poor man. The phantom moans and groans of John the Jibber were heard coming out of this cave ever afterwards. And his spectre was seen too. The ghost still appears on dark nights when a storm is blowing up.

Rather more active at the pub is the Man in Black phantom. Nobody really knows who he is. One story has it that he began his hauntings only after a former landlord installed a set of carved pillars to support the roof of a bar excavated from the rock. They were brought from the Lambton estates and are decorated with faces of the different Lords Lambton. They are said to be cursed.

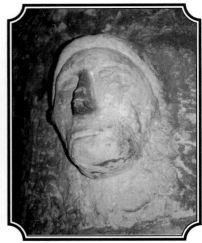

THE MARSDEN GROTTO PUBLIC HOUSE,
WHICH IS HAUNTED BY SEVERAL SPECTRES
AND IS FAMOUS FOR A NOW VANISHED
CURSED TANKARD.

ONE OF THE HEADS CARVED ONTO
THE PILLARS THAT SUPPORT THE
CAVERN ROOF IN THE MARSDEN
GROTTO.

A waitress who saw the ghost recently reported: 'He is a tall man and wears a long black cloak and has got long dark hair. I didn't see his face, just his long black cape as he ran down the spiral staircase beside the restaurant.'

There was once a cursed tankard at the Grotto. The waitress explained: 'Back in the 1830s this young chap from Marsden was drinking in the Grotto. As he drank more and more, he talked too much. He let slip that he was a smuggler, which was a problem as the revenue men were in and were keeping their ears open. They moved to arrest the young man, who put up a fight. In the struggle the young man was shot dead.

'The only thing left upright in the bar after the fight was one table, on which was perched the tankard from which the smuggler had been drinking. The landlord, Peter Allan, emptied the remaining ale and hung the tankard on a hook over the bar. Nobody must ever drink from it again, he declared, for it was surely cursed. Only the landlord of the pub was allowed to touch the cursed tankard. Whenever anyone else picked it up, bad luck struck within hours. Once a rockfall almost destroyed the pub.

'In 1998 the Grotto closed and stood empty for nearly two years. When it opened up again, the tankard was missing. Curse, or no curse, it has not been seen since.'

* * *

Not far inland from Marsden is Boldon, where there is another haunted pub, the Black Horse. Joseph Briggs, the landlord, recently saw the ghost quite clearly one summer's morning.

'No doubt about it,' said Joe. 'Now the Black Horse is an old place, you know. At least 400 years, maybe more. And it is from the early days that this ghostly man comes. There was a battle fought

THE BLACK HORSE IN BOLDEN, WHERE THE SCEPTICAL LANDLORD BECAME A BELIEVER IN GHOSTS AFTER A SUPERNATURAL ENCOUNTER.

AN APPROPRIATELY NAMED DRINK AT
THE BLACK HORSE IN BOLDON.

over on Nanny Cow Hill, you see. In the Civil War, I think it was. Or it might have been against the Scots. No, the Civil War. Anyhow, one of the soldiers was badly wounded and his friends brought him here to care for him. I suppose they must have laid him in the bar, as that is where we see him. And here he died a day or two later.

'Now I was not a believer in ghosts and such when I came here,' declared Joe. 'Not me. I thought it was all nonsense. But now I'd give credit to anything, I would.'

What caused his change of mind?

'Well I was in here opening up one day. Lovely day it was and I had the front door open to let the air in. Then I saw this man sitting by the door looking out the window. He was quite solid, not see-through or anything like that. He was wearing a long dark cloak of a very rough texture. Funny how you remember details. It was coarse and woollen; I felt I could just reach out and touch it. And he had a big dark-coloured hat on with a wide brim. I think he was wearing boots as well, but wouldn't swear to it. He looked about 45 or 50 to me and was pretty heavily built, definitely not a thin man.

'Anyway, I thought he was an early customer come in to wait for us to open. So I called across "Can I help you?" or words to that effect. The man turned to look at me and I suddenly thought how sad he looked. Then he was gone. Just like that. He did not walk off, he did not fade away. Nothing. He was there, then he was gone.

I tell you, I left this bar in a real hurry. The hairs on the back of my neck were sticking right up.

'At first I wasn't sure what to do. I mean, you wouldn't be, would you? I didn't tell anyone what I had seen. Then some time later one of our girls mentioned the pub was meant to be haunted and told me about the soldier and all. So then I knew that I had seen the ghost. Like I said, I didn't hold with all that when I came here. But I do now.

'The other ghost is upstairs in the private rooms. She is a little girl, about nine years old I guess. It's very sad. She's from Victorian days, apparently, and she lived and died here. She doesn't appear as often as the man, but she's real enough. You hear giggling and laughing coming from the end room upstairs. And then it goes cold, and I mean really cold. Not just a shiver down the spine, but like you have walked into a deep freeze. And there is this real feeling that something is not right. Spooks me, I tell you.'

* * *

It is, of course, the Americans who have put the town of Washington on the tourist trail. The first President of the United States of America was George Washington, whose family came from County Durham. The American Washingtons had moved to the New World in 1656 after getting into some political difficulties during England's Civil War.

Washington Old Hall, once the home of the Washington family and now in the care of the National Trust, is the focus of the hauntings in the town. Joe, the general maintenance man, was clear on the subject. 'Definitely haunted,' was his verdict. 'Most people see the ghost in the Panelled Room. Back in the old days that was the private chamber of the lord and his family. Out in the main hall was where all the farm workers, servants and what have you ate their meals and did their work.

'We see her about four or five times a year, I think. She usually sits in the centre of the room on a chair. Just sitting there minding her own business like. Though she does seem to make the

WASHINGTON OLD HALL, A BEAUTIFUL JACOBEAN MANSION THAT IS THE HAUNT OF MORE THAN ONE PHANTOM.

temperature drop. People who see her say the room gets suddenly very cold and they look round to see if there is a draught or something, and see this lady sat in a chair. But sometimes she walks about. And here's the thing. She walks straight through the north wall of the room. And that tells us how old she is, you see.

'After the Washington family sold up and moved out, the Old Hall passed through the hands of various families and by around 1840 it was all divided up into tenements and rented out to poor families. Right state the house was in then. They just pulled down interior walls and put up partitions, as they liked. This end of the ground floor was made into one big room, from front to back. That wall was not there. Then, in 1951, the house was bought up by a trust that wanted to restore it. They put this partition wall back in where it should be and bought up a load of oak panelling from an old house that was being pulled down. So the ghost must date from the time when that wall wasn't there. That's why she could walk right through it.

THE PANELLED ROOM AT WASHINGTON OLD HALL WHERE THE GREY LADY IS MOST OFTEN SEEN.

THE DOOR AT WASHINGTON OLD HALL THAT WILL NOT STAY CLOSED.

'And one other thing. The door that leads to the main hall can never be kept shut. You can shut it as firmly as you like, but when you come back it is wide open.'

Sarah, a lady helper at the house, had come across a very different ghost. 'It's odd really. More strange than frightening. I've not seen anything, you see. But we do hear someone running up and down the stairs a lot. But when the ghost runs downstairs, it doesn't just run, it jumps. Thump. Just like that. It's as if it leaps from one landing to the next with a terrific thump. You can't miss it. We always know when the ghost is about.

'The staircase isn't from here really. The original staircase was lost years ago and there was some horrible falling down Victorian thing when the restoration work began. This staircase came from an old hotel in Guildford in Surrey. It was given to us by Lord Gort, the general that got our boys away from Dunkirk in 1940. We think the noisy ghost came with it.'

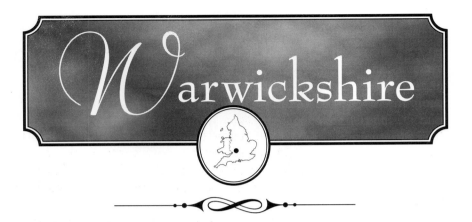

Warwickshire

Not only was Warwickshire the birthplace of William Shakespeare, the greatest playwright in the English language, it was also in Warwickshire that he set some of his plays and here that he penned his first lines. In those days it was a rural county, with some stretches of wild country where law-abiding folk wandered only in armed groups.

Today much of the area is still rural, though it has all been safely tamed. Even the formidable Forest of Arden is now little more than a stretch of farmland slightly more wooded than that which surrounds it. Elsewhere the landscape has changed out of all recognition. A little place is described in Domesday Book thus: 'Richard holds of William four hides. The arable employs six ploughs; one is in demesne. There are five villeins and four bordars with two ploughs. There is a wood half a mile long and four furlongs wide. It was worth 20 shillings in King Edwards time, and the same now.' Thus it was summed up in 1086. Today it is Birmingham.

But though the landscape may change, the ghosts remain pretty much unaltered. One phantom that persists despite developments to her surroundings is the lady who haunts the Old Mill Hotel at Baginton. This building was originally two quite separate structures – the mill beside the river and a house some five yards distant. When the place was converted into a hotel early in the 20th century, the gap between the two was infilled so that what had been the carriageway by which flour carts got to the mill became the bar and reception hall. As the 20th century came to a close, the building was altered again when a large block of bedrooms was added to the eastern end of the hotel.

All these changes were done with much sympathy of design and it can be difficult to see where the original ends and the new begins. Perhaps this is why the Pale Lady has not been disturbed. She haunts what was the old house, which now contains the main dining area and some offices. She is said locally to have died here – some say been murdered – in the 18th century, though no name has been preserved.

One member of staff who saw the ghost not long ago recalled: 'It was all over in a second, really. I came through the door at the foot of the stairs in the old house to take some linen up to the store cupboard. There was somebody coming down and these are narrow stairs with not much room to pass. I caught a glimpse of a lady in a pale dress and assumed it was another member of staff. So I stepped back to one side, but when I looked up the stairs again they were completely empty. Like I say, I only saw her for a second, may be not even that long, but there was definitely somebody on those stairs. I'd stake money on it, I would.'

* * *

Undisturbed by even more drastic changes are the ghostly monks of Kenilworth. They built themselves a fine monastery, dedicated to St Mary the Virgin, after the house was founded here in 1129. When King Henry VIII took over and closed down the monasteries as part of the Protestant Reformation of the English Church, Kenilworth Abbey was shut with speed and efficiency. The buildings were stripped of anything that could easily be sold by the agents of the king. Dressed stone, glass windows, lead from the roof, wooden beams – everything of value was removed and sold to the highest bidder. Most of the building materials found their way into the houses and barns of Kenilworth and nearby villages.

All that was left of the once mighty abbey were some piles of rubble, discarded stonework and foundations that were more trouble to dig out than they were worth at auction. Within a very few years grass and weeds had covered over the sad remnants, and by the early 20th century the exact site of the different buildings had been forgotten, though they were known to lie in the field beside the parish church.

But the ghostly monks had not forgotten. Time after time, they were seen processing along the avenue of trees outside the parish church, turning left at the end and then vanishing. One man who encountered the ghosts when a choir boy in the 1970s said: 'We had finished practice and I had to stay behind to help put some stuff away so I was the last boy to leave the church. I came out in a bit of a hurry to get home and there was this man in a long black cloak down the avenue. There was something odd about him – can't say what really, he wasn't transparent or anything like that. Just odd somehow. I stopped to look at him and suddenly he wasn't there. Just like he had gone poof or something. I was really frightened, I can tell you. I ran all the way home.'

When archaeologists came to Kenilworth to unearth the lost abbey, they dug trial ditches, scanned the soil with instruments and studied old maps for clues. They eventually found the foundations of the old abbey church exactly where the phantom monks were in the habit of vanishing. The archaeologists could have saved themselves a lot of trouble if they had paid more attention to the ghosts.

* * *

The village of Bearley, north-west of Stratford, is a nice enough place, but quite unremarkable and much like others in Warwickshire except for one feature. There is a ghostly miller here who guards a buried treasure of great value. It is said that this miller lived here some centuries ago, working the windmill that formerly stood on the hill just outside the village. He was a secretive soul and not much given to being pleasant to his neighbours.

In a very un-miller-like fashion he kept in his stable six powerful black stallions. He was never seen to ride them himself and flew into a furious temper if anyone ever approached the horses. Once each day, the miller led the great steeds down from his hill to drink in the stream at the valley base, then led them back up again to graze beside his mill.

Of course, there were all sorts of ideas as to why the miller had these horses. Some said he was in league with a highwayman, others that smugglers were his colleagues. One or two whispered that the powerful horses belonged to the devil. But whoever the horses were used by, they obviously paid the miller well for his trouble in caring for them. The man always had plenty of ready cash.

Then one day the horses and the miller were gone. The miller's belongings had been packed up in a hurry and the building left deserted. The man was never seen again, at least not in human form. Some weeks later as a full moon climbed into the night sky, his ghost was seen leading the great black stallions down to drink at the stream. His spectre has been seen periodically ever since, always walking down to the stream followed by the ominous black shapes of his mighty horses.

Wiltshire

Wiltshire is an ancient county. The light soils of the chalk uplands were among the first to be farmed in England. More than five thousand years ago our remote ancestors were using wooden ploughs and digging sticks to turn over the soil and prepare it for crops of wheat, barley and beans. These ancient peoples left their mark in the form of standing stones – none more spectacular than at Stonehenge or Avebury – and as burial mounds that lie scattered all across the region.

The ghosts of Wiltshire are not much younger. High on the chalk downs beside the modern A4 stands the West Kennett Long Barrow. Built about 3,000 BC, this is one of the largest and best preserved burial mounds in England. It measures some 350 feet long and is surrounded by a ditch and a string of small, upright stones. The façade is most impressive with massive upright standing stones forming a small courtyard and guarding the entrance to the chambers within the mound.

When the dawn sun comes up over the hills, it shines directly onto the entrance of the West Kennett barrow, its rays piercing the gloom to bathe the sarsen uprights in a glow that can be both warmly orange and somehow eerie. It is at such times that a tall man may be seen standing in front of the barrow, facing the rising sun. He wears a long, cream coloured cloak and has at his heels a tall white hound. The man appears to watch the sun for a while, then turns and disappears into the interior of the mound.

Who this enigmatic figure might be and why he haunts the ancient stones we cannot know. Perhaps he is a priest from long ago, still conducting his ancient rites according to the beliefs of his time.

* * *

Still ancient, but modern by comparison, are the ghosts that haunt the great Tudor mansion of Longleat. Today this magnificent stately home is as famous for its tourist attractions as for its history. It has the world's longest hedge maze and an extensive safari park with lions, tigers and a host of other wild animals. It is the 16th century Renaissance house, however, that remains at the heart of the estate and the centre for the hauntings.

The best known of the ghosts is that of Louisa Carteret, who married Thomas, 2nd Viscount Weymouth, in the early 18th century. Lady Louisa was strikingly beautiful and it was generally agreed that Weymouth had made a good match. As was the custom then, the bride brought to her new marital home her own servants, whom she knew and trusted. Among these was a particularly good looking footman. For some reason, Weymouth became suspicious of the servant, suspecting that his devotion to the new Lady Weymouth was not entirely innocent.

One night Weymouth found the footman in an upstairs corridor close to Lady Louisa's bedroom. Ignoring the man's protestations of innocence, Weymouth drew his sword and after a violent fight killed his supposed rival. The dead body was dragged downstairs by Weymouth and hurriedly buried in a shallow grave. Lady Louisa never really believed her husband's tale that the footman had been called away suddenly on some business to do with his family. She spent long hours wandering the corridors of Longleat trying to find some clue as to the whereabouts of her faithful servant.

She wanders them still – in spectral form. She is seen often in a green dress, passing quietly and sorrowfully along the corridors, sometimes pausing as if to listen and at other times peering through doors into rooms.

THE BEAUTIFUL 16TH CENTURY MANSION OF LONGLEAT HOUSE PLAYS HOST TO SEVERAL PHANTOMS.

When central heating was being installed at Longleat just before the Second World War, the floor of the cellar was taken up to install boilers and piping. The workmen discovered a skeleton with its feet still encased in boots of the type worn by 18th century footmen. It seems there was some truth in the old story. The bones were given a decent Christian burial, ironically, close to the grave of the Lord Weymouth who had killed the footman.

* * *

The four ghosts of Manningford Bruce, on the northern edge of Salisbury Plain, always appear together, dressed in the fashions of the mid-17th century. These gentlemen, for clearly they are such, are deep in conversation with each other and are without doubt discussing a subject of great importance. This village was, in 1651, home to a lady named Jane Lane, who was a staunch Royalist at a time when such overt political sympathies were dangerous.

Parliament had won the Civil War and executed King Charles I. That summer his son, the exiled King Charles II, tried to win back his throne, but was defeated at the Battle of Worcester and went on the run. If his enemies had caught him there can be little doubt what his fate would have been. For weeks after the battle there was no news of the fugitive's whereabouts. Then a friend sent a letter to Jane Lane asking if she would help a man on the run. Guessing the man to be a fellow Royalist, Jane agreed but was startled when the man arrived and she recognised Charles himself. Before accepting responsibility for the king, she demanded to know the plans for his escape. The men who had escorted him to Manningford Bruce went into a desperate huddle with the young Charles to discuss matters before being forced to announce that there were no plans.

Suddenly aware of her danger, Jane dressed the, as she hoped, unidentified man in the nondescript clothes of a servant and 'employed' him as her valet. Together they rode over Salisbury Plain to Farley, where Jane lodged the king in hiding with Royalist friends while a route was planned to get the fugitive to the coast, where he might be able to get a boat to safety abroad.

While at Farley, the king became so annoyed at being shut up in an attic that he persuaded his host to let him go out with the local forester to do some work in the woods on the estate. A troop of Parliamentarian cavalry suddenly arrived searching for Charles and other fugitives. They were at first suspicious of the tall 'forester', but were satisfied that he was a humble workman by the strength with which he wielded his axe.

Charles eventually got to safety and nine years later returned to England as monarch. But it seems his phantom and those of his friends remain at Manningford Bruce. The four men mentioned before, in Cavalier attire and talking so seriously, are said to be the king and his supporters discussing how to arrange his escape.

247

Worcestershire

The beautiful Malvern Hills dominate western Worcestershire, rising to impressive heights above the villages and towns that share the Malvern name. The natural springs that are found here were famous for their medicinal properties as early as 1700 and today their water can be found in bottles in most supermarkets across England.

East of the Severn and Avon, the county descends to the Vale of Evesham, one of the broadest and most attractive valleys in western England. This is a fruit growing area as fertile as Kent and producing fruits of equally high quality. Unlike Kent, however, Worcestershire does not produce apples mainly for eating, but mostly for turning into cider. Varieties such as Cap of Liberty or Slackmagirdle are crisp and acidic, perfect for fermentation, while the much more famous Worcester Pearmain is one of the few eating apples grown here.

One pub that does a nice line in local cider is the Fleece Inn at Bretforton. It also has paranormal activity of more than one kind. Nigel Smith, the landlord in 2005, knew all about the ghostly presence of former landlady Lola Taplin. 'There is definitely somebody around,' reported Nigel, 'and a lot of the manifestations take place around the settle in the Pewter Room.'

The pub began life as a farm in the 14th century, opening as an inn in 1848. From 1400 to 1978 it was owned by the Taplin family, and Lola was the last and most formidable of her line. She was very

THE FLEECE INN AT BRETFORTON IS HAUNTED BY A FORMER LANDLADY WHO
SIMPLY CANNOT BEAR TO LEAVE.

proud of her old home, preserving the old cockfighting room and
as much of the fabric as she could. On her death it passed to the
National Trust, though it is still run as a pub.

'We've still got Lola's shoes,' says Nigel, 'and we've found they
are best left alone. If anyone moves them or interferes, we get a bit
of bother. Saucers have flown off tables and I saw a glass jump off
a shelf in the bar, fly across the room then land on a table quite
gently. It did not break despite travelling at least 12 feet through
thin air. Very strange. Oh, and Lola was always very insistent about
certain chairs and where they should go. I moved them when I
started here, as I thought they would work better that way, but
every morning they were back how Lola wanted them. I don't move
them any more. Finally, I must mention our witches' marks by the
chimney. There were some witches here in the 1920s, apparently,

THE FLEECE INN BOASTS 'WITCHES MARKS' IN THE BAR FIREPLACE.

and they made those marks for whatever reasons they had. Lola left them there, so I reckon that is probably the best thing to do. They are still there.'

The Fleece Inn is not the only haunted place in Bretforton. The church plays host to a phantom funeral. It appears complete with black hearse drawn by a pair of black horses with black feather plumes on their heads. The hearse advances slowly up the road from Weston Subedge, arrives in front of the lychgate and vanishes. Whose funeral this might be nobody seems to know. Nor is it clear whether or not it is linked to the gruesome ghost that frequents the nearby fields.

Again, the identity of this ghost is unknown. This is odd, as she takes the form of a headless woman dressed in fine clothes. It might be thought that such a stark apparition would have a story behind it, but apparently not. She simply manifests herself, frightens those who see her, then vanishes.

* * *

By contrast the headless woman of Huddington is very clearly identified. She is Lady Winter, who died there in the early 17th century. Along with her husband, Thomas Winter, Lady Winter was a Catholic. At this date Catholics were treated with suspicion in England, a staunchly Protestant kingdom. The Pope had issued a religious decree that Catholics in England owed no allegiance to their monarch, but should wage ceaseless war to try to return England to the Catholic faith. Most Catholics ignored the orders from their religious chief, but a fanatical few took the Pope at his word. Thomas Winter was one.

Along with Robert Catesby of Warwickshire, Winter came up with a plan to force England to become Catholic. They arranged for fellow conspirators to seize Prince Charles, the young heir to the ruling King James I, while others were to grab control of the huge stocks of weapons in Warwick Castle and still more would commandeer the cash wealth of the City of London. Before any of this could happen, however, King James had to be killed and the main figures of government killed or put out of action. Winter and Catesby decided to achieve this by blowing up Parliament when it met with the king at Westminster on 5 November 1605. They hired a soldier and explosives expert named Guy Fawkes to do the deed.

The plot was discovered just in time, and at 4 am on 5 November Fawkes was arrested by men searching the cellars under Parliament. The plot rapidly unwound when Fawkes was tortured to reveal the names of his fellow conspirators. Winter was arrested, dragged to London and hanged.

His distraught wife returned to her home at Huddington Hall and spent the rest of her life there in sadness and despair. Her ghost remains, being most active in January, the month when her husband was executed.

* * *

The centre of Worcestershire is, of course, Worcester and it is a city as full of ghosts as might be wished. The best known phantom of the city appears with startling frequency on the green outside the cathedral. The ghost's first appearance seems to have resulted from the most traumatic event in the building's history. The church had been founded in AD 680, though the oldest surviving part is the crypt of 1080. A 13th century rebuilding was followed by the construction of the famous 14th century tower. King John is buried here, as is Arthur, eldest son of Henry VII, who died before he inherited the throne.

The cathedral escaped the Reformation relatively unscathed, but in 1642 disaster struck. The English Civil War was just getting under way, with towns and shires being forced to choose between King and Parliament. Both sides claimed to be the legitimate government of the realm and sent out demands for payment of taxes and appointed their own sheriffs and other local officers. Worcester declared for the king, Charles I, and defied Parliament to do its worst.

This Parliament proceeded to do. A large army was collected and sent west under the command of the Earl of Essex to enforce taxation and obedience from places that had refused. As the army approached Worcester it unexpectedly encountered a small body of Royalist cavalry under the command of Prince Rupert, a nephew of the king. Rupert recovered from the shock first, ordering his men to mount and leading a dashing charge that swept the Parliamentarian advance guard away from Powick Bridge.

Rupert could not hope to face the entire Parliamentarian army, but he had won the first battle of the Civil War. Essex came up next day with his main body and Rupert retreated. Two days later, Essex and his army were in Worcester, intent on revenge. The cathedral was desecrated and much ornamentation smashed, while troops ransacked the houses and taverns, stealing what they liked at swordpoint. Essex set up his headquarters in the cathedral close, and surrounded the place with armed guards.

It was one of these guards who in the early hours of the morning fled his post and ran into the cathedral screaming, then collapsed into a gibbering wreck. When he recovered his senses, the man said that he had been attacked by a gigantic bear, but that when he shot at it the bear had vanished into thin air. The unlucky sentry was assumed to be drunk and punished accordingly, but this same phantom bear has been seen many times since. It is, they say, a most disturbing and bizarre spectre to encounter.

Yorkshire

Covering 6,100 square miles, this was once the largest county in England. In 1974 Yorkshire was carved up by interfering bureaucrats into three new counties. But the proud folk who live there refuse to recognise the change and still prefer to say that they live in Yorkshire as if the whole were still united.

But Yorkshire is a highly varied county. The Pennines of the north-west are composed of grey limestone, covered by short green grass and dotted by sheep. The moors have their foundation on older, harder rocks, which support heath and heather as much as grass. The lowlands of the Vale of York embrace a vast area of rich alluvial soils able to grow impressive crops of vegetables and grain.

But it is the rivers that define Yorkshire and its borders. The Aire, Ouse and Don pour into the Humber, their drainage basins defining most of Yorkshire. None of these pushes as far to the west as do the headwaters of the Aire, which at Skipton are three times closer to the Irish Sea than the North Sea.

The imposing castle at Skipton was begun in Norman times and has been enlarged, altered and improved many times over the centuries. It is, today, a magnificent home that retains much of its medieval grandeur and is open to the public throughout the year. For most of its existence the castle was owned by the rich and powerful Cliffords. The family rose to prominence in the 13th century and John, the 9th Baron Clifford, gained an evil reputation for utter ruthlessness during the Wars of the Roses. Despite being a

THE GATEWAY TO SKIPTON CASTLE, SCENE OF ONE OF THE MOST SPECTACULAR HAUNTINGS IN ENGLAND.

Yorkshireman he fought for the Lancastrians, which may account for his unpopularity in Skipton.

In the 17th century the castle passed out of ownership of the Clifford family when the 18th Baron died without a male heir, but that did nothing to put off its spectral manifestation, which remained as active as ever. This is one of the most spectacular ghostly happenings that Yorkshire has to offer, though one of the most rarely seen. On the day that the owner of the castle is to die a phantom black carriage comes to call for his soul. The carriage drives slowly up the wide High Street of Skipton pulled by four black horses. When it arrives at the mighty gatehouse of the castle, the doors swing open by themselves and the carriage enters. It then moves slowly on to the castle entrance, where it stops and gradually fades from view.

* * *

Another haunted castle stands at Richmond, where the towering keep built in 1071 still dominates the town and countryside for miles around.

In the 18th century a party of bored soldiers came across a long forgotten passage at the castle. Remembering old stories about hidden treasure buried deep within the rock on which the castle is built, the soldiers were keen to explore. Unfortunately the entrance to the passage was too narrow for any of them to enter. They quickly enlisted the help of a drummer boy and pushed him into the hole, shoving his drum after him. They told the lad to beat his drum as he progressed along the passage, allowing them to trace his route above ground.

The soldiers followed the sound of drumming out of the castle gates, across the Market Place and into Frenchgate. As the men approached the edge of the hill, where it drops down to the River Swale, the drumming stopped. The unfortunate boy never emerged from the passageway and nobody was ever brave enough to retrace his steps. The passage was blocked up, but that did not stop the ghost of the lost drummer boy from returning to Richmond. On still nights, when the hum of daytime traffic has stilled, the eerily distant sound of a drum being beaten underground can still be heard coming from the rock beneath Richmond.

* * *

Just as grim are the ghosts that haunt Clifford's Tower in the city of York. This stone tower set on top of an artificial hill, or motte, was built by the Normans to protect the eastern approaches to the river crossing here. In 1190 the tower was built of timber, but despite this was the stoutest and most easily defended building in the city. It was less than a year since Henry II had died and his magnificent son, Richard the Lionheart, had come to the throne.

Richard at once announced that he was off on a crusade to rescue the holy places of Christianity from fanatical Moslems who had been killing innocent pilgrims whose only wish was to worship at Christian shrines in Jerusalem and Bethlehem. Events in the Holy

Land were not quite that simple, but England was fired with religious fervour.

On 3 September Richard was crowned in Westminster Abbey. He had given orders that only Christians were allowed to attend. When a number of rich Jews arrived to offer him gifts, the soldiers on guard beat them up and threw them out. The citizens outside took this to signal a persecution of the Jews and began a massacre that claimed the lives of nearly every Jew in London. The anti-Jewish riots spread rapidly, faster than the armed men sent out by the king could stop them.

At York the Jews responded by barricading themselves and their wealth into Clifford's Tower to await the arrival of the king's men. The mob outside was not to be denied, however, and brought up siege machinery to break into the fortress. In desperation, the Jews inside committed mass suicide, then fired the tower above their heads. There were no survivors.

It is this terrible event that is recreated in spectral form at Clifford's Tower. Terrifying screams will suddenly pierce the air while the unmistakable smell of burning timber fills the air. Those who experience this report an odd sensation rather like falling through thin air for the few seconds that it lasts. Then everything returns to normal.

CLIFFORD'S TOWER IN YORK WAS THE SCENE OF A HORRIFYING MASS SUICIDE THAT HAS LEFT ITS SPECTRAL MARK.